Vicuy

Bound in Silver

Solis Invicti: Book III

JOSIE JAFFREY

© Josie Jaffrey 2016

Cover illustration by Martin Beckett Art.

All rights reserved.

The right of Josie Jaffrey to be identified as the author of this work
has been asserted by her in accordance with the Copyright,
Designs and Patents Act 1988.

All characters and events in this publication are fictitious and any
resemblance to real persons, living or dead, is purely coincidental.

ISBN-13: 978-1548145514
ISBN-10: 1548145513

By Josie Jaffrey

The Solis Invicti Series

A Bargain in Silver
The Price of Silver
Bound in Silver
The Silver Bullet

The Sovereign Trilogy

The Gilded King
The Silver Queen
The Blood Prince

Short Stories

Living Underground

For Vicky

PROLOGUE

But the ungodly by their words and deeds summoned death;
considering him a friend they pined away and made a covenant
with him,
because they are fit to belong to his company.
For they reasoned unsoundly, saying to themselves,
"Short and sorrowful is our life, and there is no remedy when a
life comes to its end,
and no one has been known to return from Hades.
For we were born by mere chance, and hereafter we shall be as
though we had never been,
for the breath in our nostrils is smoke, and reason is a spark
kindled by the beating of our hearts;
when it is extinguished, the body will turn to ashes, and the spirit
will dissolve like empty air."

- The Wisdom of Solomon

The guild hall rang with the sound of the gong as it struck the bells of midnight, the echo demonstrating the cavernous

1

extent of the space where the light of the few candles had failed to do so. From their faint glow I could see the ranks of faces lined row after row around the sides of the room. They watched with eerie stillness as we awaited our judgement.

My palms were damp with sweat, the satin of my dress sticking to my skin as terror clenched my body into a ball of nerves.

I knew what the verdict would be.

I knew that they would send me to the dawn ceremony, and I knew that the turning would fail. I wouldn't become Silver; I'd turn Weeper instead. I'd become a monster.

The throne at the far end of the room was occupied by an anonymous figure in a dark, hooded cloak. The attire gave it the appearance of an executioner, a black judge of we lucky humans nominated for this honour. But what had started out as an opportunity had become an obligation that would take my life and turn it into something else: something dark, infected and twisted.

Eight cloaked figures stood between us and the throne, a strip of naked flesh visible on each of them from neck to waist. Drew was among them somewhere. It would be his teeth in my neck, his hand at my throat and his conscience weighed by the sum of my life.

I wondered whether he would care at all when he saw me fall at his feet and break apart.

I felt sick with anxiety, the blood loss making me so weak that I wasn't sure I'd be able to stay on my feet I had to breathe through my mouth to keep the nausea that was rolling in my stomach at bay.

I just had to keep it together for a little while longer, I thought, and then it would all be over.

I'd be done.

I could give up.

My name's Emmy, I'm twenty-eight and I'm still human.

For now.

CHAPTER I

Thursday

The gate of the Silver city slammed shut behind us, the bolts shooting home with force as the pick-up truck pulled out onto the road beyond, driving slowly through a breach in the barricade that circled the towering perimeter walls. The rain was pouring heavily from the leaden sky, thudding into the open truck bed with thunderous force until Oliver and I were sitting in streams of water that washed the mud from the trailer around us.

I braced myself as best I could against the jerky movement while the truck thundered onto the road, the barricade falling behind us quickly as the buildings reared up on either side.

"Look," Oliver said, pointing off to our right.

I followed his gesture and saw that Weepers were lining the sides of the street, queuing in their thousands to watch our progress with apparent interest as their eyes streamed with the bloody tears that gave them their name. I shuddered. One bite from a Weeper and we'd be transformed into one of them, but if they managed to carry us off for their lunch then there wouldn't be enough of us left to turn anyway.

But they were keeping their distance from the truck, doubtless having spotted, or perhaps having sensed, that the driver was a Silver: one of the vampiric race that had created the Weepers with their failed attempts to make more of their own kind.

They had unleashed the Weeper plague on the humans and now they were the only ones who could keep us safe from it, apparently able to repel the Weepers simply with the force of their presence, so they were in charge. We humans gave the Silver our blood and worked for them for the privilege of their protection, a bargain many of us found difficult to swallow. The humans' refusal to submit to it was the reason Oliver and I were in this mess, caught in the fallout of a failed rebellion.

Oliver was topless except for the bandage that wrapped around his torso to hold the dressing onto his shoulder injury, but in this rain a shirt wouldn't have done him much good anyway. I was still wearing my T-shirt and mini skirt, both shredded from the explosion the night before, and for all the protection they were affording me I might as well have been naked. Goose pimples crawled along my skin as my body tried to keep itself warm, but at least my feet were snug in my knee-high boots.

I stared out at the ranks of the Weepers, following them with my eyes as they followed us, their fluid and undulating movements seeming to roll us along as we went. They were a sea of intent faces peering out from the shade of the alleys and buildings crowding in over the road, huddled under overhangs and in doorways in a half-hearted attempt to keep the daylight from their weeping eyes.

"They're not hiding like they used to," I said.

"Who? The Weepers?"

I nodded.

"They used to stay indoors, in the shadows. They're pushing the limits."

We both watched them for a moment in silence as the trucked bumped onwards.

"The sky's clouded over," he replied. "But maybe they're

getting hungrier too."

I wrapped my free arm around my knees and curled into a ball, pulling myself as far into the centre of the truck bed as I could. With the Weepers encroaching further and further into the street, I didn't want to tempt fate. I knew we were safe with the Silver close by in the driver's seat, but being locked out in the open air like a sacrificial offering whilst we thundered past thousands of hungry Weepers was utterly terrifying.

"At least they didn't send us out here alone with the rebels," Oliver said.

It was a small mercy, but I could have done without the reminder of the events of earlier today.

A group of fifty-odd humans had blown up some of the buildings in the safe zone last night, in the Silver city. A lot of people had died, and a couple of the Silver too. Little wonder, then, that the ruler of the Silver, the Primus, had sent them on a short walk outside the perimeter wall to meet the Weepers.

We'd driven across the bloodstained tarmac on our way out of the gates.

"I'm not sure it will make much difference to me in the long run," I replied, my teeth juddering as I shivered.

"You're thinking about the Casting?"

I nodded.

The Primus had decided to offer an opportunity to all of the remaining humans: the opportunity to turn Silver. I'd let myself be convinced into signing up, a decision that I had come to regret bitterly.

"Will that really still go ahead?" he said. The rain had plastered his curling hair to his face and neck, turning its light brown a darker shade. The water dripped off his long lashes, ran down his stubbled cheeks and poured off his chin.

"I assume so. I don't know. Maybe not after last night."

Oliver and I had tried to stop the explosions and save some of my friends who had been trapped in the blast zone, but in the process we'd been implicated as rebels by a couple of Silver who were trying either to end my life or to make it miserable. The Primus, Solomon, had sentenced us to indefinite punishment duty on Silver Farm, where all our food was produced and stored.

I couldn't imagine that it was going to be a barrel of laughs, but with the Casting scheduled for Wednesday I didn't think I'd have to suffer through it long. It would all be over soon.

We sat upright in the trailer watching the transfixed Weepers until, after what felt like an age, we reached the edge of their multitude and saw the limits of their silent vigil disappearing into the distance as the truck sped on. There were millions of them, crowding patiently around the city walls, waiting for the Silver to leave their human flock unguarded, for their opportunity to break in. We watched them until they were out of sight, unwilling to let our guard down until we felt that we were out of their range.

I exhaled heavily, relieved at escaping their normally unseen and yet oppressive embrace of the city. The stark spectre of my own future was not something on which I wanted to dwell.

The cuff that chained my right hand to the metal floor was chafing on my wrist, the wet skin already blistering under the constant movement caused by the truck's poor suspension. I shifted to try to get comfortable, and found that the only way to stop it from rubbing was to lie down in the truck bed.

I was soaked anyway, so what did it matter?

"Why did you even agree to it?" Oliver asked me, his bright, grey eyes narrowing in incomprehension as he looked down at me.

"What? The Casting?"

"Yeah," he said, lying down beside me. "Tell me you don't want to be Silver."

"Of course not. I've seen how they are, how twisted they can become. I don't want to be like that."

"Then why?"

"At the time, it seemed like the only option," I replied mournfully. We were now less than a week away from the Casting and it was looming in the forefront of my mind. If I made it through the selection process, then I would have to go through with the attempt to turn Silver. And I would fail.

"Tell me," he said.

"It's complicated."

"It must be," he replied.

"It's a long story."

"We have time," he said.

I was unsure whether or not to trust him. Everything we had gone through together in the past twelve hours had formed some kind of connection between us, but so much had changed during that time that I was no longer sure where my loyalties lay. I thought of Drew and Sol, of Cam's distraught face as the gates of the city closed behind us, shutting me out of their world. But what did I owe to the Silver who had sent me away? I thought of everyone I had lost and realised that Oliver was the closest I had to a human friend at this moment.

"Tell me about what happened with the rebels," I replied.

"I think you know most of it."

"Tell me from the beginning," I insisted, looking for a story to distract him, and to distract me from my chattering teeth. "Tell me your Revelation story."

Two weeks ago, when the Silver had first made themselves known, it had been in response to the arrival of the Weeper plague, which swept through the streets rapidly and relentlessly. In populated areas it spread quicker than wildfire, the infection originating from a single Weeper converting an entire city within minutes. Of course, we knew now that the timing of the Silver Revelation was no coincidence, and that the arrival of the Weepers had been caused by the Silver, but back then many saw them as our saviours and deliverers, albeit requiring more in terms of payment than we might have offered otherwise.

That moment had become a defining one for all the humans who had survived this far; a common experience lived and suffered in so many different ways.

"It's a bad one," he said quietly.

I shielded my eyes with my free hand and looked up into the sky, through the rain at the buildings falling away on either side of us as we moved through the city. The structures were starting to shrink as we left central London, the towering faces of the broken office blocks giving way to beautiful old terraces, their balconies strewn with new horrors I didn't want to contemplate. I closed my eyes, but my mind was filled with horrors of its own.

"So was mine," I said.

There was a moment of silence before he responded, each of us shut in the walls of our own memories.

"Another time, then," he said.

Oliver had just lost his brother to the failed rebellion, so I could understand why he might not want to talk about the Revelation. I imagined that they would have been together. It had probably been insensitive of me to ask about it, but it was difficult to find a safe topic of conversation these days.

"I hate to push you on this," he said, "but is there anything I need to know before we get to the Farm? We're in this together and, well, there have been a lot of rumours about you being some kind of pet of the Primus…"

I groaned aloud. I really didn't want to talk about Sol, didn't want to confess my sins to Oliver, to relive the rush of adrenaline aroused by the scrape of the Primus's teeth on my skin.

"Look, Emmy," he said, "I already know about the choker and the brand, though I admit I'm starting to doubt that my information about either of them was accurate given that it came from Benedict. But forget that. What I'm saying is that you can talk to me. I'm hardly in a position to judge you, after all. You wouldn't be here if I hadn't gotten involved with the rebels. You wouldn't have lost the choker, or the protection of the Primus. This is my fault."

I turned my head to the side, my cheek lying along the cold, metal trailer bed as the rain pounded down around us, and looked into his grey eyes.

"It's my fault too," I said with feeling.

"Tell me," he said again as he rolled onto his side and pulled me, shivering, into his arms, my face cradled against his shoulder. After all we had been through last night and having spent the morning helping him to limp around the city, I was accustomed to his proximity, and it felt comfortable and calming to feel him close. His warmth settled into my chilled flesh, my limbs slick with rain on the bare skin of his torso.

"It all comes down to Ben," I said quietly. "Benedict, the Silver's third in line in England. You know that's who he is, right?"

"I knew he was one of the Solis Invicti," Oliver answered, naming the Silver's elite military and the Primus's personal guard.

"Yeah, well, he's a bit more than that. Solomon is Primus, Andrew is Secundus and Benedict is Tertius. If Sol and Drew were out of the picture…"

"Oh," Oliver said. "But they're Silver," he continued after a moment, "and they're old. Even the explosion at the Palace only killed a couple of the younger ones. I knew Benedict was planning to overthrow the Primus, but are you saying he was going to kill them? How?"

"I think he was planning to depose Sol with intrigue rather than strength, but Drew… Well, long story short: Ben has been trying to kill me because it would kill Drew, but all of that's kind of irrelevant now that the bond has broken."

"So that much of what he told us was true? That the bond links people's lives and lets a Silver heal their lover? That's how you got the brand?"

"Yes," I said quietly, "it's true."

Drew had silvered for me, delicate silver threads suffusing his irises, an extension of the silver filaments in the whites of his eyes that the Silver were named for. With that superficial change came something deeper, a love that formed a bond from him to me that tied his life to mine, dooming him to die with me. The bond also gave Drew the power to heal me and even to bring me back from the brink of death. When Ben nearly succeeded in his mission to kill me, Drew was able to save me, leaving a shining Silver handprint over my heart: a brand that pulled me to him, that tied me to him as he was tied to me.

But I didn't love him. The emotion was compelled from me, forced by intangible magic. It wasn't real. It didn't mean anything.

And I knew what it felt like when it was real, when it burned in your veins and cowed you with its realisation, crushing your pride and leaving you weak. Admitting to that and feeling something that humbling meant casting yourself not as the heroine or the victim of the play of your life, but as the fool: human, fallible and wrong. The feeling I had known was visceral and brutal, its object terrible and uncompromising.

But I had left it behind me, along with everything else in my life, and there was no way that it would ever be mine again.

"The bond and the brand… they're both gone now," I said.

Everything was gone.

"Something… odd happened last night," I continued. "I was hurt in the explosion, badly hurt, maybe dying. The next thing I know I wake up covered in bits of shrapnel that have apparently been pushed out of my skin, the brand's gone and then Drew tells me the bond's broken too."

"So, what? Something broke the bond?" Oliver asked.

"I don't know. As far as I can work out, the brand burned itself out healing me, and that's what broke the bond. Either way, they're gone now."

"Hmm."

I remembered a conversation I had had with Oliver earlier in the week and a thought struck me.

"You said you had a way to break the bond," I said.

"Yeah, I did," he agreed, reluctantly.

"Well? Would it explain this?"

"No," he said. "Well, actually, maybe, but I wouldn't recommend taking it as gospel given that Benedict told me it. He said that we could stop your heart for a few seconds, and that it would break the bond, but that we could bring you back quickly enough that the bonded Silver wouldn't die. I didn't know which Silver we were talking about, of course, but I wouldn't be surprised if Benedict was just spinning me a line to get to you."

"I guess," I said, "but it could explain it." I looked into Oliver's eyes for a moment, the rain running along his cheekbones and across his lips. "Maybe I died, and the brand brought me back."

"Maybe," he conceded.

"Did you really think I would ever have trusted you and Ben to bring me back after stopping my heart?" I asked incredulously.

"Ha! Yeah, maybe that was a bit of a stretch. I hope you trust me a bit better now, though. I meant it when I said we're in this together."

He pushed a sodden lock of hair away from my face and pulled me close against him, trying his best to shield me from the downpour. I didn't know how to respond to the intimate gesture, but it hadn't felt awkward, so I just kept quiet and let him shelter me.

"And it was the Secundus?" he asked after a few moments, the sound rumbling through his chest and against my cheek. "He's in love with you?"

The blunt question took me by surprise.

"He was, or so he said. I don't know."

It hadn't felt like love should. Love shouldn't blink out in a second, just because the magic is gone. But apparently that was exactly what had happened with the bond, a love built on nothingness crumbling and dissipating like sandcastles in the tide. And I had no idea how it had happened.

The way Drew had spoken to me last night had made it perfectly clear to me that there was nothing between us now, just the ghost of lost emotion for him to mourn.

"And the Primus protected you because of the bond to the Secundus?" Oliver asked.

"Perhaps," I replied.

I didn't know how to explain my relationship with Sol. He'd given me the choker to wear, a mark of his protection, a beautiful piece of black lace threaded with a lily pattern picked out in silver. It wasn't the only one he had given away, but if I was to believe him then it was the only one that had mattered, the only collar that marked possession of more than simply the blood running in the veins of its wearer.

And I had wanted to be possessed by him, had been set on fire by his voice, by his scent, by his touch.

Until he had silvered for someone else.

"Either way," I continued, brushing aside thoughts I didn't want to deal with, "the bond should have kept me safe through the Casting. It should have guaranteed that I would turn Silver rather than Weeper. It was supposed to have kept both me and Drew safe from Ben; I wouldn't have been so easy to kill as a Silver."

"And now?" he asked quietly.

"I don't imagine Ben will have any interest in me anymore."

Much like the rest of the Silver, I thought.

"So there's some good news," he said, "but I meant with the Casting. What will happen now that the bond has broken?"

There was no way to back out. I had been signed up, my name sealed onto the Casting ledger with Drew listed as my sponsor, bound to participate.

"In six days' time," I said as reality settled in with crushing finality, "Drew will turn me into a Weeper."

CHAPTER II

After about half an hour the rain slowed and then stopped entirely, the sun breaking dramatically through the dark clouds that eventually cleared to reveal bright, blue skies beyond. We were through the remains of the city now, the truck moving quickly along well-travelled roads that had been cleared of debris. I tried to sit up in the lee of the cab, but the speed of the slipstream battered at me, catching at my hair and whipping it around my face. Instead, I lay back down next to Oliver, propping myself up on my elbows, and peeked over the edge of the truck bed at the landscape falling away behind us.

I could just make out the city skyline falling away in the distance, but the street along which we travelled was lined with rows of suburban houses fronting directly onto the main road, abandoned cars and other detritus stacked up against them as if they had been bulldozed to clear the way for our passage. The terraces on our left suddenly gave way to a large, tree-lined park, ominous shapes moving in the shade of their leafy avenues. However many Weepers had been drawn into the city, there were still more gathering in the spaces in between.

They raised their heads as we passed them by, following the motion with their bloodied eyes, before moving to trail us along the sheltered edges of the street. Raising myself higher on my elbows, I saw with dismay that they were not the only ones following us.

"We've been picking up stragglers since we hit the outskirts of the city," Oliver said as he followed my line of sight. "They're sticking to the dark where possible, but I've seen a few walking out on the pavement rather than risk losing us."

"Shit."

"I wouldn't worry; we're going too fast for any of them to stay with us for more than a couple of blocks. These ones probably just follow the farm trucks first one way, then the other, stuck in the middle between the city and the Farm, too slow to find either or to catch the vehicles on the road."

"Until we have to stop," I said, then wished I hadn't.

"We won't have to stop," he said, "but even if we do then they won't come close, not with the Silver at the wheel."

The park disappeared behind us, the Weepers left in our wake, but Oliver was right: they were gathered in this limbo in greater numbers, not knowing which direction to choose, their faces peering out from between the buildings and cars that we left behind us.

After a while the buildings thinned entirely, and we were driving through the countryside, birds calling and singing over our heads as they darted between trees and hedgerows that marked the boundaries of the road. We saw no Weepers at first, the open fields too exposed to hide them in the day time, but as the road plunged into dense woodland the light dimmed and suddenly they were massing around us.

My pulse raced, my eyes darting from one side of the other as I tracked their swarming movements. There were so many of them, pushing inexorably towards us, closing the circle.

I pushed myself tight up against the cab, as close to our Silver driver as possible with my hand still chained to the floor. The truck slowed to a crawl as the Weepers crowded in on every side. Oliver pulled me close to him and tried to push my head down onto his shoulder, but there was no way I was taking my eyes off the Weepers.

When I had last been this close to them, when Cam had been walking me through the city outside of the walls, the Weepers had never come nearer to us than about fifteen feet. I knew that they would stop at a distance because of the Silver behind us, knew that they would be backing off as the truck pushed forwards, and knew that they would not approach any closer, but as they clustered around us my nerve faltered.

There were hundreds of them coming out from behind the trees and bushes, pushing through the foliage towards the road. There were men, women and children in every state of health and decay, their clothing ranging from crisp, clean suits to ragged cotton clinging to emaciated frames, but they all had one thing in common: blood weeping from their eyes and hands dirtied with gore and filth.

I looked around in a panic and saw with horror that they were climbing the trees to either side of us and, following the branches until they arched over the truck, that they were poised directly above us. They were silhouetted against the sun above the tree canopies like sinister crows, waiting in an eerie stillness that was foreign to the normal, fluid movements of the Weepers, ready to plunge down to pin their prey.

We crawled on along the road as they orbited around us, but although we were pulling away, those behind us still seemed to be closing the gap.

"They're not stopping," I said in a strangled whisper.

"They'll stop," Oliver said, turning to point through the cab window at our backs. "Stop panicking. The driver is right there."

I looked around and reassured myself that our driver was, indeed, still in his seat, but that was little comfort when I felt a gentle thud on the back of the trailer. I spun around to see that one of the Weepers, a girl of about twelve wearing a ragged, floral dress, had climbed onto the bumper of the truck and was hanging on to the truck bed. As I watched, she swung one leg over into the trailer and perched on its edge, less than six feet from me, staring me down with a gaze that was so intent and full of hunger that I found it impossible to look away.

"Can I panic now?" I whispered snidely to Oliver.

As the girl stared me down, he hammered urgently on the window in the back of the cab. She was joined by a woman and a man, both clambering up onto the bumper and hanging off the edge of the trailer.

"Hey!" Oliver shouted. "Little help, here? Can you go any faster?"

The Silver looked around at us and then, shrugging nonchalantly, turned back to the road.

"Guess that's a no, then," I muttered under my breath, returning my attention to our unexpected hitchhikers.

The man's skin was so bruised and torn that it was impossible to tell how old he had been when he had been turned into a Weeper. His hair was thick and had been cut longer on top than at the sides, so it now hung in lank, matted clumps along his forehead. He was wearing a shirt, possibly white once upon a time, that was now dark with grime and ripped of its buttons, exposing horrific gashes across his hollowed stomach in a configuration that suggested they had been made by busy, digging fingers.

But it was the woman who drew my gaze. She had long, brown hair that fell in dirty waves around her scratched, bare shoulders. The remnants of a black dress with spaghetti straps covered her body, and she was wearing knee-high, flat-soled boots on her feet. I felt like I was looking into the future, a mirror of the woman I would become after the Casting: myself as a Weeper, a monster.

I clutched at the rings that hung on four silver chains around my neck: my parents' wedding rings and my mother's engagement ring. Their familiar weight and shape in my hand centred me. I wasn't a Weeper, not yet, and there was still time to change my fate, somehow.

The seconds ticked by in agony as the truck crept forwards, the Weepers staring across the horrifyingly short distance at us. They didn't seem to be in a hurry to come any closer, and the Weepers to either side of us were still keeping a pace or so away from the truck as it rolled along, so we hunkered back in the trailer as far as we could and tried to stay as central as possible.

A few minutes later the truck burst out of the woods, out of the circle of Weepers and into the daylight, the sunshine glaring against the chrome of the trailer. Our hitchhikers hung on for a few seconds, blood streaming freely from their eyes in the brightness, before dropping off the back of the vehicle as it sped off along the clear road. The woman was the last of the three to slink away under the shade of the trees, and I watched her turning back to follow our progress until a bend in the road obscured her from view.

Oliver and I shared a glance then slowly relaxed, uncoiling ourselves from the tight positions in which we had been holding ourselves.

"Shit," I said.

"Well, that was intense."

He ran his fingers through his hair, pushing the damp curls away from his face. The sun was heating the air around us, but not quickly enough to have dried us out yet.

"I've never seen them come that close before," I said, my eyes fixed on the dirty, bloody smears at the end of the trailer where they had climbed on board. "They can't have been more than about eight or ten feet from the Silver."

"Don't touch the blood," he said. "If it's theirs, then it's infectious."

"I know," I said irritably, before I registered the haunted look on his face. He was looking at the blood on the metal, but he was seeing something else entirely, his eyes staring wide and full of horror.

"Oliver?" I said gently.

He shook his head as if he were snapping himself back to the present.

"I wonder how far away we are?" he said, turning in his seat to look around us.

I followed his gaze and we both saw it at the same time:

another wall reaching across the landscape, this time in chains rather than stone. Through the links of the high perimeter fences we saw fields stretching off over the hills, huge hangers that looked like warehouses and breezeblock buildings laid out over a compound that spread beyond the distance to the horizon.

The road sloped down into a valley then climbed up the other side to the gate in the first of a series of three fences that bordered the Farm. They had looked flimsy from a distance, but as we approached we saw that they were reinforced with layer upon layer of metal bars driven into concrete footings. Given how many Weepers were gathered in the woods nearby, doubtless ready to congregate outside the fence as soon as the light dimmed, I found the scale of the fortifications reassuring, if a little intimidating. The stark, institutional atmosphere of the place made it feel like a prison rather than a farm.

I glanced over at Oliver and thought from his expression that he seemed to share my concern, but he quickly schooled his face into nonchalance when he saw me looking.

"I know you can take care of yourself, but I'll be here to look after you too," he said.

"You don't know that," I replied quietly, suddenly feeling as if I wasn't at all prepared for this. Sol had told me that I would survive this exile, but it had sounded more like a hope than a certainty. I was no longer under Sol or Drew's protection, and even if we weren't separated, how could Oliver stand against the Silver? We were utterly in their power, and I had been disowned by their Primus after the rebellion.

I wondered how big that would make the target on our backs.

The truck slowed as we approached the outer perimeter fence and I looked anxiously over my shoulder to see the gate sliding to one side to admit us. We drove through then stopped in front of the second fence about forty feet away from the first gate, which slid and slammed shut behind us on some kind of automated lock. There was a building to our right and in between the first two fences, a concrete and metal fabrication that looked like a huge garage. A truck similar to the one in which we were chained drove out from around the side of the building and drew up alongside us, the doors of the cab opening to disgorge two female Silver dressed in the utilitarian style I had come to associate with the Solis Invicti. Both had their brown hair tied back and away from their faces, bodies and expressions hard as stone.

"These are the rebels?" the taller of the two asked our driver as he stepped out of the truck.

I was tempted to object to the title, but Oliver caught my eye and indicated with an economical gesture that it would be a suicidal move, so I capitulated. It was probably best to keep our mouths shut until we worked out what the score was.

"Yeah," the driver replied. "We had a couple of the Weepers up on the truck bed through the woods, so we'll need to get the vehicle washed down and these two quarantined."

"They're not bunking with the others anyway," said the second of the women.

I glanced over at Oliver anxiously, thinking that this sounded suitably ominous.

"You want a hand loading them out?" the driver asked as all three of them came round to the side of the trailer.

"No, thanks, we've got it. Truck five is loaded up and ready to go back to the city when you are."

"No problem. Here are the handcuff keys. Oh, and before I forget," he added, pulling a piece of paper out of his pocket, "here's a letter from the Primus for Ada. Important, I think."

"She'll be delighted," said the shorter of the two, sharing a meaningful look with the other woman.

"See you tomorrow, then," he said, waving at the women as he walked off towards the hanger.

"Okay," the taller woman said, turning her attention to us, finally acknowledging our presence. "First thing: life here is going to be difficult for you. I strongly advise you both only to speak when spoken to, and to make yourselves as unobtrusive as possible. You make life easier for the guards, and they won't make life harder for you. That's pretty much the only concession you're likely to get."

Punishment duty at the Farm was starting to sound a lot like imprisonment after all. I felt that my worst fears had been confirmed: they were going to destroy us here.

"Second thing: the Casting's coming up next week and we've been told one of you is signed up. We're not allowed to know which one of you it is, or who the sponsor is, until the Casting itself, but we're making provision for whichever one of you it is to see your sponsor daily, as required by the rituals."

Oliver and I shared a glance: so the Casting was still going ahead after all, and they were still keeping the roster sealed, but I hadn't realised that I was going to have to see Drew on a daily basis. That was going to be awkward as hell.

"In the circumstances," she continued, "I can't imagine that you'll make it through, but rules are rules. Third and final thing: quarantine. For the next twenty-four hours we can't let you come into contact with the rest of the humans here, but in any case you'll be isolated for most of the time that you spend in this facility. Questions?"

I had plenty of questions, and I imagined that Oliver did too, but none that I felt at liberty to ask. We both kept quiet and shook our heads.

"Good, then let's get you set up," she said, reaching over me to unfasten our handcuffs. "I recommend that you avoid the rear of the trailer and jump out over the sides of the truck if you don't want to be joining the Weepers by sundown."

The metal pulled mercilessly at my abraded skin as I slipped it out of the bracelet. It had rubbed a welt across the tattoo on the inside of right wrist, the stylised 'SI' that had been the mark of the city, the sign that I was part of Sol's house. I wondered whether that was still the case, or if the Farm had its own house, its own ruler.

Hopping down onto the damp grass while the two women helped Oliver out of the other side of the truck, I went to his side as quickly as I could and took his uninjured arm over my shoulder so he could walk without assistance from the Silver. He smiled at me gratefully and we made our way slowly towards the building together, the women leading the way through a door set in the side facing the outer fence.

The building was set up for decontamination: a large open room for hosing down vehicles and a smaller room with showers for hosing down humans. We were led past rows of trucks and armoured cars to a door at the far end of the building that opened into a changing room with benches on one side and a row of showerheads on the other. There were no niceties here like hot water, and the room was open plan and unisex. We were both unceremoniously stripped of our ragged clothing and Oliver was relieved of his bandages, which was no great loss since they were soaked through.

Neither of us protested, but I looked away awkwardly as Oliver's trousers hit the floor, fixing my eyes on the wall of the shower area as the shorter of the women cut the remaining scraps of material from my body and tossed them into a plastic bag. I wrapped my arms around myself in an attempt to cover my nakedness, but it wasn't much use.

"You'd better get used to it," the taller Silver said to me. "You're going to have to get comfortable with each other pretty quickly where you're going."

The other woman laughed once, a hard sound that reverberated sharply around the unfurnished room.

I shared a glance with Oliver. This was sounding less and less promising.

"Necklace," the shorter woman demanded of me brusquely.

I stared back at her, curling my fingers around the rings that were hanging at my neck, and shook my head desperately. There was no way I was handing over my parents' rings.

Her expression softened slightly and she pulled a small envelope from her pocket.

"I'm sorry, but we have to take it. We'll keep it safe for you until you're released."

I shook my head again, fisting my hand until the precious metal cut into the skin of my palm. Even if I managed to get out of the Casting alive, there was no way I would ever be released from here. Our sentence was indefinite, which I figured was just a euphemism for 'forever'. If I handed it over now, I was certain I would never see it again.

"Emmy," Oliver said quietly from behind me. "They have to take it."

I looked over my shoulder at him, his torso stripped from its bandages to reveal the raw, stitched wound underneath, and he nodded at me slowly, willing me with his eyes to hand the jewellery over.

"Okay," I whispered as I turned back to the Silver woman, but when I raised my hands to unfasten the clasps of the chains on which the rings were suspended, I found that my fingers were trembling too much to cooperate.

"Let me," Oliver said, taking a step further towards me so that I could feel the heat radiating from his chest against my bared back. He gently released the silver chains from my neck, each of them falling one by one into the palm of my hand until I held all four chains and the three rings. I passed them reluctantly to the Silver woman, who slid them into the envelope and tucked it away into her pocket.

I wondered what would happen to it now, where they would keep it.

Oliver rested his hands on my shoulders and squeezed them gently, an otherwise comforting gesture that felt starkly intimate in our current state of nudity.

"Right," said the other woman, "showers."

The water was freezing, stripping the warmth from my body and raising goose pimples all over my skin, so showering next to Oliver wasn't as awkward as it could have been. Both of us were preoccupied with the desire to get the experience over with as soon as possible. We soaped and shampooed quickly, sluicing the mud and grime from our bodies and hair until we were clean enough to satisfy the Silver.

After we had towelled down they examined every inch of

our skin minutely for any wounds or scrapes, presumably looking for evidence of Weeper bites, whilst we stood opposite each other with our limbs outstretched, trying not to look at each other's bodies. That was awkward.

I was declared clear after only a minute or so, which was unsurprising given that the brand had healed up everything except the cuts on my wrists from the chafing of the handcuffs, but Oliver was still covered in grazes and puncture marks from the explosion. The Silver who had been examining me handed me what looked like a pair of blue hospital scrubs, then went to help her colleague checking Oliver's cuts whilst I pulled them on.

I sat down on the bench and turned to the side to comb out my wet hair with my fingers in an attempt to give Oliver some privacy as they continued their examination, prodding and squinting at each scratch on his skin, but after a few minutes my gaze drifted back over towards him. He was watching me, the corners of his mouth twitching up into a smile when he saw I was looking his way.

It's okay, he mouthed at me. Relax.

I wasn't sure how he expected me to do that in the circumstances, or how he was managing it himself, but I forced a smile back at him as the Silver finally brought their scrutiny to an end and passed him his own set of scrubs.

They asked us each our shoe sizes then passed us canvas trainers and socks to put on before leading us back out of the building and into their truck, handing us up into the trailer bed. This time they didn't bother cuffing us to the floor. After all, where were we going to go?

The gates in the perimeter fences were staggered, so we were driven round the edge of the Farm between them for a few minutes before we reached the second gate. The journey brought us past fields and warehouses, moving us ever closer to the cluster of buildings that appeared to be the heart of the compound. The second gate, unlike the first, was opened by a Silver guard who operated it manually rather than remotely.

"Are these the prisoners?" he asked the Silver women as

we drove through.

"Yep, going round to the new block," came the reply.

"Ada wants to see them before you put them in."

"Is she going to come out to the gate?"

"I think so."

"Alright then."

We drove on between the second and third fences until we reached the final gate, which was marked by a huge, single-storey, breezeblock building. We were unloaded on the other side, finally within the confines of all three fences, and were shepherded into the squat building, Oliver limping along with his arm around my shoulders. Inside, it was a bizarre labyrinth of corridors and corners that made me wonder whether it had been deliberately designed that way to ensure that anyone brought within it would lose their way.

The thought was unsettling.

We were led through the twisting passages until I was utterly disorientated. Our destination was a plain, wooden door, just like tens of others that we had passed on our way here. One of the Silver women knocked briefly then opened it, ushering Oliver and me through and closing it behind us.

We were on our own, apparently.

"Sit down, please."

The room was small and clinical in nature with a doctor's couch against one wall and a desk against another. There were a couple of chairs off to one side, in which the man who had spoken indicated that we should sit. He was perhaps in his late forties, hair greying at the temples, with a New Zealand accent that surprised me in the context. More surprising still, he appeared to be human, apparently an exception to the 'no human contact' rule during our quarantine.

"I'm Dr Tanner," he said, "and I do the admissions here. I need to clear your blood to make sure you aren't carriers, get you booked in to the system and then give you a quick checking over. Who's first?"

"I don't mind going first," Oliver volunteered with a shrug, so I helped him into the chair nearest to the doctor before sitting down next to him.

Dr Tanner turned to his work swiftly and efficiently, putting a small, cylindrical device to Oliver's fingertip and pressing a button at its end. It was the same sort of gadget that the Silver had used in the city to test our blood for infection, and to identify us. The doctor turned the device on its side and read the information that appeared on a small screen.

"You are Oliver Faulkner, and you last donated just after the Revelation. Correct?"

"Yes," Oliver answered.

"Good," the doctor said as he plugged the device into his computer, apparently downloading the data. "Well, you're not a carrier, so that's good news, but we'll have to quarantine you until tomorrow to make sure you aren't infected. Hop up on the couch and let's take a look at your injuries."

The Silver clearly didn't care much for human modesty because, as in the showers, there was no privacy curtain in the room. Nevertheless, Oliver didn't seem at all abashed as he stripped out of his clothes once more. The doctor re-dressed his shoulder wound for him and pronounced that his leg would heal on its own, but gave him a pair of crutches to help him get around.

As Oliver swung his way back over to the seats, fully-clothed once more, I shifted over so that I was now in the seat closest to Dr Tanner. He took my right hand and pressed the device to my finger, but when he turned it to the side to read the screen he frowned with confusion.

"You're not a carrier…" he said, shaking the device in frustration.

I sighed. This wasn't the first time I had been through this.

"My blood's not in the system," I said.

"Oh?" he asked.

Shame bubbled up through me as I tried to think of a way to express myself without sounding like I had been some kind of Silver prostitute. Nothing came to mind.

"I was one of the Primus's chained girls," I said, trying to suppress my frustration as my cheeks flushed. Apparently my shame reflex could cope with nudity just fine, but the admission that I had been a blood bag for the Primus was too much for it to handle.

"Ah," the doctor said quietly. "So you would be Emilia, then."

Oh, god. Apparently I was famous, and not in a good way. I cringed and nodded at him.

"I'm afraid there's been a broadcast, a recording of what happened in the city earlier today. You might find yourselves the centre of attention for a while. The Silver here... well, they're not happy."

"We did everything we could to stop the explosions, you know," Oliver chimed in vehemently. "What's happening here is Emmy being thrown under the bus by a couple of homicidal Silver with a grudge."

I was touched by the protective outburst, but it wasn't going to help us now. The doctor looked from one of us to the other then sighed heavily before replying.

"That's as may be, and I can well believe it knowing what goes on in this place, but I wouldn't go around repeating what you've just told me. It won't make either of you popular, trust me."

I took Oliver's hand in mine and he settled down, holding his anger and frustration simmering beneath the surface.

"We'll keep our heads down," I said quietly.

"Well, let's get you properly admitted. I'm afraid we'll have to take a donation from you as well since you haven't given one before."

"It doesn't count when it goes straight to the Primus, then?" I asked derisively. He'd twice taken my blood, and Drew had taken it once, not to mention the night Ben had arranged for me to be drained by one of his chums, so all told I felt that I had already given more than my fair share.

"I'm sorry; your blood screen shows you're in good shape, so I can't try to argue that you've donated too recently," he replied as he plugged the device back into his computer.

"However, I'll check with my counterpart in the city, so we can delay it until tomorrow. Full name?"

"Emilia Nelson," I said.

"Age?"

"Twenty-eight."

"Birthday?"

"Twenty-seventh of June. If you need my star sign too, it's Cancer."

The doctor raised a sardonic eyebrow at me.

"Any medical conditions?" he continued.

I wondered whether to mention the magic healing brand, but decided that it was probably irrelevant at this stage.

"Not that I'm aware of," I replied.

"Okay, then let's have a look at that wrist. Any other injuries?"

I shook my head as I offered him my right hand so he could examine the wound that cut across the tattoo. He cleaned and bound it for me, and as he did so I noticed that he bore a twin of the tattoo on the inside of his own wrist.

"The Farm is the same house as the city, then?" I asked.

"Oh, yes," he replied. "We're all subject to the Primus here, although we see less of him. He visits a couple of times a week."

My stomach flipped with excitement. He'd be here. Maybe I'd get to see him. But reality chased close in on its heels with the realisation that he had sent me away, that he had a consort now to occupy his time. He had thrown me aside, an old toy that failed to hold his attention any longer. He was in love with someone else.

CHAPTER III

Making their rounds in the city the sentinels found me;
they beat me, they wounded me,
they took away my mantle,
those sentinels of the walls.

- The Song of Solomon

The taller of the Silver women was waiting outside the room for us when we left Dr Tanner's office. She led us further into the labyrinth, or perhaps out of it; by this point I had no idea where we were in the building. Oliver was now able to make his way under his own speed, swinging himself along on his crutches, but after a short trial run he left one of them behind with the doctor because using both pulled at his shoulder wound.

This time the Silver woman accompanied us into the room to which she ushered us, acknowledging its occupant with a respectful nod of the head. This room was much grander than the first, more like an audience chamber than an office, but the furnishings still had a military air about them, chosen for strength and practicality rather than for appearance.

"Ada," our Silver escort said as she closed the door behind us, "these are the human prisoners. Also," she added, handing over an envelope, "here is a letter for you from the Primus."

The woman stood from her seat behind a large desk to take the letter and indicated that Oliver and I should take the two seats opposite her. She was dressed neatly in a skirt suit and looked as if she were in her early fifties, but as she was Silver her apparent age had little bearing on her actual years. She had greying blonde hair that was cut into a gentle bob, a fringe sweeping back from her face in a style that looked as though it required a lot of hairspray to appear so effortless. Her blue eyes fixed on the letter in her hand with an avaricious glance, excitement flaring in her gaze for a second before she forced it away, composing her features into a suitably neutral expression.

"Thank you, Martha," Ada said to our escort. "Will you be heading straight back to the city?"

"As soon as Mr Faulkner and Ms Nelson are safely installed in their quarters," she replied.

Watching Ada carefully, I saw interest flicker momentarily in her eyes, perhaps noting the formality our escort had used when referring to us. I was surprised myself at the Silver's respectful tone, and wondered what she hoped to achieve by it.

"Very well," Ada replied. "We are always honoured to receive a visit from the Invicti, but of course we understand that the Primus has need of your talents elsewhere."

"Indeed."

There was a pause, the atmosphere stretching tensely around us, and I wondered what Ada was waiting for. It felt as if there was an undercurrent of which we were unaware, a subtext to the exchange that we were unable to understand. Was Ada expecting Martha to leave? Martha had pointedly taken up a position behind us, against the back wall of the room, and it was clear that she was going nowhere.

"Very well," Ada repeated, turning to Oliver and me and

reclaiming her seat once more. She glanced at Oliver briefly before moving her attention to me. I felt as scrutinised as I had whilst Martha and her friend had been examining me for cuts, Ada's eyes raking over every inch of me as if she were cataloguing each flaw. She pressed her lips together, clearly unsatisfied with what she saw, and cleared her throat delicately before speaking.

"I am the director of this facility, with oversight and control of everything that goes on here. In terms of your confinement, you will be kept in a separate building from the rest of the inhabitants of the Farm. That building will also serve as your holding area whilst you are quarantined, so you will remain there for the rest of the day until tomorrow lunchtime. Your duties will begin tomorrow afternoon, as will the visits from the sponsor of whichever of you is participating in the Casting. Any questions?"

She smiled at us, but there was a predatory edge to it that made my skin crawl, and I felt like she was holding back because Martha was here with us. Suddenly, I very much hoped that the Invicti would be visiting us regularly.

Oliver and I both shook our heads silently. If I had been unwilling to ask questions of Martha, I was doubly reticent in this face of this new Silver. Something about her was off. There was an edge to her tone that made me want to get out of her presence as soon as possible.

"Very well," she said again, standing from her seat once more. We took her cue and did likewise. "I will leave Martha to see you to your accommodations."

As it turned out, the cell into which we were eventually escorted had been somewhat oversold.

It was a small, rectangular building set close against the internal perimeter fence, maybe five or ten miles away from the gate. It was surrounded by three fences of its own, each spaced about fifteen feet apart. However, unlike the perimeter fences, these curved over to form a dome above the building, completely enclosing the space. The building itself was a simple concrete and breezeblock construction with two doors, one on each side of its longest face, and a couple of barred windows. It was planted in the centre of a circle of grass with perhaps a hundred feet of space on each side between it and the innermost of its surrounding fences.

"I don't know quite how they're expecting you to ninja your way out of here," Martha said to us as she helped us down from the trailer, "or where they think you would go, but you should be aware that these fences are electrified."

I eyed the chain links cautiously and took a step further away. I didn't feel like frying today.

Another truck had approached from the centre of the compound, apparently coming to meet us, and it parked up next to ours. A couple of Silver dressed in a green uniform stepped down from the cab, one woman and one man.

"Good afternoon, Invicti," the woman said as both of the new arrivals snapped off salutes. Oliver and I shared an apprehensive glance. It looked like these two were taking their guard responsibilities a bit too seriously, which couldn't bode well for us.

The woman was too thin for her moderate height, her dark hair scraped back into a severe bun at the base of her skull and her sharp features jutting from a face that looked cold and unkind. In contrast, the man had a dissolute appearance: his belly hung over his belt, his clothes looked as though he had slept in them and his balding scalp and double chin made his pointed head resemble nothing so much as a boiled egg nestled in a dollop of mayonnaise.

"Mark, Tessa," Martha said, acknowledging them with a nod of her head.

"The gates and electric charges are on a time lock," said the guard called Mark, "but we've radioed ahead and they should be activated shortly."

As he spoke, the gate in the first of the three fences slid open to admit us. Mark gestured expansively towards the entrance and the shorter of the Invicti stepped through first.

"After you," Martha said to Oliver and me, so we obediently walked into the first ring of the fences. Once

Martha and the two guards had stepped in behind us the first gate slid shut, the second one opening shortly afterwards to admit us into the next ring.

"They're set so that each gate will only stay open for a prescribed period," Mark explained as we stepped through towards the third and final gate, "and no two gates can be open at the same time. Each fence is reinforced and electrified, and the walls of the cell block are reinforced concrete."

Martha was right: this was complete overkill to hold Oliver and me. What did they think we were, superhuman? Even if we did turn Weeper overnight, there was no way we would have been able to get through the walls of the block, let alone even the first ring of the fence.

It had me wondering who this cell had really been designed for. The thought that it might ultimately be intended to hold the Silver was a worrying one in this politically unstable environment, but what could really contain the Silver if they wanted to break out? I had little doubt that certainly the older amongst them would make light work of escaping from our holding cell, but maybe it was a different story for the younger Silver, the newest Silver. With the Casting fast approaching, I had to wonder whether they were worried about what they might create.

"So this is your new home," Mark announced to Oliver and me with a snicker as we walked through the final gate and into the caged arena that held the building. "Let me show you around."

He led us across the grass to the door set towards the left side of the building, punching in a code to release the lock.

"This door is not only time-locked," he said proudly, "but it also requires direct code entry for added security."

I couldn't see what purpose double-locking would serve, particularly when any of the Silver could simply smash through the reinforced wall, but I smiled politely and played along. It seemed to be what he wanted, apparently not recognising that it was strange to expect your prisoners to approve of the strength of your security system, but then we weren't really his intended audience. His eyes raked Martha up and down, making no effort to hide the fact that he was taking in the snug fit of her black shirt and the way her charcoal cargo pants flared to accommodate her hips. I watched with amusement as she tried valiantly to quash a sneer of contempt.

"Impressive," the other of the Invicti interrupted, coming to Martha's rescue, "but I'm afraid that we really must be getting back to the city."

"Of course, of course," Mark crooned at her.

Tessa stepped over to the door, holding it wide, and jerked a thumb over her shoulder.

"In you get," she said to Oliver and me. "See you in the morning."

The moment we had stepped through the door it was slammed quickly behind us, the code lock clicking shut, followed by the bolt of the time lock sliding home a few seconds later. We could hear them working their way back through the gates, the clunking and whining of the mechanism filtering through the air vent set into the thick, metal facing of the door.

We looked around, taking in the Spartan nature of our new accommodation. One thing was abundantly clear: the cell had only been intended to house one prisoner at a time.

The central room was small, a square box about eight feet across, with a single bed and a thin mattress. A small pile of threadbare sheets and towels had been put on top of it, together with a paper bag holding a bar of soap, some bread, a couple of apples and some cheese, but there were no pillows or blankets. There were a couple of narrow windows at head height, one next to the door and the other on the wall opposite. Although it looked like they would open inwards, they were small and there were bars blocking the frames on the outside.

There didn't seem to be any lights in the building, but there was a small speaker set into the ceiling, presumably to carry broadcasts to us in the same way that they were transmitted within the city. I wondered how much we had missed during our journey today and our absence last night. What had been said to the world about us and our role in the events of the past twenty-four hours?

On the wall to our left a door led into a tiny bathroom about four feet wide with a toilet, a tap and a showerhead sticking out of the walls. There was a drain set in the centre of the floor, but no sink or shower tray.

On the wall opposite the bathroom was a locked door that we couldn't open. Judging from the dimensions of the building, the room on the other side would be about the same size as the central room in which we were standing. I wondered whether it was a mistake, if we were supposed to have a room each, but there was a panel set into the top of the heavy, metal door that looked as though it might be a hatch that opened from the other side.

"Do you think it's an observation room?" I asked Oliver as I prodded at the panel to see whether I could make it move. It was stuck tight.

"Who knows?" he said. "That Silver wasn't wrong about us having to get comfortable with each other, was she?"

We eyed the bed. It was small for one person, but for two it was going to be a challenge.

"We could top and tail," I suggested.

"Your feet in my face? No thanks."

"Ha! I think I should probably be more worried than you about smelly feet."

"Yeah," he said with a look of mock concern, "that's what I'm trying to tell you."

"Well, I think you're just going to have to get used to them," I said, surveying our claustrophobic cell, "because you're stuck in here with me."

Although maybe not for long, I thought. Oliver was more than likely to find himself without a cellmate in a week's time.

"What's wrong?" he asked.

With the mess that we had found ourselves in, I was

surprised that he would ask.

"What isn't wrong?" I replied.

"Well, we're alive, which is more than I can say for the rest of the humans who were sent outside the city walls today. And I know you're worried about the Casting, but we've got time to figure something out."

He hobbled over to me, dropping his crutch down onto the floor, and pulled me towards him with his good arm.

"We'll get through this somehow," he whispered as I wrapped my arms around him and laid my head on his chest, taking the comfort he offered. Beneath the laundry detergent from the scrubs, I could smell the sunshine on his skin; a warm, clean scent of gentle citrus and salt.

"We've come this far," he added.

"Further than most," I said, thinking about everyone I had lost: Sarah, Jeff, Danny and, most recently, Alice. Then there was Mary. I never found out whether or not she had made it out of the explosion alive, whether her teenaged girls had lost their mum.

But I wasn't the only one who had lost friends and family. Oliver had lost his brother, Graham, who had been gunned down in retaliation for shots fired against the Silver by the rebels. I suspected that the shooting had been orchestrated by Ben in order to manipulate the humans, and I wondered whether Oliver had yet come to terms with the fact that it was likely his own alliance with Ben that had designated his brother as the target.

And I had no idea how many others he might have lost in the Revelation, how many other deaths weighed on his conscience.

He squeezed me tight for a moment then released me, hopping over towards the bed.

"Come on," he said. "Let's get the sheets on this at least, and then we'll have somewhere moderately comfortable to sit."

I hung the towels on the back of the bathroom door then helped Oliver to put a sheet on the bed. There was only one other in the pile, so we left it folded for the moment, ready to use as a cover when night fell. Oliver plunked himself down on the mattress and stretched out his leg, clearly glad of the respite from limping around on his injured limb, but I was restless and I couldn't settle.

The room was heating up quickly, so I opened the windows to let a breeze through, but after that there was nothing to do. I stared through the close-set bars on each side of the building, hoping to see some kind of activity, any movement, but there was nothing. There were no vehicles moving around, no people visible, and the aspect of the windows was such that I could see only the fence and the fields stretching into the distance.

"What time do you think it is?" I asked Oliver.

He shrugged.

"About five o'clock, maybe?" I said, trying to guess from the angle of the sun.

"Maybe. Maybe a bit later."

I sighed and sat down next to him on the bed, shucking my shoes. I propped myself up with my back against the wall as I ran my fingers through my hair, trying to tease the knots out as it dried in the warm air. Once I'd done the best job I could, I plaited it back and away from my face, leaving the end loose. It would come undone eventually without a tie, but it would do for now.

"How's the leg?" I asked.

"Feeling a bit better, actually. Maybe it's all relative, because my shoulder is killing me."

A few minutes passed in silence, each of us lost in our own thoughts.

"Tell me about yourself," I said.

"Like what?"

"Well, what did you do? Where did you live? Where did you grow up and what was your childhood like? Anything; everything."

So, as we ate the bread and cheese, he did.

He'd grown up on the coast near Bournemouth with a

younger brother and sister. He told me about their summers on the beaches, their beautiful home set in a wild expanse of windswept countryside, and an upbringing that seemed idyllic until their father's long hours away at the office eventually drove their mother to an affair, and divorce. He told me of childhood arguments, playground bullies and career aspirations, and how they all crumbled into insignificance in the face of the acrimonious disassembly of the family that had raised him and his siblings.

They had gone with their father to live in the city, and from there Oliver had moved himself to Birmingham to study engineering. He'd been very successful, securing funding for a doctorate and then post-doctoral studies, followed by a good job in the midlands. But then his father suffered a minor stroke, which although not completely incapacitating had left him unable to manage on his own, bringing Oliver back to London just a month before the Revelation.

And there his story stopped, abruptly. So, as the light coming through the windows dimmed into the evening, I told him my own.

I told him about my studies in Oxford, about the deaths of my parents in a car crash and about Sean, the paranoid boyfriend who had left me, disappearing from his job and our home to escape a pile of debts that I hadn't known he owed. I started to talk about the club as it was before the Revelation, about Parker's and all the friends I had made and cherished during my short time there, but the aftermath of the explosion was too fresh in my mind for me to face mentally digging through the pile of rubble that the club had become to drag out the memories of the time before the Silver.

I trailed off into silence, unable to continue. Oliver pulled me towards him and down onto the bed, holding me close against him to stop me from falling off the narrow mattress.

"We don't have to talk about it," he whispered in the darkness.

A cool breeze blew across the room between the open windows, raising a chill on the exposed skin of my arms.

"It's all gone now," I said, "destroyed in the blast, and they're all dead. Everyone I knew is dead."

I felt numb, the enormity of the statement thudding into my chest. It wasn't as if I hadn't been aware of it before, but now my heart had suddenly recognised the reality of it. The past fortnight had felt like nothing so much as a nightmare, a dream peopled with demons and angels, fighting in a fantasy setting that bore a passing resemblance to a world I had once known. My family and friends had been a memory lingering in that place, filling it with a sense of warmth and familiarity that had been destroyed along with the club and the Palace.

Our new world was harsh and cold, shaded in grey and silver, missing the colour and light that had made it shine. But where everything else was dull and muted, there was one Silver who had burned through it, sharp and hard as ice.

"Everyone I knew is gone, too," Oliver said quietly. I put my hand over his where it lay over my stomach and squeezed it gently. He intertwined his fingers with mine, holding on to me as though my hand was a lifeline.

Oliver was right: all we had in this place was each other. There was no point in thinking about next week, about the Casting and what it might bring. Either I'd turn into a Weeper, in which case I had only a week left to live, or Martha was right and I wouldn't make it through the selection process. Either way, now that we were on our own, pushed out of the nascent society that had promised to protect us, we only had each other, in this room, and it was pointless to hope that we would be able to get out of it.

We just had to find a way to make that enough to last us for the rest of our lives, however long they might be.

CHAPTER IV

When I woke it was dark outside, but I couldn't tell how long we had been asleep, whether it was the evening or the following morning. Oliver's arms were still around me, but he'd shifted a little during his sleep so that his wounded shoulder was stretched back and away to rest against the wall. Without the benefit of a pillow, my head was hanging down at an awkward angle that had put a colossal crick in my neck.

I rolled onto my back, balancing precariously on the edge of the mattress, and tried to get comfortable.

Then I realised what had woken me up.

There was a noise coming from the open window above the bed, a quiet scratching that was determined and rhythmic, rasping and squeaking. I froze still, straining my ears to pick up the sounds above the quiet rush of Oliver's breathing, and realised that it wasn't only his breathing that I was hearing.

"Oliver," I whispered urgently as I slid off the mattress and out of his arms, crouching down next to the bed to shake him awake. "Get over here."

The scant moonlight from the window opposite the bed shone on the surface of his eyes, and as soon as I realised he was alert I grabbed his arm and pulled him off the bed towards me.

"What's wrong?" he mumbled.

"Something's outside."

I felt him crouch down next to me, my eyes fixed on the window as I tried to make out shapes in the darkness. I could see the gentle glow of the moonlight reflecting off the pane of the window that was opened inwards high above the bed, and I could just about make out the darker square of the window itself, but from this perspective I couldn't see the bars or the outside world beyond them.

"I can't hear anything," he said.

Then there was the scratching again. It sounded like something was scraping and tapping at the window frame and the bars covering it.

"Can you see it?" I whispered, squinting into the darkness.

"No."

We both fell silent and listened for a few seconds, both holding our breath. But someone else wasn't.

"It sounds like there's someone out there," he said.

He moved beside me, and when he spoke again his voice came from above my head.

"Who's there?" he asked loudly.

An unearthly howl filled the room and the scrabbling noise from the window redoubled, joined by clanging thuds as something battered against the bars.

"Shit!" Oliver shouted over the noise in a panicked voice. "Close the other window!"

I rushed across the room and slammed the window shut quickly, latching it tight as Oliver did the same with the one above the bed. Unfortunately it didn't block out the noise, muffling it rather than silencing it.

"Bloody hell," he said incredulously as the creature outside thumped against the building. "They've put fucking Weepers in here with us."

"What?"

"Well it's not like it could have got in here on its own. How far apart were those bars?"

"Er, I don't know," I said, feeling pretty shaken up, "about an inch I guess."

"Well why the fuck did they go to the trouble of quarantining us if they're just going to shove a fucking Weeper outside where it can spit blood into our cell?"

He was pacing around the tiny room, gesticulating wildly in desperate fury.

"I don't know," I said redundantly as the pounding outside seemed to shake the building. That had to be my imagination, I thought. I sincerely hoped that the Weeper wasn't actually capable of hammering through the walls.

"Fuck!" Oliver shouted as he walked back over to the window above the bed. "I can't see enough to tell whether or not there's any blood here. We're going to have to wait until the sun comes up."

"It'll be okay," I said calmly.

"How can you say that? You don't know that. I was right under the window. It could be on my skin. I could get infected."

"And if you do, then what exactly do you propose that we do about it?" I asked angrily. "We're stuck in here together, so either both of us are going to be Weepers or neither of us will. That's just the way it is."

He was quiet for a moment, and then I heard the bedsprings creak as he sat down on the mattress.

"I don't want to hurt you," he whispered, barely loud enough for me to hear over the Weeper's racket. "I don't want to turn into one of them."

"Neither do I," I said as I took a seat next to him and put my arm around his shoulders. For me, though, it was practically inevitable. Even if we got through the night safely, I didn't have long to remain human.

"I think chances are good that we're clear," I continued. "I didn't feel any blood."

"We'll see," he replied.

We sat together in tense silence for five minutes or so as the Weeper battered at the bars of the window. Eventually, as it became clear that it wasn't making any progress in breaking through, I started to relax. I was crashing hard in the aftermath of the adrenaline rush from our rude awakening, the tightness dissipating from my muscles to leave me shaky and exhausted. I felt like I really needed to lie down.

"Let's move the bed away from the windows and try to get back to sleep," I said. "It's been a long day and I can't imagine tomorrow's going to be any better."

Also, I thought, if I was going to turn into a Weeper then I'd rather that it happened while I was sleeping.

Oliver didn't protest, and after a lot of cursing in the darkness we finally got the bed turned around and pushed up against the door that led to what we were thinking of as the observation room. I clambered in and pulled Oliver after me, dragging the spare sheet over us to ward off the worst of the night's chill. He settled onto his back and put his good arm around my shoulders, turning me onto my side so that my head was cushioned on his chest, one arm lying across his stomach.

The Weeper outside was still throwing himself against the window, but with less force and frequency. It was loud enough to stop me from falling asleep, but it had gentled sufficiently that I had hopes that it would quieten down soon.

Oliver's reactions to the Weepers were puzzling me. The Weepers themselves didn't seem to concern him more than they did anyone else, but he was paranoid about the blood, almost hysterical at the thought that either of us might become infected by drops from the window or from the smears on the end of the trailer.

"You've seen it happen, haven't you?" I whispered, struck by a sudden insight.

"What?"

"You've seen someone turn into a Weeper."

I felt his body fall still next to me, his muscles taut.

If I hadn't been distracted by our new neighbour then I might have thought a little harder about asking him the question in the first place, and perhaps then I might have done so with a bit more tact, or not at all.

"Sorry," I said quickly. "I didn't mean to pry."

"No," he said after a moment, "it's okay. It's just not something I've told anyone else, my Revelation story."

"I don't expect you to."

"No," he whispered, "but it's about time I did, now that Graham… well, it's just us now."

"I'm sorry."

I felt him shrug.

"If I have to be imprisoned in a cell for the rest of my life, the company could be worse."

"Charmer," I whispered.

"You just wait. You have no idea how charming I can be, particularly in these attractive blue pyjamas."

"They certainly make a statement," I teased, playing along in an attempt to dispel his anxiety.

"And they're very convenient. You wouldn't believe how quickly I can get in and out of them."

I laughed softly, thinking back to the various states of undress I had seen him in over the course of the day.

"I've got a pretty good idea."

"I knew you were watching, you minx."

"Yeah," I replied dismissively, "but there wasn't much to see."

"Now that's just offensive," he said in an affronted tone. "You wait until it's light enough in here for me to refute that statement."

He pulled me closer, rolling me over his side so that my leg rested on his own, and stroked my hair back from my face. The thudding from outside was quieter now, the Weeper apparently losing energy or motivation, or both.

"I never thought you'd be like this," he said quietly.

"Like what?"

"I don't know. You were the girl who was always with the Silver, the Primus's pet human. I suppose I expected you to be vacuous, a nothing person."

"You've never met Sol if you think that's what he's into," I said.

"No, but now that I have, it makes sense. I don't think I really understood what Benedict meant when he said that you were like me, that you wanted to escape this. You're fun, but at the same time you're serious as death."

I wasn't sure that his description was entirely accurate, but I tried to take it as a compliment.

"Is that how you think of yourself?" I asked.

"I don't know," he said. "Maybe. But I chose the wrong thing to get serious about, fixated on the wrong cause, and now here we both are."

"I made the same mistake," I said quietly.

"Oh?" he asked.

So I told him my Revelation story. I started at the beginning, telling him how Drew had saved me from a Weeper attack and, unbeknownst to me, had silvered for me almost instantly. I told him how I had run from admission to the safe house, finding my way back to the club and to Sarah, Jeff and Danny, and how we, like the rebels, had planned to make our way outside of the walls of the safe zone to find a way to live on our own terms.

"But," I said, "Benedict got in the way. He found out that Drew had silvered for me and he followed me. He snapped Danny's neck while I watched, then he drained Jeff and Sarah and convinced me that Drew had killed them. We thought we could make a better life for ourselves, but if I had just done as Drew had asked in the first place, if I had just submitted at the start rather than attempting to rebel against the Silver, then all three of them would still be alive. They would never have been a target for Ben, and they would have been brought inside the safe house to live with the rest of the humans in the city.

"So do you see why I can't judge you for your failed uprising?" I said. "You never meant for anyone to get hurt either."

I thought about the hundreds of people that had died in the explosions in the city, of Graham, shot in the head to send a message to the rebels, but most of all I thought of Ella and

Alice, their feet swaying in the breeze as they hanged in chains on the front wall of the club. Those deaths were on both of our heads.

"Strange how much damage we can cause without even trying," I added in a whisper.

"None of us have a rule book for this situation," Oliver said. "The world's falling apart and we're just trying to find a way through. The biggest mistake we made was trusting the wrong Silver."

"The same one," I said wryly.

"And maybe we should have trusted some of the others a little more."

He was quiet for a minute or so, but just when I was starting to think that he had fallen asleep he spoke again.

"So here it is," he said, "my Revelation story. Ready?"

"Sure."

He paused, as if he were marshalling his thoughts.

"Well, it was Thursday evening, two weeks ago. You know that.

"So I had moved back in with my dad, and my brother and sister were there too. Lucy was just visiting for the night, staying over for an early meeting in the city the next morning, but Graham had come back for good about a week ago. He'd had a messy break up and he didn't have anywhere else to go, and dad was glad of the extra company.

"We were all watching TV with dad after dinner when the broadcast came on, interrupting a film we were watching. At first, we thought it was some kind of sick joke and just ignored it, but through the night we started to hear noises out in the street, and then in the early hours of the morning there was a pounding at our door. Apparently our area had been overrun by Weepers more quickly than had been expected, and the Silver were clearing us out and bussing us straight to the nearest safe house in Clapham. We didn't have any time to pack; we just walked straight onto the transports. I think part of me still thought it was a hoax until we heard the first howls of the Weepers following us as we drove away."

I shuddered a little as I thought about the Weeper outside the building, and of the howl that had ripped through the cell around us. Now it thudded softly, a beating drum that seemed to add urgency to Oliver's story.

"When we arrived at the supermarket," he continued, "a temporary safe house, the streets were jammed with vehicles and people crammed in all over the place. The Silver had set up a perimeter to get us all inside safely, but there had clearly been Weepers around earlier in the morning because there was blood everywhere. It was in pools on the street and dripping down the walls of the buildings. And we had no idea how infectious it was, so no one was avoiding it."

He shifted a little, adjusting his arm around me to relieve the pressure on his injured shoulder.

"Still," he continued, "we were unlucky. Graham and I helped dad out of the bus we'd been driven in and we headed for the supermarket, Lucy leading the way, but when she stepped up onto the pavement her heel got caught on the kerb and she went down. She saved herself with her palms, but not before one of her hands had slid through a puddle of blood. She looked over at us and then something changed, like her face was breaking, and her eyes went wide and filled with blood. I guess she must have grazed her hands when she fell, and the Weeper blood got into her bloodstream."

So that was where his paranoia about the blood came from. I could hardly blame him for being twitchy about it when he'd watched his sister become infected. I could well imagine the horror that the experience must have held for him, to see someone he loved turn into a stranger, a monster, before his eyes.

"I'm sorry," I whispered.

"I wish that was the end of the story," he said, his voice shaking a little as he spoke. "But dad didn't see too well, so he can't have seen her face change, and before we could hold him back he was there checking that she was alright. She howled, just once, and then her face was at his neck, her jaws clamping down. Graham started to run towards them, but I pulled him back and dragged him into the bus, slammed the door shut behind us.

"It spread through the crowd, but the Silver didn't stop it. They told our driver to take us away, and we reversed out while the infection surged like a wave across the street, hundreds of humans just… gone in seconds."

He paused.

"It was the craziest thing I've ever seen."

We lay quietly for a moment in the dark, listening to the noise from outside as it softened from thudding to knocking, knocking to tapping.

"Do you blame them for it, then?" I asked.

"The Silver?"

"Yes."

"I don't know," he said, then added: "Yes. I think I do. I know they couldn't have done much to save Lucy and dad, and it's not like they had time to clean all the blood off the streets just in case, but knowing what I do now I can't help but feel that they could have stopped the spread of the infection through the crowd, could have saved hundreds of lives. I mean, there were options. They could have zipped over to them as soon as it started and taken them away from the crowd, or they could have just stood as a barrier and scared them away."

"That doesn't seem to be working for them so well right now," I observed, thinking back to the diminishing ambit of protection that the presence of the Silver had provided us from the Weepers on our journey to the Farm.

"But it's worked fine up till now," he said, "and they must have known that."

"Maybe they didn't," I speculated. "Maybe this is all as new to them as it is to us. It's not like any of us had ever seen a Weeper before the Revelation."

"Well, we hadn't seen a Silver either," he said.

"No, we had. They can hide the silver in their eyes, so to us they would have just looked human, but the Weepers can't pass as anything other than Weepers. If they'd been around beforehand, we would have known about it."

The tapping from outside was barely audible now, a muffled sound that I could only hear because I was listening for it.

"Maybe," he said.

He was quiet for a moment.

"It was why I joined up with the rebels, I think," he said. "After seeing dad and Lucy change like that, twisted versions of themselves, I needed to be able to blame someone for something. I think I needed a target, and the Silver were an easy one. So that's what we did, me and Graham: we made them our target to try and take our minds off what we'd lost."

"I'm sorry," I said, hearing the catch in his voice as he talked about his brother. It was as though he had dealt with the deaths of his father and sister, maybe because he had had his brother to help him through it, but losing Graham was something he was having trouble processing.

"Graham seemed to be more upset by it than I was. He just stopped talking to me. I think he resented me, blamed me for what happened and for holding him back. Maybe I was trying to compensate for that, trying to be his mouthpiece."

He exhaled heavily.

"I don't know," he said. "I'm sorry for the way I spoke to you."

"When?" I asked.

"Back when we first met, back in the city. I judged you."

I remembered the way he had sneered at me, how he had mocked me in front of the rebels for letting Sol bite me.

"You talked to me like I was an idiot, like you were better than me."

"I was wrong."

"Yes, you were."

But I wasn't certain that he had been wrong about the situation I had got myself into with the Silver.

There was nothing I could have done about Drew silvering for me, although I probably could have handled it better. That had marked my card as far as Ben was concerned, but it was harder to explain away the time that I had spent with Sol, the things that we had done together. At first, it had been nothing more than his otherness that had attracted me, because in all honesty I had been a little star-struck. With all I knew about him now it was a little easier to see where that attraction might have come from: the power he wielded, the respect he had earned, and his status as a king and god to humans and Silver alike in the millennia he'd watched pass him by.

But whilst that might have been a small part of it, it had very little to do with the fascination he held for me now. It wasn't why I had given in to him, why I had offered him my body and my blood, and it was difficult for me to rationalise that. There was nothing rational about it. He intoxicated me, calling to and satisfying a part of me that I didn't know existed.

But he had known it was there.

He knew me better than I knew myself, and he knew how to give me everything I never realised I needed, offering it to me if I would only admit that I wanted it. It opened up the horizon before me, and it had terrified me into pushing him away.

"We're both idiots," Oliver said.

"Yes," I whispered into the silence, "we are."

CHAPTER V

Friday

The next time I woke the sun was pouring through the windows, the temperature in the room already starting to rise until it was slightly uncomfortable. Oliver roused beside me as I lifted my head from his chest.

"We're not Weepers yet," I murmured.

"Not yet," he replied sleepily, rolling me into a brief hug before pulling his arm out from under me. He moved his shoulder in circles as he stood from the bed and walked towards the window opposite the door.

"Looking for blood?" I asked.

He stood close to the window, minutely examining the space between it and the bars. I stood up and joined him, peering over his shoulder. The ledge was about seven inches deep, and the first three inches were smeared with gore, presumably where the Weeper had managed to push its fingers through the spaces in the bars. The outside of the glass was spattered with a spray of blood, but it looked like it had all been left there after we had already closed the window.

"It doesn't look like there's any inside beyond the

windowsill," he said, but the tension was still coiled in his body.

"Do you think it's still out there?" I said, walking into the tiny bathroom to get a drink. Of course, there were no glasses, so I just cupped my hands under the tap and made do.

"Where else would it go?" Oliver shouted over the noise of the running water.

I wiped my face and hands on one of the small, grey towels I had hung from the bathroom door and walked back into the room.

"But with the sun up…" I said.

"They don't seem to like the sun because it makes their eyes bleed," he acknowledged, "but does it really hurt them?"

"Well, they stay out of it where they can."

"But not so much anymore. I don't know what we can expect to find out there, whether it'll be dead, or incapacitated, or just walking around like normal."

"Can you see it?" I asked.

He pressed his face against the glass, turning his head from one side to the other, up and down, trying to get the widest possible view. After a few seconds, he crossed the room and repeated the routine with the other window.

"I can't see any sign of it," he said, "but that doesn't mean it's not there. The perspective's pretty steep."

He sat back down on the edge of the bed, running his fingers through his brown curls.

"I mean, seriously," he said, "what are they trying to achieve here? As if the fortified cell and the three electrified fences weren't enough, they think they need to throw a Weeper into the mix to keep us locked up tight? Do they think we're magic or something?"

I sat down next to him and shuffled backwards, leaning my back up against the locked door that led into the other side of the building and stretching my legs out in front of me along the mattress.

"Maybe it's not just about us," I said. "Maybe they're watching the Weeper too."

"What," he scoffed, "like we're an experiment? Throw the Weepers and the humans in together and see what fun ensues?"

"I don't know. I hope not."

"Me too," he agreed with feeling.

"Maybe it's just a convenient place to keep the Weeper, like a multi-purpose prison."

I remembered what Sol had told me about the Weeper virus. The Silver had been trying to find a way to kill or contain the Weepers safely, but they'd also been looking for a way to neutralise the infection.

"I know they've been experimenting with the virus," I said.

"They have?"

"They're looking for a cure."

Oliver turned around to face me, swivelling to sit sideways along the bed, his expression serious and intent.

"Do you mean a way to restore Weepers, a way to turn them back into humans?" he asked.

I saw the light of hope sparking in his eyes and I thought about his father, his sister.

"I don't know," I said gently, "but even if we could find a way to do that, I think that, for a lot of them, coming back wouldn't be a possibility." I remembered the man from the truck yesterday, with the rips slashed across his stomach, and wondered whether that was something a human could survive. "Most of them are starving," I said, "and injured. I think they're probably beyond repair."

He nodded sadly, but there was no anguish in his expression, and I realised that he hadn't needed me to tell him that it was a vain wish, but that he had wanted to hear his reasoning confirmed, the words spoken aloud.

"I think the Silver's priority is to preserve those of us that are left," I continued, "rather than to bring back the ones we've lost."

"They've got a funny way of showing it by throwing us in here."

"Yeah, well, apparently some of us have lost our value," I

said, reflecting as I spoke on just how accurate that was as far as I was concerned. "In any case, I imagine they're focussing on finding an inoculation rather than an antidote. I don't know much about it, but I'd think it would be easier to inoculate than to cure."

Oliver's stomach grumbled, the sound amplified by the emptiness of the room.

"I wonder if they're going to bring us more food, or just let us starve," he said.

"I'd rather not think about it, personally. We've still got the apples," I said, picking up the paper bag from under the bed and passing it to him. Maybe we should have rationed them, but I couldn't see that an apple was going to make much difference one way or another.

"So," Oliver said through a mouthful of fruit, "what do you think they're going to have us doing for our punishment duty?"

I shrugged as I bit into my own apple.

"I don't know," I said. "Breaking rocks? Peeling potatoes?"

"Making licence plates is also traditional."

"I don't think our society needs those anymore. Anyway, we're on a farm. Won't there be... farm-type things to do?"

"Like what?"

"I don't know," I said, "milking cows, ploughing fields, feeding chickens, that kind of stuff."

"They probably have machinery for all of that. And anyway," he added, "they said we'd be kept away from the other humans. They'd be idiots to let us into the general population if they're going to keep exposing us to Weepers."

"So, what then?" I asked.

"Who knows? But it'll be a good few hours before we find out."

He wasn't wrong.

The morning passed quickly, both of us so tired out by the interruptions of the night and the events of the past couple of days that we dozed off together shortly after our makeshift breakfast. We figured we had better make the most of it while we could. When we woke again the room was stiflingly hot, so, after checking that the coast still appeared to be clear, we opened the windows again and let the breeze blow through the building.

I braved the shower to wash away the sticky heat from my skin, carefully avoiding the bandage at my wrist, and was unsurprised to find that the water was freezing cold. In the circumstances it was welcome, but bracing rather than refreshing. I dried myself with one of the tiny towels then climbed reluctantly back into the same scrubs, wondering whether a change of clothes and a toothbrush would be out of the question. Probably, I thought.

By the time Oliver had also showered, barely managing to keep his own bandages dry, we decided from the position of the sun overhead that it was approaching midday, so we expected that someone would be coming to collect us for our duties soon. After half an hour or so I was feeling restless, gradually becoming more impatient through the afternoon until I developed serious cabin fever.

Oliver tried to distract me by telling me the entire plotline of his dad's favourite television soap, which he had apparently been forced to watch and in no way enjoyed himself, but I just couldn't calm down. I couldn't shake the feeling that something awful was coming, and until I knew what we were going to be doing every day, what our punishment duty was, I was running through the worst possible scenarios in my head over and over. Add that to my anxiety about the Casting and the Weeper outside our door, and I was fit to burst.

Oliver was bringing me up to date on Rob's relationship with Jade, the one whose house had burned down in a revenge attack orchestrated by the jealous Vicky, whose sister had just found out she was pregnant after sleeping with Jade's estranged husband Carl, who had a brain tumour, on the night before their wedding, when we heard the outer gate of the fences sliding open. We shared a glance and walked over to the window to see Dr Tanner and the two guards, Mark and

Tessa, walking through the gates towards us. The doctor was carrying a large, metal briefcase and Tessa was holding a paper bag.

"More food?" I said quietly as we watched them pass through the gate in the last fence.

"I hope so. I'm ravenous."

"Let's hope the guards aren't," I joked, but it didn't seem as funny when the words were out of my mouth. They were the only Silver around to protect us, and who was going to object if they were feeling a little peckish? This wasn't like the club or the Palace. I didn't wear Sol's choker here or carry his mark, and the Invicti weren't around to save me now. Without the bond, there was no reason for them to be concerned for my safety anymore. I didn't mean anything to anyone important. I was just another human, a rebel as far as the Silver were concerned, and my only worth to them was as a food source.

"Do you think they're bringing the doctor to replace the bandages?" I asked.

"I don't think so," Oliver replied darkly. "We could do that ourselves if they gave us the dressings, and I don't think they really care that much."

"Then are they here for the blood?" I wondered, realising that it was the only reason the doctor would come here, inside the fences and the locks that sealed us in.

"That would be my guess."

I expected them to come to the door to our cell, but instead they walked to the side, to the second door that led into the building, and a moment after it opened we heard footsteps in the room next to ours. The hatch in the interconnecting door between the rooms dropped open, and I could see Tessa's dark, brown eyes gazing at us through the gap. She looked us up and down briefly before slamming the panel shut again and opening the door, swinging it wide into the room in which she was standing.

Oliver and I quickly pulled the bed out of the way of the doorframe, sliding it back against the wall under the window, but the Silver didn't make any move to step into the room.

"Walk this way," she said, holding the door open for us.

The room beyond was actually a little larger than our cell, with four chairs and a table set at its centre. It felt odd to be in the extended space, the connecting door wide open, after having spent so long confined in just a portion of the building.

Oliver limped a little as he walked into the room, but left his crutch where it was on the floor of the cell.

"Glad to see the leg is getting better," Dr Tanner said to him.

"It is," he replied, "thank you."

I nodded my own greeting at the doctor.

"Please," he said to me, "sit."

I pulled out one of the chairs from under the matching table, a plastic-topped set with rickety metal legs, and sat down as Dr Tanner put his briefcase down opposite me. Oliver sat protectively in the seat next to me, but the guards remained standing: Tessa by the connecting door and Mark by the door behind the doctor that led outside.

"You're here to take my blood?" I asked as he unclasped the metal case and lifted the lid.

"Yes," he confirmed. "I've spoken to the Chief Medical Officer in the city. I'm afraid we do need to take a donation from you."

"They've been messing about sorting this out all day," moaned Mark, "so between this and the sponsor visit, you're not going to be doing any work today."

So Drew was coming for the first time. I was expecting it, but I had no idea how I'd react when he turned up. I didn't think there was anything we could do to bring the bond back, to prepare me for the Casting, so the requirement that I see him every day seemed a little redundant.

The doctor pulled out a laptop, which he connected up to a mobile phone as he sat down in front of it and opened the screen. He reached across the table to take my wrist and, seeing that he had taken the familiar cylindrical device out of the briefcase, I offered my hand to him palm-upwards. He pressed the device to my finger and there was a brief, sharp pain as the needle pricked through my skin.

"Why is there a Weeper outside?" Oliver asked abruptly.

The doctor looked up, his gaze moving between us before resting on Tessa.

"There's a Weeper outside?" he asked.

"It was throwing itself up against the building all night," Oliver said, rage simmering beneath the controlled surface of his voice, "pushing its bloody fingers through the window bars." He glared at the guards like he was trying to burn holes through their skulls.

"Thought you might enjoy the company," Mark replied jovially. "Must get a bit lonely in here with nothing to do except that miserable bitch."

He laughed smugly, as if he had just made a wonderfully witty quip. I felt Oliver tense beside me, his muscles bunching in anticipation. There was a moment of terrible calm and then Dr Tanner looked at Oliver pointedly, giving a miniscule shake of his head. The doctor returned to his task briskly, the movement breaking the mood and bringing us back from the brink of an altercation.

Mark laughed again and turned to Tessa.

"Uppity little bugger, isn't he?"

Tessa nodded, but kept her eyes fixed on the doctor as he read the screen on the device. He squinted at it briefly and a look of concern crossed his face. He plugged the device into the laptop and typed for a few seconds before looking up at me again. For a moment I thought the data was missing and that we were going to have to repeat yesterday's twenty questions.

"I'm afraid there's a problem," he said.

"Problem?" Tessa asked.

"Yes. There's a hold notice on Ms Nelson's record," he replied, unplugging his mobile phone from his computer and tapping in a number, "so I can't take a donation from her until I've called back to the city."

"You said you'd already done that," Mark said impatiently.

"Just get on with it."

"I spoke to my counterpart," the doctor said as he held the phone to his ear. "Now I need to call someone different."

"Who?"

"Hello, yes," the doctor said into the handset, "I'm terribly sorry to disturb you, but this is Dr Tanner calling from the Farm. I was about to take a donation from a..." He looked up at me. "Yes, that's right."

Mark leaned over the doctor's shoulder to look at the computer screen and his face paled a little as he read.

"You're calling the Primus?" he whispered with equal parts disbelief and reverence.

Tessa and Mark shared a glance, doubtless wondering what interest Sol would have in my donations. I was pretty curious myself, given that he'd disclaimed his rights to my blood when he ripped off my choker yesterday so publicly.

The seconds passed in silence, just a faint noise audible at the other end of the line, but from across the table I couldn't hear what was being said or determine whether or not it was Sol doing the talking.

"Yes," the doctor said after a minute or so. "Of course. Understood. Give me one moment."

With that, he put the phone down on the table and pressed a button to activate the speakers.

"Can you hear me, Primus?" he asked.

"Perfectly," came Sol's voice over the line. "Thank you, doctor."

His voice was like an electric current under my skin, lighting up my nerve endings and shocking my pulse into overdrive.

"I understand that I am addressing two Silver guards, as well as the two rebels and the good doctor," he continued.

"Yes, Primus," Tessa answered, but Mark appeared to be lost for words, as was I.

Did Sol really consider us to be rebels, after all he knew of what had gone on with Ben and Tamsin, of their plot to send me into the explosion, to murder Drew by orchestrating my death? Of course, their plan had had the bonus of making the incident seem accidental, so no blame would have attached to Ben or Tamsin, and of implicating me by putting me in the rebels' den. But surely Sol knew that I had nothing to do with it and that I had just been trying to save my friends?

Then again, Tamsin was his consort's BFF, Laila's confidante and collaborator. I wondered how much influence Laila had over Sol now that he had silvered for her. Maybe it was enough for her to be able to make him believe their version of events. After all, what had I been to him? A two-time blood bag and a one-time lover. Not much competition when I was stacked up against the Silver he had bonded with, whom he loved so much that the bond had marked him as hers, whose death would mean his death.

I couldn't bear the thought of it. Part of me wished that he would leave me alone to get on with my life sentence, but the treacherous part just longed to hear him speak again.

"And you are the two guards who will be attending to the rebels during their detention?" he asked, his voice as clear and melodic over the phone as it was in person.

"We are, Primus," Tessa replied.

"Yessir," Mark chimed in, finding his voice, "that's right."

His cheeks flushed as he spoke, a sweat breaking out on his forehead, and I decided he was the least Silver-like Silver that I had ever met. Unlike the rest of them, he was constantly moving: putting his hands in and out of his pockets, shifting his weight from foot to foot, and wiping his finger under his nose. It was a bizarre contrast to Tessa, whose bearing was as still and controlled as that of the Invicti, so motionless that she seemed to fade into the background. I wondered whether Mark was a relatively recent addition to the fold.

"Good," Sol continued. "Then I want to make it clear that this conversation is to go no further than us."

"Yes, Primus," Tessa said.

"Primus, yessir," said Mark, wiping his face on his sleeve.

"You are aware that the female rebel was one of my chained," said Sol, "but that she has now been stripped of my patronage in light of her recent betrayal."

My mouth dropped open. Apparently Laila had really done a number on him, but betrayal? That was rich in the circumstances. He was the one who had sent me to this place for participating in an attack I had tried to prevent. I tried to tell myself I was angry at the injustice of it all, to get up a head of righteous indignation, but in reality I was just crushed. He had dismissed me to the extent that I didn't even merit a name anymore, and that cut me like a knife to the heart.

"However," he continued, "I have fed directly from her veins, so it is not proper that her blood should be tasted by another Silver. Accordingly, you will separate her donations and send them directly to me through my Invicti. Is that clear?"

The guards chorused their agreement.

"Primus," Tessa said, "if I may ask a question: do you object to our informing Ada of this arrangement?"

"I have already done so," he replied. "I thank you for your service."

And with that, he severed the connection.

There was a pause before anyone spoke.

"Shit," Mark murmured, "you've got some powerful enemies, girl."

Wasn't that the truth? I nodded quietly to myself, too stunned even to object to being called 'girl'.

Dr Tanner took my blood quickly and efficiently while I was still dazed, filling a bag before shutting it away in his briefcase with his various electronics. It seemed like a recipe for disaster to me, but I let him get on with it.

The guards ushered us back into our half of the building and Tessa passed me the paper bag she had been holding before shutting and locking the connecting door between us. We watched the them from the window as they escorted the doctor out through the gates and away to their car, driving him back towards the centre of the complex.

"What was all that about?" asked Oliver as I rooted through the bag: more bread, cheese and apples, and some cereal bars this time too. "Why isn't it 'proper' for any of the other Silver to drink your blood? I'm not saying that they should be going to town or anything, it's just… odd."

I shrugged.

"Sol's got this whole divinity thing going on," I said, "so I imagine it has something to do with that. Some of the Silver think he's their god."

It sounded like he was starting to believe it himself, and I wondered how much of that was down to Laila. I couldn't believe the arrogance of it; that no one else should be permitted to touch what he had touched. He was like a child not wanting to share his toys, even when he never played with them anymore.

"That's…" said Oliver. "Well, I was going to say it was crazy, but I can kind of see it."

"Boy crush?" I asked.

"Honestly? A little bit. It doesn't mean he's not an evil bastard, but there's no denying that he's a snappy dresser."

"Like you in your blue pyjamas?" I teased.

"Well, of course, style this effortless takes years to cultivate," he said, putting his hands on his hips as he struck a pose.

I laughed and threw an apple at him, which he caught deftly.

"You're such a clown," I said, tucking one leg under me as I sat down on the edge of the bed. "Anyway, I guess it doesn't much matter to me where my blood ends up. He can have it if he wants."

But part of me cared deeply and, although I didn't want to admit it, that part of me was hoping that Sol had demanded it because he wanted it for himself, not just because he didn't want anyone else to have it.

And that was creepy. Wanting someone to want your blood just isn't normal. Besides, even if he did want my blood, it didn't mean that he wanted me.

I had to get past this.

"I'd kill for some toothpaste," I sighed as I bit into my

apple.

"Well," said Oliver, "you can always ask the Secundus when he comes to see you later."

I laughed bitterly.

"Yeah, we'll see," I replied quietly. Given how he had behaved towards me yesterday while we were sentenced and sent away by Sol, I couldn't imagine that he could have very much to say to me. He had completely ignored me, as if I were invisible to him, just a ghost of someone he had cared for. Despite everything, despite all my mixed feelings about the bond, it had hurt.

"I thought you were going to lose it at Mark in there for a moment," I said.

"So did I."

"You don't have to go into battle for me, you know."

"I know." He sat down next to me on the bed, his eyes cast downwards as he turned the half-eaten apple around in his hands. "But I don't want you to think that's what this is about, that I'm just trying to get into your pants."

I reflected briefly on his use of the word 'just'. Was he trying it on with me, or had it just been a slip of the tongue?

"I don't," I said, "so chill out about it."

But I wished he hadn't brought the subject up. It stretched a thread of tension between us, and I was suddenly aware of how close he was sitting to me, in a way that I hadn't been before. His proximity had been so easy and relaxed, fraternal almost, but not anymore. My mind was racing backwards through all of the gestures of intimacy that he might have intended me to construe otherwise: sheltering me from the rain as we drove away from the city, holding me close to him while I slept, stroking my hair away from my face as we lay together in the dark last night.

And then there were the jokes. Had he been flirting? Had I been flirting? It had felt so natural to be close to him, and it had been comforting to have him hold me in his arms in this isolated place, as if we were the last two people in the world.

I cleared my throat awkwardly and bit into my apple again.

"I mean it, Emmy," he said as he turned to face me. "I'm not expecting anything from you here."

"Okay," I said, feeling like I was getting the message loud and clear. I looked at my hands and fidgeted a little, shifting my weight so that my hips moved a fraction further away from him.

"Then stop being… weird with me."

I sighed.

"I can't help it," I said. "You've made me feel uncomfortable."

"I'm sorry. I shouldn't have said anything."

I didn't respond, fervently wishing that he hadn't. How was I supposed to know how to behave around him now? It was like Drew and the bond all over again, the guilt of his emotion making me feel pressured into reciprocation I wasn't ready to offer. And we were stuck in here together, so there was no way to escape the atmosphere.

After a few seconds' silence he spoke again.

"Look, I like you. It's out there. And you don't feel the same way, and that's okay. Sure, I'm a bit disappointed, but it doesn't have to be a big deal."

He took my hand in his.

"Emmy," he said. "Look at me."

I did as he asked, raising my eyes to meet his.

"I'm your friend, and that's it. End of story. Don't overthink this and end up ruining our friendship, okay? Just be flattered by the attention and let's move on. We've got bigger things to worry about."

Could it really be that simple? I decided to give him the benefit of the doubt, hoping this wasn't going to turn into another emotional saga like it had with Drew.

"Okay," I said. "But I reserve the right to be weird for a while."

"You're always weird anyway," he said as he bit into his apple again.

"You like weird."

"Damn right I do," he said with a grin.

He pulled me into a quick hug then walked over to the window and posted his apple core out through the bars.

"A little snack for the Weeper, if it's still there."

"Pretty sure it's not interested in a vegetarian diet," I replied.

"Well, it's going to have to get used to it, because I'm not feeding it anything else."

I finished my apple quietly, hoping the guards wouldn't make a liar of him.

CHAPTER VI

We had eaten half of the bread and cheese, saving the other half for a late dinner, when we heard an engine outside. We watched from the window as a car approached, driving slowly through the gates one at a time as they opened for it, and then pulled up right outside the building. It didn't look like they were taking any chances with the identity of my sponsor, and in the circumstances it was probably wise. The leader of the Solis Invicti was not an appropriate choice as a sponsor for the Casting, the whole point of which was to try to form a bond between the Silver and the human so that the transformation to Silver would be successful. I was all too aware of how much of a target Drew's position made him and, by extension, had made me.

We heard a car door open, but from our vantage point we couldn't see who entered the door to the observation room. Nevertheless, I could make a pretty good guess as to whom I would be seeing.

Sure enough, a few seconds later the hatch in the connecting door opened and I saw Drew's eyes looking in at us. Since almost the first moment I had met him, his emerald irises had been threaded with the silver that marked his bond to me. It was strange to see them without it, the clear green colour appearing oddly dark without its highlights.

He looked away and shut the hatch, opening the door a moment afterwards. He was dressed more casually than usual in jeans and a long-sleeved t-shirt, one hand hanging from his pocket. His dark, mid-length hair fell forward scruffily over his face, his expression grim but uncertain.

"Emilia," he said quietly.

"Drew," I replied awkwardly, "hi. This is Oliver. Drew, Oliver. Oliver, Drew. You sort of met the other night after, you know…"

The explosion, I added mentally. It hadn't been the best possible introduction: Drew carrying Oliver's bleeding body to safety.

Drew nodded an acknowledgment at Oliver and he nodded back. I could almost smell the testosterone.

"We need to talk," Drew said to me, holding the door wide as he stood aside to let me through.

I exchanged a glance with Oliver, smiling briefly to reassure him that it was okay, and then followed Drew into the room, turning over my shoulder to watch him slam the door firmly closed behind us. He couldn't have made it any clearer that Oliver was not involved in this conversation.

"So," I said, taking a seat at the table, "you're here to discuss the Casting?"

He sat down opposite me and took my hand in his own, staring into my eyes with determined intensity, as if he was trying to find something he had lost. He looked bereft, empty and hollowed out, and I remembered the grief I had seen on his face that night when he told me that the bond had broken. I was still there, right in front of him, but as far as the bond was concerned I had died in the tunnels under the city. It was gone, and there was nothing to hold us together anymore.

"Drew…"

After a moment more he blinked, his face a mask of suppressed emotion. He broke eye contact as he released my hand and sat back in his chair.

"I'm going to kill you," he said tonelessly.

"What?" I whispered. He was detached, staring sightlessly through the surface of the table, and it was starting to scare me.

"The Casting," he said. "You know what's going to happen." He looked into my eyes again and said: "If you get through the testing, then I'm going to kill you."

The statement hung heavily between us, the blunt acknowledgement of a fact that we both already knew. If he tried to turn me Silver without the bond, then I'd turn into a Weeper. I probably would have preferred death to that.

"It's not coming back," he continued quietly. "I'd hoped that maybe when I saw you I might silver again, that…I don't know, things would click back into place."

I shook my head in resignation.

"There was no reason for the bond in the first place," I said. "You didn't love me, didn't even know me, not when it happened. It wasn't real."

His reaction was unexpected and terrifying. It was as though my words had lit a fuse in him, fury suffusing his expression instantaneously. His eyes darted sharply to mine and he slammed his hands down onto the table top, making me jump.

"Will you stop telling me it isn't real?" he said, anger rising in his voice as he clenched his teeth in frustration. "It was real. I felt it every moment of every day since the second I met you, the most... right thing I'd ever felt. It was everything to me. It gave me a purpose, and just being near you, just thinking of you was enough to make me feel fulfilled. It was like I had found my place in the world, and suddenly it's gone.

"Can you try to understand how that feels?" he said, shouting at me now, his tone so full of vitriol that it set my heart pounding in my chest. "Do you know how it feels to have it tear pieces off me, ripping at my insides every time I remember it's not there anymore?"

He stared me down, aggression rolling off him in waves as he leaned over the table towards me. His face was full of rage, twisting his features until he was someone I didn't recognise.

But I couldn't look away, frozen in terror in the crosshairs of the Silver who had apparently loved me once.

"Stop telling me it wasn't real," he growled, so close to me that I could feel his breath on my skin, "because nothing in my life has ever felt so real to me. Do you understand me?"

He lifted his hand from the table top and I flinched away, not sure whether he was going to hit me, or bite me, or worse.

There was a hammering at the connecting door and Oliver's voice filtered through.

"Emmy, are you okay in there?"

Drew dropped his hand and moved away slowly, sitting back down. I had a white-knuckle grip on the sides of my chair, my fingernails clawing into the plastic, and my muscles were trembling, ready to run, for all the good it would have done me. I swallowed painfully to moisten my dry throat.

"I'm fine," I shouted back at him, barely controlling the tremor in my voice. "It's okay."

"Good," he yelled back, his voice rough and raw, "because if he lays a finger on you then I swear I'll break every bone in his body. I don't give a shit if he's the fucking Secundus."

Drew snorted derisively and stood up from his seat, slamming it roughly under the table so that the metal legs clattered on the concrete floor, and turned his back to me as he ran his fingers through his hair.

"I don't know what you were hoping to achieve here," I said quietly, "but I think you'd better go."

He looked over his shoulder at me and saw my face, saw my hands gripping the edges of my seat, and walked slowly to the outside door with his eyes fixed on the floor, his expression still tight with anger. He brought a device out of his pocket and pressed a few buttons on it, then the bolts released and he pulled the door open. The latch clicked shut softly behind him as he let himself out of the building without another word.

I waited in silence, frozen to the spot, until I heard the last of the three gates shut after his retreating vehicle. The moment he was gone, I gasped with relief and a tear ran down my cheek. I let go of the chair and tried to relax my hands, but the muscles were clenched tight, shaking uncontrollably in the aftermath of the confrontation.

"Emmy?" Oliver called through the door. "Are you there?"

I tried to reply but my shout came out as a whisper.

"Let me in," he yelled.

I stood up from the chair and made my way unsteadily to the connecting door.

"If that bastard has taken you away then I'm coming after him," he shouted as he thumped against the door.

It took me a moment to work out that there were just a couple of simple latches on this side of the door to keep it locked, but eventually I managed to release them both and swing it open. Oliver practically fell inside, scooping me up into his arms and cradling my head against his shoulder. I broke down as he held me, great, wracking sobs crashing through me until my chest ached and my voice cracked.

It wasn't pretty, but he just gathered me up and limped his way to the bed carrying me in his arms. He held me close until I was all cried out, his top soaked with my tears, then lay down with my head on his chest and stroked my hair until my breathing calmed and I started to relax into his warmth.

"I don't like your ex," he said.

"No," I said with a hollow laugh, "I don't think I do either."

I lay still for a few minutes, trying to absorb the shock of what had just happened.

"I thought he was going to…" I whispered, trailing off into silence.

"What?" Oliver asked quietly.

"I don't know. I've never seen him like that before. He was so angry, and angry at me. I mean, I've seen him angry before, but with the bond I always knew with this crazy certainty that he would always do what was best for me, and that he would never, ever hurt me."

"I gather that he's not someone who deals well with

rejection."

"It's not that," I said. "He doesn't want me anymore because the bond isn't there, but he wants it to come back. I suppose he's angry with me because he thinks I broke it, and he misses it. I don't know."

"He blames you because he doesn't love you anymore?" Oliver asked incredulously.

"I don't know. Maybe. But that feeling I used to get, knowing in my heart that he would always protect me? Well, that's not there anymore."

I thought about the rage in his eyes as he had leaned up in my face, how his whole bearing had been full of threat and menace, and I shuddered.

"He scared me," I whispered.

He had made me feel powerless, like a fragile thing that he could take and do what he wanted with, and there would have been nothing that either of us could have done to stop him. I supposed that he had always had that power over me, but I had never before believed that he would use it.

I had done exactly what Danny had warned me against, back when we were trying to find a way out from under the rule of the Silver. I had forgotten that they weren't human, and that expecting them to act human was naïve in the extreme. I had forgotten what Drew was, what they all were: killers.

"He's changed?" Oliver asked quietly.

"He's like a completely different person," I said, "and I don't know whether it's that the bond was stopping him from being himself or that losing it has made him lash out. Maybe a bit of both."

"Did you love him?"

The question caught me off guard, but I knew the answer without thinking.

"No. No, I didn't."

I thought about how he had been when we first met, inveigling and persuading me with his touch, insinuating himself into my life when I had wanted him out of it. He had been single-minded about it, determined, but never aggressive. He had been frustrated, begging me to give him a chance, desperate to the point of obsession, but he hadn't been violent. Even when Sol had kissed me, bitten me, leaving his mark on me in the most proprietary way, Drew's anger had all been directed towards Sol rather than at me.

But that had changed now.

"The bond made him fixate on me," I said, "and he was constantly trying to win me over, always trying to demonstrate how sincere his feelings were. With the bond broken, it's like that fixation has shifted, so he's obsessed with the emotion itself rather than with me."

I had been all there was in the world to him, and he had acted as though protecting me was an all-consuming need that had taken over his life. Now that emotion was disconnected, divorced from its object like an intangible thing that he was unable to ground in reality, and it was making him frantic.

"That kind of obsession can make people dangerous," said Oliver.

"The problem is that it never had anything to do with me, not really. It came out of nowhere, this ridiculous intensity of feeling that pointed itself at me, but he thought it was the other way round: that it had started with me. Now I guess he's realised he had it wrong because he can't bring it back, can't make himself feel it again. He wants the bond, but he doesn't want me.

"Who I am never mattered, but that kind of undermines the validity of everything he's felt over the past couple of weeks."

"And he doesn't want to accept that," Oliver said.

I wondered what had triggered the bond in the first place, wishing that another Silver had been around to save me that night, anyone but Drew. Hell, I could probably have escaped from the Weepers on my own and run back to the safety of Parker's if he hadn't interfered.

"I don't know why he silvered," I sighed. "I don't know why it happened that way, but there it is. The bond breaking has spun him out of control, and he's not trying to prove anything to me anymore. By the time the Casting comes round he'll probably want to kill me anyway."

He'd probably enjoy it too, I thought, remembering the malicious look on this face as he loomed over me.

"Don't say that," Oliver said.

"And he'll be back tomorrow," I said in a hollow tone of voice, the horror creeping up my spine and turning my stomach. "And the day after, and the day after that…"

"Shh, Emmy," he whispered. He shifted back until he sat up against the wall and then pulled me into his lap, curving his body around me and holding me tight.

"Worst break up ever," I muttered into his shoulder.

"Really? I've had worse."

"I don't believe you."

"What can I say?" he said. "The crazy ones can't get enough of me. I've had it all, from 'I heart Ollie' tattoos to Valentines cards written in real blood. One time a girl I'd broken up with sent me an actual heart with an actual knife stuck through it. I think it was something she'd seen on TV. I had to call the police and everything."

"Really?" I asked in disbelief.

"Really. Of course, turned out it was a cow's heart, but they still weren't happy about it."

"I can imagine."

A few moments passed in comfortable silence as I relaxed in his arms, all of the awkwardness from earlier this afternoon absent. He was right: things between us could be easy. There was no guilt here, no pressure, and I could just take the comfort he offered me without feeling the weight of expectation or obligation crushing me down.

"Do you normally go by Ollie rather than Oliver, then?" I asked. He hadn't mentioned it before.

"Sometimes, mostly only to people I'm close to. I guess it would be nice if you would call me Ollie, but don't worry if it's weird."

"No," I said, lifting my head off his chest to look up into

his grey eyes, "I like it. Ollie suits you better."

He raised his eyebrows at me and then, after a second, he smiled.

"Okay then."

CHAPTER VII

I will rise now and go about the city,
in the streets and in the squares;
I will seek him whom my soul loves.
I sought him, but found him not.

- The Song of Solomon

We had the rest of the bread and cheese for dinner, making the most of the expanded space by eating at the table in the observation room. There were still the cereal bars and a couple of apples left for breakfast in the morning.

"It's like having our own private dining room," said Ollie as we sat across the table from each other, ripping the bread up into chunks and breaking the cheese onto it.

"The height of luxury," I agreed, but if I was honest with myself I wasn't yet comfortable sitting in here after the drama of Drew's visit. I had deliberately taken a seat on the other side of the table from the one I had occupied earlier, but being there still reminded me of what had happened, the scene rolling through my mind unstoppably: his hands slamming onto the tabletop, his twisted expression as he asked 'Do you understand me?', biting out the words through his clenched teeth, the hatred in his eyes as he shouted me down.

I knew rationally that he had been completely out of line and I kept telling myself that it was his problem and not mine, that he had massively overreacted to a perfectly reasonable statement of mine, but I couldn't shake the feeling of shame that rose up inside me every time I replayed it in my head. In my heart of hearts, a scared little girl took the blame for provoking him and wished that I hadn't been so dismissive of his feelings, wished that I'd treated him with a bit more respect, and then maybe none of it would have happened and I wouldn't be feeling so terrified and worthless. He had made me feel cowed and I should have hated him for it, but instead I was filled with self-loathing and regret.

And I dreaded him coming back again tomorrow.

Ollie must have seen me glancing around nervously, because he asked me whether I would be more comfortable moving back into our cell, but I wanted to stick it out. I was worried that, if I didn't, I'd imbue the room with a sinister quality in my mind that would just mean I would get even more upset when I was next here with Drew.

"Do you think they've all got it in them, that anger?" I asked Ollie.

"What," he replied, "the Silver?"

"Mmm," I said, nodding as I chewed.

I was thinking about the parallels I could draw between Drew and Ben, both of them superficially pleasant and caring, but with a terrible rage bubbling under the surface that had an edge of madness to it. With Ben I knew that his veneer had been deliberately deceptive, but maybe it had been a show with Drew as well, albeit an unintentional one put on by the bond.

"I think it's probably in us all," he said. "I don't think they're much different from us at the end of the day, it's just that their world is smaller, they live forever and they're more powerful, so maybe they have to live life a bit bigger than we do."

"You're saying the Silver are drama queens?"

He shrugged.

"If the shoe fits."

"Did you see it in Ben?" I asked, wondering why Ollie had trusted him. It wasn't that I was in any position to judge, but I was intrigued because I hadn't had any idea of the nightmares that he had been planning behind his pleasant exterior until he'd revealed himself as a murderer to me.

Ollie paused in thought for a second before he answered, putting down a piece of cheese that had been halfway to his mouth.

"I'd like to be able to say no," he said, "but I'm fairly certain I'd be lying if I did. You could tell he was on a mission, and he didn't try to make a secret of that. Actually, it was what made us talk to him."

"He approached you?"

"No, he got us to approach him. Well, me anyway. He was at the broadcast, the one where the Primus announced the Casting. Graham was mouthing off about it when we were walking back to the club from the Square. There were Silver everywhere, so I was about to tell him to keep his voice down when I noticed Benedict walking a little way behind him, nodding to himself like he agreed with every word. He gave me this sympathetic smile, as if he was trying to make me understand that he supported us.

"I wasn't enough of an idiot to start telling him about our plans just because of that, but everywhere I went that day I kept seeing him, as though he was just waiting for me to take the opportunity to talk to him, which I suppose he was. And then at the end of the afternoon I went over to the Palace to check the kitchen rota for the next day, and he was there again.

"Did you ever go in the kitchens at the Palace?" he asked.

I shook my head.

"I went in the restaurant," I said, "but not the kitchens."

"Okay, well, you walked in through these swing doors, then about eight feet along on the right hand side there was this alcove that was a sort of office with a load of books and a pin-board with the work rota on it. So I'm tucked away out of sight while I'm copying the rota onto a piece of paper to take back to the club for the others, and Benedict walks in through a door at the far end of the room, right over on the other side of the ovens and work stations, opposite the swing doors. He's in the middle of an argument with a woman, and they're really going at it, him saying how she's crazy to want to be a sponsor for the Casting and that it's just going to end up hurting the humans, and how it's their duty to protect us, how the Primus was oppressing us and all that."

"An obvious ploy," I interjected.

"Yeah, well," he said, "it's easy to see that now, but back then we were desperate. We'd talked about trying to find a Silver who was on our side, who could champion our cause, and then there he was: the answer to our prayers. The woman screamed back at him for a bit, then she walked through the kitchen, past the alcove and out through the swing doors, leaving me alone in the kitchen with Benedict. So I stepped out and introduced myself."

"You made a deal with the devil," I said.

"Yes," he said, "I did. He told me he wanted to change the world and that he could help us. He said there were a lot of Silver on his side, and that he had enough support to displace the Primus and put things right so that humans had the position they deserved in our society."

"Right," I said. "If Ben had his way then our place would be grovelling on the floor at the feet of the mighty Silver. He'd take away what little freedom we still have. Well," I added, remembering where we were, "had."

"Yes," Ollie said ruefully, "again, I know that now. But we'd got ourselves stuck in the mindset of the old world, and it was so self-evident to us that the Silver should do the fair and decent thing that we couldn't believe that he planned to make things even worse.

"I could see he had ambition from the way he spoke about it. There was this rapacious look he got about him when he talked about taking down the Primus, and I knew there was a touch of megalomania in him. But I thought we could use it for our own ends. I got caught up in it, and I told myself it would all work out, that he'd give us some influence when he came to power. He promised us equality if we helped him."

"I don't think equality is something we'll ever get from the Silver," I said. "It just doesn't make sense. It's not as if they're benevolent overlords, after all."

Ollie nodded his quiet agreement.

Although there was an element of symbiosis in the bargain we'd made with them, because we each needed the other to survive, it wasn't an equal partnership and the Silver were overwhelmingly more powerful than the humans. The truth was that while we needed their cooperation to protect us from the Weepers, they just needed our blood, and they didn't need to keep us happy to get it. They could achieve their ends by simply taking what they needed from us as and when.

The Silver weren't parasites, they were predators, but they came in such familiar packaging that it was easy to forget it. Just as I had with Drew.

I remembered a conversation I had overheard the previous week at the club, two men discussing how they could become the inner circle when the time for change arrived.

"I heard you out on the fire escape that night," I said.

"You did?"

"My bed was right by the window. One of you was smoking, and it woke me up."

"Yeah," Ollie said, "that was Johnny. He was one of the others."

"The rebels? One of the forty-seven?"

He nodded.

"He died yesterday."

"I'm sorry," I said.

"I'm not. He was an evil bastard. He was one of the ones who tried to kill you, who murdered your friends."

"Alice and Ella?" I asked, my voice cracking a little as I spoke.

"Yes. Good riddance to him and his idiot friends. He had a cruel streak in him, and he enjoyed having a gun in his hand a little too much for my liking. I was worried about that from the start, worried about who was going to get caught in the crossfire, but I kept my mouth shut until after the protest at the gate. And then when Graham died everything changed."

He looked away, taking a bite of bread as he blinked away the tears that had been threatening to interrupt him.

"I know Benedict killed Graham," he said through gritted teeth. "I knew it in my gut the moment I saw the blood on his bed, just like I knew it was my fault. I'd been worried about the direction we were taking and I started expressing those worries to other people, so I think they decided to send me a message.

"When Jane and Mia joined us, I still thought we were going to make things better. I was prepared for there to be some violence if it would be worth it in the long term, but there had been this shift in the dynamic of the group, and I felt like the people who were being listened to were suddenly the wrong ones, the ones that should never have been trusted with any kind of power."

"Ben was probably looking for exactly those people," I said.

"Well," Ollie continued, "he found them, and they starting taking over. Slowly but surely, I was inched out. Killing Graham was a way of keeping me in line, keeping me quiet. I wondered why they didn't just kill me instead, but I decided some of them were the sort to enjoy watching me suffer, a kind of petty-minded vengeance for the influence I'd had over the group at the start. And, of course, Benedict was using me to get to you."

He looked at me apologetically.

"I never realised that you were at this centre of all of this," he added.

"I wasn't," I replied. "None of us are. It's all about the Silver and their power struggles. We're just the pawns they're playing with."

"You're right there," he sighed.

The night was drawing in when we finished our food, and I thought about moving through into the next room.

"We'd better lock up for the night," I said.

The two windows in the observation room were closed, but we'd left the ones in the cell open to let the breeze through. With the light fading fast, I didn't want to find a Weeper at the window by the time I came to shut it, and after the spray of blood we had found on the glass this morning I knew Ollie wouldn't want to risk leaving them open. We took one window each, Ollie taking the one over the bed and me taking the one by the door, but as I went to close it I heard the furthest gate opening and squinted out into the dusk.

"What is it?" he asked me, latching his window closed before coming to stand next to me.

I slammed the window shut quickly and made triple sure it was securely locked.

"They're bringing more in," I said, running through the building to check the other windows and doors.

"What?"

I wasn't even sure whether the door had locked behind Drew as he left earlier, and I hadn't thought to check because even if last night's Weeper had gone, there was no way for us to get beyond the fences. But it looked as though the second door was on the same double locking system as the one to our cell, and they were both bolted shut.

When I arrived back at Ollie's side, the innermost gate had opened and Mark was stepping inside our enclosure dragging a couple of Weepers behind him. It was difficult to make out in the gathering dusk, but it looked as though he was holding on to the end of ropes that were tied around their waists. He let go of them, stepping back out of the gate as it closed, and waved to us expansively.

"Brought you a couple more friends!" he shouted, the noise faint through the closed windows.

With our faces at the glass, it didn't take them long to work out where we were. By the time we saw the headlights of

Mark's car blaze into life, they were throwing themselves at the bars, eclipsing our view as he drove off back to the centre of the compound. We stepped away from the window hurriedly.

"I fucking hate that bastard," said Ollie with feeling.

"Me too," I agreed.

We debated using the building as two separate bedrooms, but with concrete floors and only one mattress we decided we were better off sharing. In any case, with the Weepers right outside, I would feel more secure in Ollie's arms than I would anywhere else. By silent consensus, we dragged the bed back in front of the open arch of the connecting door so we were as far from the windows and doors as possible, just in case, and then we kicked off our shoes and Ollie lay down, cuddling me in next to him on my side.

"How are the leg and the shoulder doing?" I asked.

"The leg's okay," he whispered in my ear, just loudly enough for me to hear over the racket the Weepers were making outside, "but the shoulder aches. The stitches feel fine, though."

"Does it hurt to lie like this?"

"Not at all. Are you comfy?"

"Yes," I said, surprised again to find that it was true, that there was no awkwardness in being close to him.

"I hope our neighbours shut up soon, because we've got a long day breaking rocks ahead of us tomorrow."

"I thought we decided it'd be potatoes?"

"God," he said, "I hope not. I never could get the hang of those stupid peelers. I'm rubbish at cooking."

"What were you doing working in the kitchens at the Palace, then?"

"Washing dishes. Apparently they had all the engineers they needed, but I was perfectly qualified to wash up pans."

"Sounds like it involves about the right level of intellect for your abilities," I replied.

"Oh, does it, now?" he replied archly, and then he tickled me around my waist.

He actually tickled me.

I didn't think anyone had tickled me since I was about twelve. But here, with the Weepers battering at the sides of the building, Ollie tickled me and I laughed until I cried, letting go of all the awful tension of the day and collapsing in hysterical fits of giggles until my stomach muscles started to cramp. I pushed him away, wiping the tears from my eyes, then I put my arms around him and pillowed my head on his chest as he lay on his back on the mattress, listening to his heart thump in his chest as the Weepers gradually settled into silence outside.

Bizarre though it was in the circumstances, I felt an odd kind of peace with him in this isolated place. Until tomorrow, we were outside of the world together in the darkness, and it encouraged confidences that we might not otherwise have imparted.

"I know how you feel about Graham," I said, knowing how awful it was to have to carry that kind of guilt. "What happened to Alice, her death? That was my fault."

"Why do you say that?" he asked.

I told him about the day of the protest, how I had gone to the gate even though the Silver who were protecting me from Ben had tried to keep me inside.

"Ben would never have seen Alice if she hadn't followed me there," I said. "He wouldn't even have known who she was. She wouldn't have needed protecting from him, so she wouldn't have been one of the chained, and she wouldn't have been killed. That was the point after all, wasn't it? Ben wanted to make a poetic statement by hanging Sol's chained from the window of his club."

And I was supposed to have been the third, the final character in a macabre trio of marionettes.

"Guilt won't bring them back," he said.

"No, but knowing that doesn't make it go away either."

He moved out from under me and raised himself up on his elbow, rolling me over onto my back. I could barely see him in the glow coming from the windows, just his shape silhouetted in the doorway behind him. Reaching down, he cradled my face in his hand, his thumb running gently over the surface of my cheek as he leaned towards me, his hair brushing over my forehead. He paused, his fingers hesitating on my skin, and then he withdrew, taking his hand away as he lay down again beside me.

"We have a lot in common, Emmy," he said after a moment.

"We do," I whispered back, not sure whether I was relieved or disappointed that he had moved away.

"It makes me feel… I don't know," he said, trailing off.

"Less alone," I finished.

"Yes," he whispered. "Less alone."

CHAPTER VIII

Saturday

We woke with the dawn and ate our cereal bars and apples, expecting an early wake-up call for our punishment duty, and we weren't disappointed. Our guards arrived within about an hour of sunrise. We checked the windows as they approached, looking around for any sign of the Weepers. Again, the glass was covered in blood spatter, but we couldn't see them out in the enclosure. In any case, if we were being escorted out of here then we would be safe in proximity to the guards.

Safe from the Weepers, at least.

My anxiety had returned, building ever since we had woken this morning as I speculated nervously about what we would be asked to do for our punishment duty. I thought it was a good bet that it would be some kind of manual labour, but however bad it was I didn't think I could take another day of not knowing.

As the guards entered the enclosure I had a sudden thought and, making sure the locks wouldn't catch, pulled the connecting door shut. I imagined that Drew wasn't supposed to have left it open yesterday, and if there was a chance that they wouldn't notice that it hadn't been relocked then I hoped we would be able to keep using the extra space.

"Good morning, inmates," Mark said with a laugh as he opened the door, clearly enjoying his role as prison guard. However, his mood was slightly muted when he realised that we were ready to leave, and I gathered that he had been looking forward to shouting us out of bed.

"Early shift today," Tessa said to us, "late shift tomorrow, early shift the day after, and so on."

I supposed it was probably unrealistic to expect weekends off as a prisoner.

"Come on then," Mark said, waving a fat hand at us as he stepped outside again and held the door wide open behind us. Ollie retrieved his crutch from where it lay against the wall and hopped out cautiously after him. I followed shortly afterwards and, like his, my head turned to the side of its own accord, drawn irresistibly towards the outside of the window that had been the focus of the Weepers' assault last night, needing to see what damage they had left behind them, and where they had gone.

The sight presented to us was not what I had expected; it was unimaginably worse. The two Weepers were lying in a mangled, boneless heap on the ground under the window, their bodies battered and broken open, the wall smeared with blood and gore that had dripped down from the bars across it. One of them lifted its head slightly as we passed, but there was no other movement and the only sound was a grotesque clicking gurgle, as if it were trying vainly to howl. The stench as the morning sun hit the rotting mess of their bodies was putrid, a heavy scent that was sharp and sweet in an indescribably gruesome combination.

I gagged as it hit the back of my throat, covering my mouth with my hand as I looked away.

"Stupid things," Mark said. "They're dumb as shit. I mean, what kind of mindless animals bash their own brains out like that?"

"They don't feel pain," Tessa told him quietly, "except in their eyes. Once they've been out in the sun long enough to blind them, nothing hurts them anymore."

We walked away across the grass to the gates, the odour gradually dissipating as we left the crumpled bodies behind us. There had been nothing like it when we had opened the windows the previous morning, so I guessed that someone must have taken the first Weeper's body away in the night.

"What will you do with them?" I asked, looking at Tessa, but it was Mark who answered.

"Put 'em back outside," he said casually. "Unless anyone in the lab wants them, that is."

It sounded like this was an experiment after all, but I wondered whether it was driven by the so-called lab, or if the guards were just having fun with us and providing research subjects as a by-product. Neither scenario was good news for us.

Four days left, I thought. Four days until the Casting, until I would likely be joining them out beyond the perimeter of the Farm.

We walked through the gates, the time-delay holding us in each ring for a second before letting us through to the next, and then we were loaded into the back of their vehicle, Mark throwing Ollie's crutch in after us. This time the guards were driving what looked like a cross between a van and an armoured car. It had a separate cab in front of a contained holding area in the back, a couple of bench seats lined along each side at right angles to the rear door. The walls of the vehicle were solid metal, but we could see through the grill that separated us from the cab and out through the windscreen beyond it.

I wanted to ask where we were going and what we would be doing, but I'd already asked one question this morning and I didn't want to push my luck, so I kept quiet as Tessa drove us around the edge of the enclosure, following the line of the internal perimeter fence away from the main gates and into uncharted territory.

We drove for about half an hour, bumping along a rough track that ran parallel to the boundary of the Farm. We could see the track, the fences, the expanses of scrubby grass and dirt around them, and the rolling hills in the distance, but other than that there was nothing else within our blinkered view. The ground had been cleared and levelled within and for about twenty feet on either side of the fences, so the walls and hedgerows that criss-crossed the landscape were interrupted abruptly before resuming their course within the Farm. Trees had been felled, their fresh stumps breaking the surface of the dry ground, and streams were forded so that the fences ran straight through the water and down into the riverbed below.

We stopped at a point that initially looked no different from any other section of the fence, but when Mark opened the door and we got out of the vehicle we saw that we were parked next to a second set of gates. There were just two here: one in the interior fence and the other in the central fence, whereas the external perimeter stretched unbroken as far as I could see in each direction. A pole with a red, triangular flag on it rose above the top of the middle fence.

We were standing in the centre of a large expanse of pasture land that spread around us, continuing on the other side of the fence until it ended in a line of trees in the distance. The only cattle grazing were within the Farm borders, where a new line of wooden fencing kept the animals contained away from the razed ground on which we stood.

"You're going for a nice stroll in the countryside," Mark said as he handed us both a whistle. For a moment I thought he was going to send us entirely outside the protection of the fences, but surely if he was going to do that then they would have taken us to a place where the gates went all the way through?

Tessa pulled a gadget out of the cab and pressed a few of the buttons on its face. A couple of seconds later the interior gate opened and Mark gestured us through it.

"Right to the edge," he shouted as the first gate shut

behind us and the second opened, about forty feet in front of us. We walked across the gap and through the second gate, Ollie limping alongside me with his crutch, then turned and looked back at the guards as it closed in our faces. We waited expectantly for them to tell us what we were supposed to be doing here.

"You're gonna walk," Mark said, "for fifteen miles. If you see a Weeper up against the fence, in the cleared zone, you blow your whistle and someone will come take it away. When you get to a red flag set up on the middle fence like that one there," he said, pointing at the material that hung down in the still air, "then you've done your miles, so you blow your whistle and we'll come collect you."

Ollie and I looked at each other uncertainly. I did a quick mental calculation. If we walked at a brisk pace, we could be going at about three miles an hour, so that was about five hours walking. But with his crutch, I didn't think there was any way that Ollie was going to be able to move faster than about two miles an hour. I looked down at the flimsy canvas shoes we'd been issued and wondered whether they would even last the distance.

"Well, get going then," Mark said impatiently.

We started walking away, following the same direction of travel as that in which we had been driving.

"Oh no," Mark said with an evil grin, as if he had been waiting for the satisfaction of this moment, "you're walking the opposite way from each other. That way you'll cover double the distance between you."

Ollie's forehead creased momentarily in a look of concern, but then he quickly hid the expression and smiled at me reassuringly as he took my hand, squeezing it briefly before letting go again.

"I'll be fine," he said. "See you later."

He swung off on his crutch back in the direction we had come from and I walked away from him reluctantly, worried that he was going to struggle on his own.

"Enjoy the sunshine," Mark shouted as he and Tessa

climbed back into the vehicle. "It's going to be a scorcher!" he added gleefully, and I could see from the clear, blue sky and the haze rising from the hills that he was right. Without a hat and in the short-sleeved top of the blue scrubs, I was going to burn until I blistered if I didn't get out of the sun. Since everything that could have provided any modicum of shade had been cleared from around the fence, there was going to be no way to avoid it.

Once the sound of the engine had faded into the distance, I looked over my shoulder and saw that Ollie was making quick progress away from me. He seemed to be managing the uneven, grassy surface well despite the crutch, so I turned back and tried to focus on getting my own miles under my belt. I knew there was nothing I could have done to help him anyway, but the anxiety pulled at me nonetheless.

I hung my whistle around my neck and set off quickly, walking close to the central fence to put as much space as possible between myself and the Weeper-ridden countryside beyond the external perimeter. I was unsure whether these fences, like those of our enclosure, were electrified, but I took care to leave enough distance between myself and the metal that I wouldn't find out.

For half an hour or so the going was flat and even, running through grassy fields with wide, open space in every direction, and I saw no trace of any Weepers at all. As the sun blazed down on me my original pace quickly became uncomfortable, and I had to slow it down. I could already feel the sweat helping my ill-fitting shoes to rub blisters onto my heels and toes, and the soles were so thin that despite the grassy surface my feet were beginning to feel bruised and sore.

At a stretch, I reckoned that I might have come as far as two miles. With the pain in my feet already reducing my pace considerably, I seriously started to doubt whether I was going to be able to finish the distance by sundown, and if there was one thing I knew for certain it was that I didn't want to be stuck out here in the dark when the Weepers were on the prowl. Still, it couldn't have been much later than eight in the morning, so with the long, summer days I should have at least twelve hours left. If I could go a little faster than a mile an hour then it should be fine.

But if I was finding it hard with two good legs then how was Ollie going to be feeling by now, limping along on his crutch?

At least he only had to put one foot on the ground, I thought as my shoes pinched at my heels.

After another hour or so of painful walking through the flat fields, the gradient increased gently but relentlessly until it seemed as if I had been walking uphill forever. I could see a copse of trees in the distance at the top of the incline, bisected neatly by the path of the fence, but it didn't seem to be getting any closer while I slogged towards it. The mid-morning sun was beating down on me as I crossed the exposed ground, the skin on my face and arms tingling with incipient sunburn and itchy with sweat. My top was already damp, darker patches spreading across its surface as my body struggled to stay cool in the rising heat, and with no water I worried that I was going to dehydrate quickly.

At least if I ended up with heatstroke it might give me a good reason to avoid seeing Drew, I thought, but then I realised that he'd only be back tomorrow. Another confrontation with him was the last thing I would want to deal with when I eventually finished this forced march. Seeing him was an utterly pointless exercise, and after last night I couldn't imagine that any good would ever come of it.

It felt like hours before I finally reached the top of the incline, and it may well have been as the sun was now high overhead. As expected, there was no shade to be had where I stood with the trees more than fifty feet away. The ground levelled out here before sloping gently downwards, but the copse was bigger than it had first appeared, stretching off darkly to either side of me and ahead for such a long way that, despite the width of the cleared area, the gently curving path of the fence ahead was obscured from view by the distant trees.

I knew the Weepers would be here before I saw them, crowding back in the cover of the trees outside the perimeter. I could hear the birds singing merrily amongst the vegetation to one side of me, on the side within the Farm, but to the other side there was only an ominous silence that was so oppressive that it seemed to push me even closer against the central fence. The woodland was so dense that, squinting against the brightness of the sun, it was difficult to make out their shapes, but once my eyes had adjusted I saw their movement, the constant motion changing and reshaping the shadows of the close-packed conifers. There was a howl as the first caught sight of me, but I was safe in the avenue of sunlight I occupied and they didn't approach, following me through the forest instead as I walked.

The path went on for miles amongst the trees and I became increasingly jumpy as time went on, each sound of a snapped twig or rustling leaf see-sawing my pulse into overdrive. The ground here was difficult to navigate, tree stumps and the remains of scraggly shrubs making the earth uneven and treacherous, so that I had to fix my eyes on my feet for the majority of the time. It was a mixed blessing in the circumstances: part of me was relieved that I had something to concentrate on other than the proximity of the Weepers, but another part of me wanted to be keeping an eye on them, just in case.

I compromised by stopping every ten seconds or so to check up and down the fence for Weepers, the minimum that I felt was required by my duty, but that interval wasn't short enough to prevent me from being startled when I lifted my gaze from the ground to see a single Weeper wandering up to the fence. She was so tall that she might once have been called statuesque, a giant looming about half a foot above me, her dark skin coated in a sheen of wet blood.

My breath caught in the back of my throat and I gasped. As if alerted to my presence by the noise, the Weeper seemed to sniff the air and then howled, her cry echoing back at her from the hordes gathering in the shade of the woods.

There was a breathless moment when I thought that I would be inundated by Weepers, pouring over the fence and down on top of me, but they came no closer. Instead, the single Weeper rushed at me, her eyes filled with blood so that all I could see was red. I realised that this was a Weeper that had been in the sun too long, her sight burned away so that she could walk in the daylight with no pain. If Tessa was to be believed, she would feel no other pain at all.

"Shit!"

I scrabbled at my neck for my whistle, but when I finally managed to get a grip of it and lifted it to my mouth I was unable to make a sound, too panicked to blow strongly enough to signal for help. The second seemed to stretch out for ever and I felt as though I were trapped in a nightmare, unable to cry for help, unable to scream, paralysed by fear of the approaching horror as she reached the fence.

As it happened, there was no need for me to have been concerned. The instant that she hit the links of metal she crumpled, thrown backwards to lie smoking on the ground. Apparently the outer fence, at least, was electrified after all.

I stared at her body, legs twisted under her and arms out above her head, worried that she would climb back up to her feet again and make another run at the fence. I couldn't believe that she would stay down forever. When she was still motionless after a minute or so, I crouched down to the ground and dropped my head between my knees, trying to catch my breath and slow my heart rate. I had seen altogether too many broken Weepers today for my liking.

I raised my whistle to my lips again and blew, first tentatively but then more forcefully, until the sound rang out in the cleared path through the trees. I saw the Weepers in the forest back off a little, as if they knew what the whistle signified, and I wondered how many other humans had walked these paths before me in the two weeks since the Revelation, and what they had done to deserve this patrol.

There was a sudden rush of air and the Weeper's body was gone. I never even saw the Silver who came to collect it.

I sighed and sat down heavily on a nearby tree stump. I was overheated and sweating, and I was starting to get a headache. From the position of the sun, I guessed that I must have been walking for about four hours now, so if I was lucky I might have covered twelve miles, which would leave me only three to go. But my pace had been slow up the incline, so I may have covered as little as half of that, which would leave still nine miles to go. Less than halfway there.

There was no way I was going to be able to manage another four or five hours in this heat. I could already see that my arms and nose had burnt, and my top lip and the back of my neck also felt hot and scratchy. To top it all, I saw that there was a stain spreading across the white canvas on the inside of my right shoe. I removed it and, very carefully, my sock to reveal the remnants of a huge blister on the side of my foot at the base of my big toe. It wasn't the only one, the uncomfortable shoes rubbing my feet on every side.

I was going to have to improvise some sun and foot protection if I wanted to make it to the flag by dusk.

I didn't want to compromise my T-shirt, because without it I was only going to burn my shoulders and my back, but I could do without wearing full-length trousers. I pulled at the stitching at the knees of the scrub bottoms and managed to rip off the lower part of each of the legs, leaving me with two tubes of material. The first I ripped into two pieces, wrapping them carefully around my feet to cushion them where they rubbed against the shoes. I pulled my hair out of its braid and spread it over my neck, fashioning the second tube into a makeshift hat to keep the sun off my head.

It was far from perfect, but it would have to do. My legs were going to burn below the knee, but I'd rather have a little extra sunburn than get sunstroke or cripple my feet so I was unable to complete my allotted miles.

And then it was time to set off again. I re-laced my shoes painfully, trying to pull the canvas together as securely as possible to minimise friction, and stood up to continue my patrol. The Weepers hadn't moved during this interlude, still keeping a cautious distance away from the edge of the forest, and the space between me and the trees was clear of activity.

The walk down through the remainder of the copse was uneventful. I started slowly, inching along painfully as I became accustomed to the agony of the blisters once more, but they were certainly more comfortable than they had been and when I had acclimatised it was surprisingly easy to ignore my feet. It wasn't so easy to ignore my thirst and the headache that was growing at my temples and across my forehead.

I broached the other side of the trees and walked out into a gentle valley of open fields, a brook running through its lowest point across the line of the fence. As I descended the hillside slowly, the grassy ground softer on my feet than the tree stumps of the forest, I started to hear the tinkling sound of the water running in rills through the rocky riverbed and I became more and more aware of my dry throat and tongue. It drew me down the slope quickly, hurrying my feet towards the water that would soothe my parched mouth, and I fell to my knees gratefully at its bank, stretching my hands out to plunge them into the stream.

But then there was a strange noise, a fzzzt sound that turned my attention to the exterior fence. It looked as though the electrified portion had been separated from the river here, a rubberised section forming a barrier between it and the lower portion of fencing that ran through the water itself and down to bury itself in the ground. I mentally chastised myself; I hadn't even thought to check whether or not the electric current might be running through the water before reaching out for it.

But it was worse than that. I imagined that, the way the fence had been constructed, the water shouldn't have touched the electric fence, but something had bridged the gap between them, a dark shadow lying in the water on the other side of the metal links. I climbed back up to my feet and edged my way tentatively along the side of the brook towards the fence to see what it was.

It was a Weeper. It was lying in the stream, half-submerged and bobbing in the flow of the current, batting intermittently up against the live fencing as it rose and fell in the swell of the eddies. Not only had I nearly electrocuted myself, I'd also nearly ingested water tainted with the Weeper plague.

Great move, Emmy.

Hoping fervently that someone was regulating access to the brook further downstream in the Farm, I blew my whistle again and, once more, the Weeper's body was whisked away without my seeing any trace of the Silver who had come to collect it.

Time to move on.

The fence was no longer making any noise so I thought it was probably safe to cross, but I wasn't taking any chances with electrocution or the infected water, so I took a run-up and jumped over the brook rather than wading through it, cursing as I landed heavily on my sore feet.

The next hour was a gentle walk through more open fields, crossing the occasional road, until the path climbed up steeply past a small collection of houses, the bright sun shining off the remaining glass in their windows. It must have been six or seven hours' walking by this point, and I was vainly looking out for the red flag that marked the end of my journey, but there was no sign of it so far. As I approached the hamlet I saw a dark heap piled up against the outer perimeter fence about two hundred yards away from the nearest house and realised why these patrols were necessary. The heap was comprised of about six Weepers, although it was difficult to be certain, all of whom had thrown themselves against the electric fence. If enough had gathered here then perhaps they might have been able to crest the top, but not on this occasion. They weren't moving now.

I blew my whistle again, and this time the Silver clean-up crew stopped still next to the pile of bodies. There was just one of them, an older-looking Silver woman with grey hair and a wiry frame that made her look tough as nails.

"Hello," I said as she surveyed the pile. It had been a long walk so far, and I was desperate for some kind of distraction.

She looked back at me in surprise, clearly not expecting to be addressed by a human.

"Hello."

"Do you not get electrocuted if you touch the bodies?" I asked, not sure how it worked.

She shook her head and turned her attention back to the Weepers.

"Will they recover from this?" I said.

She looked up at me impassively for a moment as if she were wondering how long I would continue to engage her in conversation. Feeling awkward and not sure what else to do, I brazened through.

"I don't suppose there's any chance of a drink, is there?" I asked. "Or do you know how far away I am from the flag?"

She simply raised an eyebrow at me then disappeared, and after a few more seconds of intense movement the Weeper bodies were gone too.

She obviously hadn't been in the mood to chat.

I passed the houses and crested the rise, seeing the countryside spread out beneath me. I wasn't sure, but I thought I could see the flag in the distance. When I turned and looked back the way I had come, the copse of trees seemed closer to me than where I imagined my destination to be, and my heart sank. Despondent, I sat down heavily on a nearby rock and contemplated my goal.

It had to be miles and miles from me, and I was hitting the end of my energy supplies. My feet were so mangled that I wasn't sure how I'd be able to walk again tomorrow, the skin so tender that the thought of standing up again filled me with absolute dread. I was utterly exhausted, and so thirsty I couldn't even seem to wet the back of my throat. When I coughed, it was dry and painful, rasping across the sensitive skin like sandpaper.

I thought briefly about seeing Drew this evening, and the Casting next week, but it was difficult to concentrate on anything other than my immediate pain. Everything else paled in comparison, and suddenly another meeting with Drew seemed like a cakewalk.

But I had another walk to finish right now if I wanted to get out of here before the Weepers were battering at the fence to get to me, so I rose unsteadily to my feet and gently covered the first few hundred yards downhill until my feet started to numb up again.

I tried to distract myself from the pain with simple games to keep my mind busy: how many different kinds of wildflower could I spot, naming all of the countries in Europe and their capital cities (an unmitigated failure) and, when I could think of nothing else, running through my times tables up to a total of one thousand. It wasn't a great success.

Every moment I thought I was going to look up and see the flag in the distance, but as time went on I was becoming less and less certain that I had seen it at all from the vantage point on top of the hill. I had lost all track of time at this point, the sun low enough in the sky that it was clearly the afternoon, but I had no idea when.

And then I saw it, the little scrap of red flashing in the green landscape.

I started to move more quickly, desperate to get back to our squalid little cell and the fresh, clear, running water in its tap, until I was finally able to raise the whistle to my lips once more, collapsing down onto the ground in a heap of sweat and exhaustion as I blew on it.

The flag marked another set of gates, again in only the inner two fences, and so it looked like I was getting out of here the same way that I got in. I figured that it would probably take them a while to come and collect me in the truck, so I lay down on the grass and closed my eyes at the sheer pleasure of having no further to walk. I could feel the afternoon sunshine adding to the burns on my face and legs, but I just couldn't find the energy to care enough to do anything about it. I'd be blistered all over by tomorrow anyway, so what did it matter?

I wondered how Ollie was getting on, worried that he

would be stuck out in the perimeter fences when night fell.

I was just starting to drop off to sleep when I was awakened by the sound of an engine approaching: the truck rolling down the hill towards me from the hamlet. By the time Mark and Tessa reached the gates I had stood up and walked around enough that my feet would comfortably hold my weight again, so when Tessa got her opener gadget out I walked through the gates quickly and got into the back of the vehicle as soon as possible, luxuriating at sitting on the bench rather than on the floor.

"You've caught the sun," Mark laughed through the partition as Tessa drove us back along the route I had spent my day walking.

It made it feel like such a wasted effort. The Silver could just drive a patrol along here, or zip along the perimeter at super-speed to check it for Weepers. I wondered whether they did that too, if this was just a way of finding us something to do that was sufficiently horrible.

"You didn't see any gaps in the fence?" Tessa asked.

"No," I said, gently feeling my ravaged skin to see how bad the burns were. They were pretty bad, but at least it was over.

Of course, there was more unpleasantness to come today, but I decided I'd cross that bridge when I came to it.

CHAPTER IX

We'd been driving along for a good while, and I was starting to doze off again when Mark began to laugh, an unattractive cackle that made him sound like a Bond villain.

"Hah! There he is, hobbling along like a bloody cripple."

Ollie, I thought. A million questions reared up in my mind, but chief amongst them was: is he okay? I wasn't sure how far we were away from the next flag, how far he had left to go before his day was over.

I pushed my face up against the partition to see him, but the truck had already gone past and I could see nothing through the grill except the unbroken line of the perimeter fence.

About ten minutes later Mark spoke again.

"There's the flag, so it'll be a good long while before you see your roomie again."

I worried that he was right. I reckoned that we had been going at about thirty miles an hour along the rough track, so that left him maybe five miles to go. If that was right, he was only two-thirds of the way through.

How were we ever going to get through another day of this tomorrow?

Mark had another surprise for me when we finally arrived

back at our enclosure: more Weepers. This time there was only one, wandering around loose on the other side of the building from where we parked up at the gates.

"Well," he said as I climbed painfully out of the back of the truck, "until your cellmate returns I thought you'd better have someone else to keep you company. Maybe you feel like playing a game with your new friend?"

He looked at Tessa and smiled cheekily as if sharing a joke, then turned the expression into a grin as he looked back at me, baring his teeth in a way that, despite his physical inadequacies, reminded me vividly that he was Silver. He was the predator here, and I was the sport.

"So let's see whether you can make it to your cell before your new friend eats you, shall we?"

I stared at him in incomprehension, flicking my gaze towards Tessa to see if this was really serious, half expecting her to intervene. But her expression was blank and stony as she leaned back casually against the driver's door of the vehicle, her arms and her ankles crossed in an attitude of apparent relaxation. Everything about her posture said she wasn't involved in this, but she wasn't going to stop it either.

"What?" I said as I turned back to Mark.

He pulled the gate opening gadget out of the cab of the truck, pushing a few buttons, and walked up to the fence, ushering me in front of him.

"I've set the gates to a quick interval," he said. "I reckon you'll get a second to go through each of them, so you better run pretty damn quick. Off you go then."

Before I had time to process this, the gate in front of me was opening and he pushed me through.

"Better run," he reminded me as I stumbled onto my knees on the grass.

The gate behind me had already shut and the one in the central fence was nearly fully open by the time I had hauled myself up into a race start and sprinted through. It slammed closed behind me and I raced through the third gate and towards the door of the cell before I realised I didn't have the code to open it.

"What's the code?" I shouted.

"Oh dear," Mark said. "Now you've told your new friend where you are. He can't see, but he hears pretty well. Here he comes."

I looked to the corner of the building and saw that he was right: the Weeper was just coming into view, sniffing at the air as he tried to track me down. I gestured at Mark frantically, trying to get him to tell me the code without letting the Weeper know where I was, fearing that he never would and that I would die here. Probably I'd get turned into a Weeper, a macabre homecoming present for Ollie when he finally finished his walk.

I panicked, my heart thundering in my chest as the Weeper came ever closer, and I was about to give up on Mark and run away from the door and around the building when he relented and shouted the number to me.

"Oh, go on then," he said. "It's 1969. It was a good year."

The second I tapped in the first number, the Weeper zeroed in on my position, turning his head towards me and howling before running at me full pelt. Desperately keying in the last numbers, I managed to yank the door open and slam it into the Weeper's body, knocking it down to the ground. That bought me enough time to run into the building and pull the door shut behind me, the two locks clicking into place securely.

I sighed with relief, leaning up against the wall with my eyes fixed on the ceiling until I could catch my breath, as the Weeper threw itself up against the door. If I had taken a moment longer to key in that code, or if I hadn't managed to key it in right first time, I would have been Weeper food. If I had thought that the guards were under any obligation to ensure our safety while we were here, I had clearly thought wrong.

One way or another, I was going to die here.

But if that was true, I thought, then I may as well do so feeling a bit more comfortable. It was time for a shower.

Before I did anything else, I walked into the bathroom to put my head under the tap, letting the cold water run into my mouth and over my scalded, sweaty, dirt-covered face. It was utter bliss.

When my thirst was thoroughly quenched, I tested the door into the observation room and found to my relief that it was still open, so I swung it wide to let some more light into the cell. I was just turning to go back into the bathroom for a shower when I realised that there was a bag on the table: another paper bag like those in which our food had been provided. Maybe the guards had realised that this door had been left open after all.

The bag held the usual apples, cereal bars, bread and cheese, but this time there was also some chocolate and a few big bags of crisps. Even more surprising, there was a stack of clothes on the table next to it with new scrubs for me and Ollie. Clean clothes! I could have cried with happiness.

I carried the haul carefully through to the cell, the rough paper of the bag grating up against my sunburnt skin, and put it all down on the bed. I meant to go straight to the shower, but now that I was no longer so thirsty my body was waking up and urgent signals started telling me that I was absolutely ravenous. After the amount of fluid I had lost, I had an extreme salt craving so I pulled out one of the bags of crisps and ripped into it, devouring half of them before I realised I was doing so. The salt made me thirsty again so I took another round under the tap before I was finally ready to strip down for a shower.

It took me about five minutes to get my shoes off. When I finally managed to do so, unwinding the makeshift padding from my feet, I found that my socks were stuck to the raw skin where the blisters had been, so I had to soak them under the tap before I could release the material. My feet were cut up badly, about six different blisters on each of them from every angle. I never wanted to wear shoes again, but I was going to have to put them back on tomorrow and walk fifteen more miles.

I shuddered and pushed the thought away, trying to concentrate on what I had to accomplish right now, and worried that at any moment Drew might arrive for his next visit. I needed to get clean quickly and thoroughly whilst I still had the chance.

When I stripped off my top and bottoms I could see the extent of the sunburn, the colour developing into an even angrier red now that I had been out of the sun for a little while. My arms were scarlet from the elbow down, my legs from the knee down. I couldn't see my face and neck, but both felt sore and hot to the touch. It was probably a good thing that our shower didn't feature hot water.

The cold shock of the stream soothed the burning of my face and limbs, but as it hit the raw skin on my feet I couldn't stop myself from crying out. It was even worse when I got the soap on it, working it into the cuts to wash out the filth of the day. I gritted my teeth against the stinging pain as the Weeper worked out where I was in the building from my yell and started thudding against the wall outside the shower. I wondered how long it would take it to break itself and whether it would be neutralised before Ollie got home. That would be a small mercy, at least.

I put the clean scrubs on after I had towelled off, but left my feet uncovered and open to the air, hoping that it would help them to heal. There was nothing for me to do now except wait for Ollie, so I sat down on the bed and did exactly that, listening to the diminishing thumps from the Weeper as the hot room started to cool towards the evening, imagining that I could almost hear its bones cracking and breaking against the concrete.

I catalogued my injuries as I combed out my wet hair with my fingers and decided they were all minor. The sunburn and the blisters were bad but superficial, and they'd heal eventually. I still had a headache, but it was improving now that I had hydrated. The raw skin on my wrist from the handcuffs was still there, but the bandage was long gone after the sweaty, grimy excesses of the day, leaving only a pale line across my skin where it had saved me from sunburn. Finally, I felt sore in my muscles, knees and ankles, but none of the twinges were particularly bad and I thought that I would likely recover overnight.

I wondered what state Ollie would arrive back in.

It was maybe a couple of hours later when I finally heard an engine outside the enclosure. The light was starting to dim a little into the evening, but the sun was still out and night had not yet fallen. I swung my feet off the bed and moved painfully over to the window at the front of the cell, praying that it would be Ollie coming back rather than Drew.

It was, but he was in bad shape. There was no race against the Weeper for him as he hopped laboriously through the gates, his arm round Tessa's shoulders as she carried the crutch for him. It didn't look like Mark was with her this time. The truck was empty with no one waiting at the perimeter. As soon as she entered the code into the door I pulled it open, taking Ollie from her and helping him over to the bed.

"Shit," I said. "Are you alright?"

He was sunburned, but his skin was darker than mine so his didn't look as bad. His face was drawn into a grimace of pain and I surveyed him quickly, taking in the spots of blood soaking through the material of his top at his shoulder, the blistered mess of his other hand and the filth caking his good foot.

"You've pulled your stitches," I said.

He gritted his teeth and nodded.

"Shit. He needs a doctor," I said as I spun round to face Tessa where she stood at the door. She nodded and handed me the crutch, then pulled the door closed behind her and was gone.

"Thirsty," he whispered.

I looked around desperately then spotted the bag of crisps. I emptied the remainder of its contents out onto the bed and then, rinsing it thoroughly, filled the bag with water and brought it to him.

"Sip it gently," I said, not wanting him to make himself

unwell. I seemed to have escaped the more serious effects of heatstroke, but from the look of him I wasn't sure that Ollie had been so lucky.

By the time Tessa got back with the doctor, I'd managed to get him to drink a few pints of water and eat the rest of the crisps, and he was looking much brighter.

"Shirt off and lie down," Dr Tanner said, and I helped Ollie do as he directed while Tessa waited in the observation room next door. Ollie winced as we manoeuvred his shoulder out of the top, but once it was free we could see that it wasn't a bad as I had feared. A couple of the stitches had pulled, but the rest were still securely in place.

The doctor cleaned the wound carefully and then replaced the stitches Ollie had torn out before helping him to strip off and get through the shower. I wasn't sure what to do with myself, feeling redundant with the doctor here to tend to him, so I just sat on the bed and waited until they came back into the cell.

When they did, Ollie was dressed in his clean scrub bottoms, his wet hair dripping trails of water from his shoulders down his torso. One of his feet, the one that belonged to his bad leg, looked okay, but the other was as beaten up as my own. The hand with which he used his crutch seemed better now it was cleaned up from the dirt of the walk, but it was still rubbed raw in places, cracked and bleeding from the exertions of the day.

"You both need to rest up and stay off your feet as much as possible," the doctor said.

"We're on patrol again tomorrow," I replied quietly.

A flash of anger crossed his face quickly before settling back into his normal, composed expression as if it had never been there.

"Then I'll do my best to seal up the wounds for you. It'll hurt, I'm afraid."

He wasn't kidding. Ollie and I sat down on the bed next to each other as the doctor knelt in front of us, pulling a bottle and some cotton wool out of his bag. He soaked the cotton wool in the liquid from the bottle and then applied it to each of our raw blisters, the astringency of the mixture so caustic and sharp on the delicate skin that it made me cry out, my eyes running with tears at the pain. I felt like I was being a girl about it until it had exactly the same effect on Ollie.

Once he had covered our injured feet and Ollie's hand, the skin did seem to be much less sensitive, and I had hopes that we might be able to make it through tomorrow after all.

"I'll leave this here for you," he said as he screwed the lid back on tight, "along with some cotton wool and some spare dressings. It looks like you might need them, I'm afraid."

He re-dressed Ollie's shoulder and my wrist before he left, handing us some cream for the sunburn as well. Tessa joined him at the door to escort him out and, once the doctor had stepped outside ahead of her, turned back towards us.

"Not a word to Mark," she whispered, and then she was gone, the door slamming closed behind her.

Ollie looked at me in confusion.

"What the hell was that about?"

I shrugged.

"Maybe we're not supposed to have any medical attention. It does seem a little at odds with the whole 'work us to death' thing."

I wondered whether we might have an ally of sorts in Tessa, despite her reluctance to intervene this afternoon. Perhaps she wasn't able to do any more for us because Mark was her superior, I thought, although I found that hard to credit.

I put most of the medical supplies away in one of the old paper bags that our food had come in, but I brought the cream over to the bed and smoothed it gratefully over the burnt skin of my lower arms and legs. Ollie did the same with his face, arms and the back of his neck and then, as I covered my own face, he shifted so he was sitting behind me. He gently pushed my hair over my shoulders before spreading the cool cream over the back of my neck, his fingers brushing at the hairs at the base of my skull in a way that sent an unexpected frisson of excitement racing through me.

"Did you see many Weepers?" he asked quietly.

"A few," I said. "How about you?"

"Just one, right by the fence where a piece of corrugated iron had fallen against it to make a sort of shelter. The Silver came and cleared it away."

"Did you see them?" I asked, thinking about my own encounters through the day.

"No," he said as he put the lid back on the tube of cream. "One minute it was there, then I blew my whistle and next thing I know the Weeper's gone and the metal's gone."

I wondered whether to tell him about the Weepers I'd seen, about nearly getting electrocuted or poisoned in the river, but I decided it would only worry him unnecessarily. I kept quiet. For the same reason, I didn't tell him that Mark had made me race the Weeper outside. He had enough on his plate with his injuries and the impending prospect of tomorrow's patrol.

In the silence, I realised that I could only barely hear the Weeper now, his assault reduced to a very gentle tapping at the wall of the bathroom.

"How are you?" I asked.

He moved forward so that he was sitting next to me and took my hand in his.

"I'm fine," he said. "I made it today, and I'll make it tomorrow, and the next day. I'm sore, but I'm sure you are too. The first few days are going to be hard, but we'll get through them and then it'll be easier. You'll see."

He pulled me into his arms, my head against his uninjured shoulder, and held me tight.

"Has your ex dropped in to see you yet?" he asked.

"No, not yet."

I wished he hadn't reminded me.

It was almost full night now, the dusk darkening quickly, but with the Weeper already incapacitated the only fear the night held for me was Drew.

CHAPTER X

We didn't hear another engine outside until about an hour later. We had eaten some dinner and curled up together on the bed, both exhausted. I could hear Ollie's breath light and even at my back as he slept, but despite the aching tiredness in my limbs I hadn't been able to drop off, anticipating Drew's visit every time I heard the slightest sound from beyond the walls of the cell. On top of it all, the blisters were stinging in an agonising way, the pain that I had been able to ignore throughout the evening coming rushing back in the tranquillity of the night when there was nothing to distract me from it.

As soon as I heard the car I slipped out of Ollie's arms and sat up to pull the connecting door shut, hoping that perhaps when Drew saw that we were in bed he might just leave us alone in peace. I listened to the vehicle moving through the gates before pulling up in front of the building. I heard the door to the next room opening, and then the footsteps crossing the concrete towards us.

The panel in the door clanked open, but there was no light from beyond it.

"Ems?"

I recognised the voice that whispered through the hatch,

but it wasn't Drew's.

"Cam?" I asked, barely able to believe that he was here.

"Yes."

"Are you alone?" I asked, worried that he might have come along with Drew.

"Yes," he said as he opened the connecting door. "I'm on my own. Are you?"

Ollie roused behind me, but I slid out of the bed and tiptoed quickly across the floor. I pushed Cam gently back into the observation room, closing the door softly behind us.

"No," I said once I was comfortable we wouldn't disturb Ollie. "Ollie's still here too. Have you got a torch? I can't see a thing in this dark."

"Er, hang on a sec."

I heard the external door open and shut as Cam left the building, followed shortly by the doors of the car outside. He was back within a minute.

"I've got these," he said, a flare of light illuminating the darkness as he struck a match and applied it to a candle wick. "It's a bit old school, but at least it'll mean I can get a good look at you."

He lined a few candles up along the table, using the flame to melt their fat ends so he could stick them upright onto the surface, then he put the box of matches down and turned to face me.

"Shit, Ems," he said, his face scrunching up in an expression of sympathy, "you look like you've had a close encounter with a flamethrower."

"It's just sunburn," I said, gently pulling him into a hug. "It'll heal."

"And your feet?" he asked as he leaned away and looked me up and down. "They look… not good."

"Just blisters," I smiled, putting a brave face on it as I hobbled over to the other side of the table and sat down. "Now tell me what's up. Not that I'm not delighted to see you, but why are you here?"

"Well," he said, "one of us has to come every day, but they

don't know who it is in the car, so here I am. Drew said you probably wouldn't want to see him."

"Drew was right," I said firmly.

Cam sat down next to me, leaning back in his chair so that it came to rest against the wall, tipped backwards at an angle.

"What happened?" he asked as he dangled his legs.

"I'm not that keen to talk about it, really. He was angry. He scared me."

"I'm sure he didn't mean to," Cam said dismissively.

"Maybe not," I said, "but he didn't care that he did. He's like a different person without the bond, someone I don't know and don't want to know."

"He's still himself, Ems. It's been hard on him, losing the bond."

"Cam," I said sternly, looking into his eyes until he fell still. "I seriously thought he was going to hurt me. He looked at me like I was nothing to him, because that's how he feels. Without the bond, he doesn't care if I live or die."

He said nothing, and I wondered whether it was because he agreed with what I had said, but didn't want to say it out loud, or admit it to me.

"It's just as well, really," I continued, "given that I'm probably going to be turned into a Weeper next week anyway."

"I could just put you in the back of the car and drive off with you," he said.

"Really? You're one of the Invicti, Cam, and I know how you feel about Sol. You're not going to commit treason against him by breaking me out of here. He put us in here, and we can't come out until he says. Besides," I added, "I can't leave Ollie."

"Couldn't you? After everything he did?"

I shook my head.

"He only made the same mistakes I did. He tried to make it right in the end."

"Maybe."

"You don't believe that?"

"I don't know," he said. "You hear things."

"From Tamsin and Ben? Jesus, not you too."

"No, that's not what I mean. It's just that with all the other rebels dead, who's left to contradict whatever story he tells you?"

"I can't believe I'm hearing this from you," I said. "He's looking after me here, and he's the only friend I have in this place. I'm going to need to hear a pretty convincing argument before I start questioning him, so unless you have something other than speculation then just drop it, okay?"

"Okay," he said, holding his hands up in a gesture of surrender. "Pretend I never mentioned it."

But it wasn't that easy. We sat together in uncomfortable silence for a minute or so before either of us spoke again. It was odd to feel awkward around Cam, someone I had always felt so at ease with. If I was honest with myself then I was finding it hard to get over the fact that he was Silver. He was one of them, a part of the system that was keeping me in this place and driving me to the Casting.

He was one of Drew's men at the end of the day.

What if he turned like him, if he snapped and started to treat me like a stranger too? Or worse, an adversary?

"We must be able to come up with another plan to get you out of this," he said eventually.

"This cell?" I asked.

"No, the whole turning Weeper thing."

"Well," I said, "can't I just fail the selection process and avoid the Casting that way? Would that work?"

"Hasn't Drew talked you through this?" he asked.

I shook my head. Of course he hadn't. He'd been too busy shouting at me.

Cam sighed.

"Okay," he said, "so there are three tests in the selection process. One is like a tailored aptitude test, to make sure you have something to offer in terms of intelligence or creativity or whatever. The other two are physical and mental endurance tests, to make sure you can make it through the transformation and that you won't have a breakdown when faced with the crushing reality of eternal life. Frankly, that's sort of a given now that you've made it this far after the Revelation, but they'll do it anyway."

"And I only go to the Casting if I make it through all those tests?"

"Well," he said, "everyone who's been sponsored goes to the Casting. It's a whole ceremonial event, so either way you'll be there. At the Casting, they'll announce who's been selected, and then those people go through the dawn rituals and, all being well, get turned Silver."

Either way, I was going to have to go back to the city, to stand in front of Sol and the rest of the Silver, and admit that Drew had been my sponsor. I wondered how many of them would put two and two together and realise that it had been me that Drew had silvered for, and how that would change the stability of his position. Maybe it was one of the reasons he was so angry with me. It wasn't supposed to have been an issue, because while the bond was there I would have been turned Silver and he would have got what he wanted. Now, not only had he lost the love he felt for me, but he also faced reproach from the Silver at his lost feelings for a human.

But he would have to worry about his reputation himself. I was more concerned with making sure I stayed alive, and now that the possibility was in my hands it seemed terrifyingly real.

"So how do I make sure I fail the tests?"

"Yeah, the endurance tests are going to be hard to fake. As far as the physical test goes, either you're suitable for turning Silver or you're not. It's more Ed's area of expertise than mine, but there's not much you can do about it either way. With the mental endurance test, you won't know what they're trying to get you to do or what they're looking for, so that's going to be hit and miss. The only one you can really control is the aptitude test."

"How?"

"Well, they're mostly common sense questions, so if you

know the correct answer then say something else instead. They'll give you the opportunity to showcase any talents you have, and you just say you don't have anything to show them."

That was actually about right anyway, but I didn't tell Cam that.

Ollie's voice came through the door from the next room. "Emmy?"

"I'm through here," I called back and he burst through the door, clearly switching into hero mode, anticipating that I would be with Drew.

"Hey," I said, "it's okay. I just didn't want to wake you. You remember Cam?"

Cam stood up from his seat and offered Ollie his hand. He hesitated for a moment before shaking it.

"Hi," Ollie said.

"I hear you've been looking after my girl," Cam replied.

Ollie raised his eyebrow at me, noting the possessive pronoun, but Cam laughed when he saw his expression.

"Not like that," he said.

"So no angry ex today?" Ollie asked.

"Not today," I said. "Presumably he'll be back tomorrow?" I asked Cam.

"He'll have to be. It's the first test tomorrow, then the second on Monday and third on Tuesday, then the Casting on Wednesday. He needs to be with you for all of them."

"Right," I said on a sigh. I guessed that I had better enjoy my brief reprieve while it lasted.

Ollie sat down opposite me at the table, but from the way his eyes scanned between us I could tell he was uncomfortable with Cam sitting so close to me. Yesterday's meeting with Drew had put him on high alert and he was watching the Silver like a hawk, making no attempt to hide the mistrust in his eyes.

"How are things back in the city?" I asked Cam. "Have you found Mary?"

I was praying that she had escaped the explosion alive. From the downcast look on Cam's face I knew what the answer was going to be before he replied.

"I'm sorry, Ems. She didn't make it out."

I thought of Jane and Mia, how distraught they must be, and hoped that there was someone back in the city to look after them and help them through this. The sad reality was that, with so many of us dead, there was nothing notable or unusual about the fact that they had lost their mother. There were people out there in far worse situations, and at least they still had each other. They were sensible, I told myself, and they'd get through it together.

"And what about Nix?" I asked him, naming the kitten Alice and I had adopted. "Has there been any sign of her?"

I dreaded his answer. Ridiculous though it might have seemed, I felt as if I couldn't have borne the loss of her on top of everything else. I had so many positive memories of her and Alice together, and having already lost one of them I felt like it would have broken me to lose the other too.

"She's fine," he said, and I sagged with relief. "Carrie found her out in the street by the rubble the morning after the explosion, and she and Ed are looking after her."

"Finally," I said, "some good news."

"Are things that bad here?" Cam asked.

"Oh, no," Ollie said, having exhausted his patience for the day, "they're treating us like fucking royalty, as you can see. Housekeeping will be round for turn-down service any minute."

"Ollie," I said, a warning note in my tone.

I turned to Cam.

"We're on punishment duty walking the perimeter for fifteen miles a day. Today was our first one, and it didn't go that well, as you can see. We're neither of us in the best mood right now."

"Are they feeding you?" he asked.

"Yes. Not well, but yes, we have food."

"And the guards?"

I sighed, not wanting to talk about the race to the door this afternoon while Ollie was sitting next to me. It would just have been another thing for him to get angry and worried about.

"One of them's a total dick," Ollie interjected. "The other one seems okay, but she doesn't rein the dickhead in."

"You saw the Weeper outside?" I asked Cam.

He nodded.

"They put new ones in the enclosure every day," I said. "I'm not sure why. They let them hurl themselves at the building until they're too broken to move, then they put them back outside the Farm. Or sometimes they run tests, I think."

"Do you want me to see if I can stop it?" Cam asked.

"No," I said, contemplating the type of vindictive person that Mark seemed to be. "I think you'll just make it worse. The one guard, he's a bully. I don't think he'd react well."

"You're probably right," Cam said. "Most of the guards here are Invicti rejects, people who wanted to join the Solis Invicti but didn't have the skills or the mental stability for the job. I'm not surprised that they're unbalanced."

"What," I said, "unlike the poster boys for mental health that you do let into the Invicti, like Ben?"

"He's not crazy, Ems. He's utterly sane, which makes him even more dangerous. He knows exactly what he's doing, and he calculates his moves every step of the way. Anyway, I hope you won't have to deal with him anymore, now the bond's gone."

No, I thought, just a raft of other problems that it caused when it broke.

"He's not going to stop trying to overthrow Sol, you know," I said.

"We know. Unfortunately, the explosions seem to have had the effect that he hoped they would. More of the Silver have moved over to Ben's way of thinking, not wanting to allow the humans any freedom at all. It's even more difficult now that the Palace and the club are gone. Everyone's bunched up together in the Square, and that's not going well. The Silver are angry, and the humans are scared."

It sounded like a recipe for disaster.

"And Sol?" I asked. "What's he doing about it?"

Cam shrugged.

"If things carry on like this, I'm not sure he'll have much of a choice. And if he's listening to Laila..."

"Is he?" I asked.

Cam shrugged again.

"We don't know. He doesn't talk to us. None of the Invicti have had a moment alone with him since he silvered, not even Drew. It's not looking good, Ems."

It sounded as if soon we weren't going to be the only ones in a cage.

There was a lull in conversation that I didn't know how to fill, and neither of the others spoke. I felt uncomfortable having Cam here, as if I didn't want him to see me in this dank place, and I couldn't work out whether it was because I was ashamed to have been brought so low or because it was our place, mine and Ollie's, and he felt like an intruder here.

"Well," Cam said hopelessly after a while, "is there anything else I can do? Anything I can get you? Anything you need?"

I laughed bitterly.

"I could make you a list. Blister plasters, toothbrushes, toothpaste, better trainers and socks for walking, sun cream, hats, water bottles, pillows, blankets, more food. That's just off the top of my head."

"Shampoo and conditioner," Ollie chimed in, "better clothes and some underwear."

Cam pulled a notepad out of his pocket and wrote down our list, promising he'd make sure everything we needed was with us in the morning.

"And how are you going to square that with the guards?" I asked. "They're going to notice when we come out wearing something other than our crappy scrubs and canvas shoes."

"Don't worry," he replied. "I've got a plan for that."

He didn't say anything else on the subject, leaving shortly afterwards to go and prepare our care package. I pulled him into a tight hug before he left and as he held me close he whispered in my ear.

"I'll get you out of this, Ems. I promise."

I pressed a kiss to his cheek and he slipped out of the door, closing it firmly behind him. The engine caught a moment later and he was gone, driving back through the gates and back to the city. I blew out the candles and we made our way painfully back to the bed, pulling the observation room door shut behind us, just in case.

"Are you okay?" Ollie asked as he lay down beside me.

"Fine," I said. "Worried about tomorrow. Today was hard. Tomorrow will be worse."

"Maybe," he said, "but it'll get easier. We'll toughen up quickly, and in a week or so you'll be eating up those miles like they're nothing."

"I'm not sure I'm going to last that long," I whispered. "Cam told me about the tests for the Casting. There's only one I can really throw, one out of three that I can control. I worry that this time next week you'll be here on your own."

"So do I, but we can't do anything about it." He rolled onto his back and pulled me onto my side so that my head was on his chest, my arms around my waist. "For the moment I have you here with me, and I'm grateful for that."

"Scared of the dark?" I teased, but his answer was serious and unguarded.

"Scared of losing you."

CHAPTER XI

Sunday

We slept soundly in each other's arms, but I still woke with the dawn the next day. Every muscle in my body was screaming, yesterday's exertion catching up with me, so instead of getting out of bed I just groaned and rolled myself more tightly into Ollie's body to steal his warmth. He cuddled me close and I fell back to sleep almost instantly.

Next thing I knew I was being awakened by the speakers in the ceiling as they fired into life for the first time.

"Good morning, this is Ada." The disembodied voice was louder than was necessary in the bare space of the cell, reverberating unpleasantly off the walls. "Today we are honoured and humbled to receive a visit from the Primus, who is conducting a tour of the new facilities. I am sure that you will extend him every courtesy for the duration of his presence here. As usual, certain exemplary workers will be privileged to take lunch with him later today. Those individuals will be informed before morning break. Have a productive day, and I look forward to seeing you all at evening prayer."

The speaker cut out as abruptly as it had begun, leaving Ollie and me bemused and slightly deafened.

Sol was coming here, and he was coming today. I wondered whether I would see him, whether he would come to see me, and then I reminded myself that things were over between us and that he had moved on. In a big way.

"Sounds like things are a little different here from in the city," Ollie said sleepily. I had propped myself up onto my elbows for the announcement, lying on my stomach, but he clearly wasn't ready for me to get out of bed yet and tugged me back into his arms.

"I wonder what evening prayer is about," I said.

"Whatever it is, we clearly aren't invited. I don't think we'll be up for the most productive worker award either. Probably for the best really. I'm not sure I want to be the Primus's lunch."

"I'm sure that's not what it's about. They'll just be eating normal food. He doesn't do blood drinking in public, and he doesn't even drink straight from his chained girls."

The moment the words were out of my mouth I realised that they were only going to make Ollie ask questions about Sol, questions I didn't want to answer. Inevitably, he did.

"But you had those bite marks…"

"Yes," I interrupted, "I know I did, but that was different."

"Different how?" he asked.

"It was just… different. Let's not talk about it, okay?"

I pulled away from him and swung my legs over the side of the bed. I hadn't told Ollie anything about what had happened between me and Sol, just letting him assume that the rumours he'd heard were true. I wasn't ready to talk about what I had felt or what we had shared, particularly not when Ollie was all I had here.

In part, I didn't want him to think badly of me for the things that Sol and I had done together, but most of all I didn't want to be made to think badly of myself for those same experiences. Ollie wouldn't understand it, and he'd think it was tawdry and twisted instead of seeing it as I had, as it had been. It had been special and precious while it lasted, and I didn't want Ollie's reproach to destroy it for me. The memories of my time with Sol were all I had left of him, and I was clinging onto them ferociously, unwilling to give them away or to surrender them up for criticism.

But I was under no illusions that there would be any way to recapture those moments or to rekindle what had been between us. The Sol who visited the Farm today belonged to someone else and he was the one who had condemned us to this place. Like Drew, he was no longer the Silver I had known, manipulated and remoulded into the image of his consort: cruel and hard. Part of me had always recognised that he had that in him, that the man who was a god to the Silver could never be a gentle creature, but the application of the more brutal side of his nature had never seemed unfair or vicious to me, always guided by an adherence to logic that appeared merciless in its ends but not in its motivations. I wished I could believe that he was still led by the same principles, but with Laila at his side his priorities had changed.

"Okay," Ollie said. "You don't need to talk about it if you don't want to."

He pulled himself out from under the sheets and came to sit on the edge of the bed next to me.

"Your sunburn looks much better today," he said as he looked me up and down in last night's fresh scrubs. I rolled up the leg of the trousers and saw that there was now no redness at all below my knees, although my arms were still a little pink.

"That cream the doctor gave us is incredible," I said. "You don't look burnt at all any more." And he wasn't. Instead, the sun had turned the Mediterranean tan of his face and arms a wonderful, radiant gold. It made him look healthy and full of life, a great improvement on his appearance yesterday when he returned from patrol.

The blisters on my feet, and on his hand and foot, had also hardened overnight so they were much more comfortable this morning. Mine were still sore, and I was sure they'd be agonising after another fifteen miles on them, but I thought they would be good enough to let us get the job done without crippling us totally.

All in all, it was an unexpectedly positive start to the day.

As I gently got to my feet, I remembered Cam's promise from last night and opened the door to the observation room to see whether our care package had arrived, but there was no sign of it.

"Do you think he changed his mind?" Ollie asked as he looked over my shoulder into the room.

"No," I said. "I'm sure he'll come through for us. It's early yet." Unless, I thought, his master plan had failed after all.

And then I noticed something odd. Both of the windows in the cell had still been sprayed with Weeper blood last night when the sun went down, but this morning the glass was clean and shiny, every trace of blood removed.

"Did you hear anything last night?" I said to Ollie, nodding towards the windows. "Was someone in here, or outside?"

He looked at the glass and his mouth dropped open as he realised what was missing.

"I didn't hear anything at all," he said. "But how did they get them clean through the bars? You think that someone was in here while we were sleeping, just to clean the windows? It seems like a lot of effort for something they never gave a shit about before."

I nodded, then had a sudden thought.

"Sol's here today," I said. "Ada said he was visiting the new facilities, which probably includes this place. I think we might have been made presentable because we're expecting company."

"Maybe," Ollie agreed. "Maybe the Primus wouldn't be too happy to find you being kept out here with the Weepers."

"Ha!" I laughed bitterly. "Don't fool yourself. He couldn't care less about me."

And as I said it I knew it to be true.

Stuck with nothing to do until the guards came to collect

us for late patrol duty, we ate some apples and cereal bars, tidying up the rubbish into a bag in the corner of the observation room. We couldn't see any sign of new Weepers outside, and we were almost certain that there wouldn't be any given the Primus's impending arrival, so we opened the windows wide to let some air through. I suppose we were conscious that we would be having a visitor at some point today and felt a vague obligation to neaten things up a little, even if we only did so half-heartedly. After all, there wasn't much to be done to make the two small rooms any more inviting.

In the end, we needn't have bothered.

We heard voices outside an hour or so after we woke up. Walking over to the window, we saw the guards and Ada escorting Sol and Tommy towards the gates surrounding our cell.

I couldn't believe Sol was actually here. His pale hair was dazzlingly bright in the morning sunshine, the light reflecting from the golden curls that crowned his head. He was like a beacon shining out across the distance towards me, but I knew he offered me no safety now, only destruction.

I hadn't seen Tommy since before Alice had died. Cam had told me that it had hit him hard, but I hadn't really believed him until that moment. He had dark smudges under his eyes and his face looked drawn and pale, as if he hadn't been looking after himself. He was standing behind and slightly to one side of Sol, distancing himself from the party as they made their way into the enclosure, a faraway look on his face.

By contrast, I noted bitterly, Sol looked remarkably well. The foreign silver of the bond shining in the ice-blue of his irises was harsh and cold, but it suited him, lending an ethereal quality to his already striking features. His expression was politely but remotely interested as he listened to Ada, as if he were intrigued that she thought he would care about what she was telling him. When they got closer and I could hear their conversation, I had some sympathy with that.

"The building itself is constructed from reinforced concrete," she said as they moved into the enclosure and the final gate shut behind them. "The door, like the gates, is on a time lock, but it is also secured by a second code-activated lock."

"Why?" he asked her, amusement rather than criticism colouring his tone.

"Primus?" she asked, confused.

"Why is it necessary for there to be a double lock on the cell door?"

Ada thought for a moment, clearly never having considered the same question that had occurred to me when Mark gave us the tour of the cell.

"Well, er," she said, "for added security of course."

Sol paused, examining Ada's face for a moment as she blushed under the force of his scrutiny.

"Of course," he said, "very wise, I'm sure."

"Thank you, Primus," she replied, her blush deepening.

"Well," he said, "this all seems to be in order. I believe you also have a new warehouse?"

Then he turned away from the building and walked back towards the gate without even sparing a glance towards the window where Ollie and I stood watching.

"Primus," Tommy said softly, indicating the large rucksack he had been carrying on his back.

"Oh yes," Sol said, turning to Ada again. "My Invictus has a few items for the prisoners, as tokens of my beneficence."

"How very gracious of you, Primus," she replied, gesturing to Tessa.

With that, Ada and Sol walked away with Mark, their conversation drifting back to us on the breeze.

If I'd thought that Mark was flustered when Sol had spoken to him over the phone, it was nothing compared with how he looked today now that he was actually in his company. He was holding his chest puffed out and his stomach in, walking in a stiff-legged way that made me wonder how much effort it was taking him to restrain his belly. His cheeks were pink, the sweat practically dripping from his forehead, and I could see that his jaw was clenched tight. In contrast, Tessa had seemed perfectly relaxed in Sol's presence.

I watched Sol disappear as they walked through the final gate, he and Ada vanishing as they sped off to god knows where, while Tessa opened the door to the observation room and let Tommy into the building. Mark stayed behind at the perimeter, waiting by his vehicle, looking back at Ollie and me with a gloating expression that worried me.

Sol was gone.

I couldn't believe that, after all that anticipation, he had been here for maybe a minute before he left. And he hadn't even looked at me, hadn't even acknowledged my presence. I was expecting him to be dismissive, to act as though I was nothing to him, but I had secretly hoped that he might catch my eye and give me a look, or whisper something to me like he had at the wall as he banished us. I was expecting some kind of indication that he still cared about me, even a little.

What a fool I had been. I didn't even exist for him any more.

"Emmy?" Tommy said from the next room.

I walked over to him quickly, finding him by the table with Tessa standing next to the closed door.

"Hey," I said.

He looked me up and down, taking in the residual burns and the cuts on my feet.

"Are you okay?" he asked.

My eyes flicked quickly to Tessa then back to Tommy. I didn't want to say much in front of her, so I opted for a shrug instead. He followed my glance and didn't push me any further.

"I've got a load of things for you," he said as he swung the bag down from his shoulders and onto the table.

"From the Primus," I said.

"Yes," he replied pointedly, "from the Primus."

But his eyes told me this was nothing to do with Sol. I wondered how hard Cam had had to bargain with him to get him to allow this.

"How very generous of him," Ollie said as he joined us.

"Tommy," I said, "this is Oliver. I don't think you've met before."

Tommy nodded at Ollie as he started to unpack the bag, pulling out shoes and blankets, food and medicines. There was everything we had asked Cam to get us and more that I hadn't thought of asking for: moisturiser, deodorant, plastic cups and a torch.

"Thank you," I said with feeling. "We're very grateful."

"I'll let the Primus know," Tommy replied.

He seemed so sad that it was almost painful to look at him, empty eyes set deep in a hollow face, as if he'd felt everything he could and was numbed to the world. It reminded me of the way Drew had looked: haunted and alone. I hadn't expected him to be so distraught. He hadn't silvered for Alice, had only spent one evening with her, and here he was in pieces over her death. But then I could understand that maybe when you've lived for hundreds of years on your own, when you think you might have found someone special the loss of that person could break you.

"I'm so sorry, Tommy," I whispered as I took his hand. He met my eyes briefly before looking away, pulling his fingers out of my grasp as he turned back to his task.

I was surprised to hear another car outside and wondered whether it was Sol coming back to collect Tommy, but that was ridiculous. He'd left with Ada and without a vehicle, and he wouldn't very well bother coming back for one of his Invicti.

"The Administrator has arrived," Tessa said.

I looked at Tommy, not sure what this meant.

"Alyssa," he said. "She's administering the Casting. She'll be here for the first of the tests."

"Oh," I said, remembering the Silver I had met about ten days ago, the one who had loved Wimbledon.

A shadow crossed over Tommy's face and I realised that he would have been helping Alice through this test today if the rebels hadn't killed her. I wondered whether he was thinking about it too.

"My apologies, Invictus," Tessa said to him, "but we will need to clear the room to preserve the confidentiality of the Casting."

Tommy knew very well that I was the one nominated, and that Drew was the one sponsoring me, but he didn't protest as he unpacked the rest of the bag's contents quickly, setting the items out along the table top.

"I'll follow you in a second," he said to Tessa, gesturing towards the door. She hesitated for a moment before nodding smartly and letting herself out of the building. Tommy watched her go, waiting until he could see her through the window as she walked into the first ring of fencing.

"With Drew needing to be here for the tests, Cam can't come again," he whispered urgently, "and I probably won't be able to find an excuse either. You're stuck with Drew, and I know he's gone off the deep end. So, look," he said, pulling a small, black box out of one of the trainers arrayed on the table, "we got you this. It's like a long-range walkie talkie, and Cam or I will always have the other one of the pair. You just press this button here to activate it, and speak into the microphone here. So if you're in danger, you let us know, okay? And we'll come get you."

"Are you serious, Tommy?" I whispered back. "You can't do this. It's way too risky. You're one of the Invicti."

"It's done," he insisted. "When Drew comes to his senses he's going to regret this, and god help us all if it's too late by then. You didn't want to be Silver, but you let him sign you up for this. You tried to do right by him, and we're damn well going to repay that debt, even if he won't."

He grabbed me up into a quick hug.

"Gotta go," he said as he released me. "Take care of her, rebel," he said to Ollie as he left us alone in the building, the lock catching behind him.

I couldn't believe what Cam and Tommy were putting on the line for me. I'd thought I was on my own here and that, despite my frequent visitors, there were none of the Silver who would fight my corner for me. But I'd underestimated them. They'd given me a lifeline, a backup plan. Even without Drew or Sol on my side, we weren't alone.

"It's like bloody Piccadilly Circus in here," Ollie said as we watched Tommy cross the grass to the gate. Alyssa's car waited beyond the fences.

"Don't worry," I said, "you'll get some peace and quiet after the Casting."

He gave me a wry look, apparently not impressed with my making jokes about it.

We gathered up all Tommy's gifts in our arms and carried them through to the cell, closing the connecting door behind us in an attempt to give the impression that we were taking the confidentiality of the Casting seriously. We took particular care to stow the transmission device safely back in one of the trainers.

Through the window, we saw that Alyssa was standing beside her car at the outer perimeter talking to Tessa and Mark. There was no sign of Tommy, so I guessed that he must have zipped away to join Ada and Sol.

Alyssa was dressed formally in heels with a navy dress and jacket that matched her Mercedes. They looked incongruous out on the scrubby track that led down to our enclosure, the sharp lines of the deep colours cutting across the rolling landscape in the same way that the uniform fencing of our enclosure cut through the multiplicity of shades of the grass and ground that surrounded us. It made them seem as though they belonged to each other, the harsh edges of the chain link, the suit and the car. They were the system, the structure that bound us in place, while we were the grass and the sky.

But the same system that separated us from the world also separated that world from us, protecting us from the Weepers. They were part of each of us: part human, part Silver, the blurred line between our two races that combined us, but the sum of which was less than either of us on our own. Together our natures mingled in the Weepers to render them savage, mindless, destructive and selfish.

We were better apart, I thought.

While Alyssa stood speaking to the guards, I quickly brushed my teeth and put on some deodorant, feeling properly clean for the first time since I had entered this building. Alyssa had made an effort for me, so I decided that I might as well make an effort for her. I had liked her when we had met, and unlike some of the Silver she seemed genuinely to mourn the events that had made the Revelation necessary. She had enjoyed all that the human world had been able to offer a Silver in disguise, and she wasn't so power hungry that she thought the current situation was an improvement.

Which made me wonder about Ben. He had seen the Revelation as an opportunity, a chance to overthrow Sol and take control. He wanted power more than he wanted peace, and I supposed that with his views about the proper place of humans in the world he had probably always yearned to subjugate us. I knew he had been human once, that he had been a prince, but there was some insecurity there, some need to see his dominance recognised that spoke of a man who was ill at ease with vulnerability.

Of course, he had loved once and that love had been thrown back in his face by the Silver who turned him. Maybe it was that offence that made him feel that he had to be indomitable.

I joined Ollie at the window as Alyssa climbed into the back of the car and was driven slowly through each of the gates towards us. I guessed that Drew would be at the wheel. It was probably for the best that they had to drive up to the building to do this cloak and dagger stuff, because there was no way that Alyssa would have made it across the grass of the enclosure in her stilettos without looking a fool. It would have spoiled the gravity of the occasion a little.

Tessa and Mark got into their own vehicle and drove away as the Mercedes pulled up beside the building. They'd surely be back to collect us later.

There was a clacking sound in the room next door as Alyssa's heels tapped across the concrete, and a moment later she opened the connecting door without checking the hatch first.

"Emilia," she said, bowing her head to me formally.

She was about as tall as me in her heels. Her long, brown hair was pinned up neatly into a French twist that complemented the smooth lines of her round face.

"Hello," I said, not sure how to respond, completely out of my depth. As with the last time I had met her, I felt outclassed and awkward, but she didn't make a big deal of it.

"Er, it's nice to see you again," I said. She smiled indulgently and I wondered whether she even remembered speaking to me in the club. She was certainly more memorable to me than I would be to her. "This is Oliver," I continued.

"Good morning to you, Oliver," she said politely.

Ollie seemed equally taken aback by this civil greeting, but after a moment he pulled himself together and offered her his hand.

"Good morning, ma'am," he said.

She reached for his hand, but instead of shaking it she draped her own over his as if she expected him to kiss it. He looked uncertain, clearly unaware of the protocol that she was following or what century it was from, but he effected a neat little bow before releasing her hand.

"Such a gentleman," she said with every sign of sincerity. "Though I am told you are a traitor?"

"So they say," he replied.

She looked him over appreciatively, her eyes lingering over his long lashes and his lips, assessing his face and torso as if she were mentally undressing him. I felt an unexpected pang of jealousy and my face twitched involuntarily. Alyssa's eyes looked my way and I knew she had caught the expression. I doubted it would make the morning's test any easier.

"A shame," she said, "but if the Primus so rules then thus it must be. And you, Emilia, I am surprised to see in this position."

"Oh?" I asked, not having expected her to have an opinion.

"You seemed to be such a favourite with Solomon, and he has them so rarely these days. We are friends, you know." She pouted prettily for a moment before correcting herself. "Were friends."

I was thrown off balance by this unsolicited confidence. I hadn't realised that anyone had noticed that there was anything going on between me and Sol beyond the blood drinking. Yes, he had marked me with his kiss, and yes, he had bitten me, but I had been sure that those traces would be dismissed by the other Silver as acts of dominance and ownership rather than of affection, a show of disdain and control rather than of weakness.

"Don't be concerned," she continued, reading the expression on my face. "I think I am one of the few who credit our Primus with a capacity for emotion towards humans. But then he is lately changed. Though I would not repeat such treasonous sentiments outside of these walls, I fear you may now be paying the penance for the attention he once showed you. I am sorry for that."

"Er, thank you?" I said uncertainly.

"So, to business," she said. "Will you join me next door, please, Emilia? Please excuse us, Oliver. It was a pleasure to make your acquaintance."

I looked back at him as I followed Alyssa through the connecting door and saw a puzzled look on his face. He had clearly found the interlude as strange as I had. Being shown respect by the Silver just felt overwhelmingly bizarre, and I couldn't work out whether it was because we weren't used to it or because something in us agreed with Ben, agreed that the Silver were superior to us and that we should be treated accordingly.

That was an uncomfortable thought.

I closed the connecting door behind me and saw that Drew was already there, standing next to the wall so that he had been out of sight until I had walked into the observation room. I jumped when I noticed him, his sudden appearance startling me, and my hand flew to my chest in shock.

"It's alright," Alyssa said in a soothing tone, "it's just your sponsor."

I glanced at Drew warily, but he didn't meet my eye. His hair was in an even greater state of disarray than normal, his stubble more pronounced and the skin around his eyes darker. He looked distinctly moody and, although I felt more secure with Alyssa here than I would have done were we alone, I was still unhappy being in the same room as him.

Alyssa looked between the two of us, not missing anything as she indicated that I should take a seat at the table. She couldn't have imagined that this hostile atmosphere would bode well for the Casting, and I wondered whether she would be more likely to fail me in the selection process as a result. Maybe Drew's anger could be turned into a positive after all.

I moved past him quickly and sat down opposite the door to the outside world. Alyssa took the seat opposite me, the line of candles from last night separating us along the table top. Drew didn't sit, but stayed where he was in the corner of the room. I was grateful that he hadn't come any closer.

"As you know," she said, looking at Drew with candid curiosity before turning back to me, "I have been appointed the Administrator of the Casting. As you have, unfortunately, found yourself… incarcerated in this place, the three tests that form the selection process will be undertaken here rather than in the city with the other candidates. I am here today to administer the aptitude test, but the second and third tests will be performed by one of our scientists in the presence of your sponsor."

She paused for a second and gave Drew an assessing look.

"I don't wish to be impertinent," she continued, "but I must say that it is highly irregular for the Secundus to act as a sponsor for a Casting, and for a human that was one of the chained no less. Has the Primus been informed?"

"The confidentiality of the Casting is absolute,

Administrator," Drew replied gruffly, "and that confidentiality has not been breached."

Given that Tommy and Cam were both well aware of my participation and Drew's sponsorship, Drew had just told a blatant lie. In the circumstances, I seriously doubted that Sol hadn't also been told. He must also have known that, with the bond broken, I stood no chance of succeeding, but I suspected that he was beyond caring.

I wondered for a brief, fanciful moment whether Alyssa would intervene here, if she would tell Drew that it was inappropriate for him to sponsor me and that we couldn't go ahead.

But that was wishful thinking from such a ritualised culture as the Silver's.

"Well," she said, "he may well get a shock, then. Ill-advised though it may be, you have thrown in your lots and there is nothing that can be done to change that now. Let us proceed."

The test itself was long, boring and more taxing than I had expected. For the first part, Alyssa pulled a few sheets of paper out of her pocket and handed them to me with a pen, asking me to complete the questions on them as well as I could. There were a lot of them, and although they were multiple choice they were complicated. They were based on the application of mental skills such as logic and spatial awareness rather than on any feats of recall, and it took some effort for me to divine the correct answer so that I could then give an incorrect one.

Alyssa looked on impassively as I worked and Drew never moved from his position in the corner. It made the atmosphere a little tense; I imagined that I could feel his eyes on me as I wrote. I had no idea what was going on in his mind, and that was terrifying to me. He seemed coiled tight like a dangerous animal, ferocious and unpredictable. I couldn't know what might set him off, so I couldn't avoid his anger.

It was a relief when I eventually worked my way through

to the end of the pages and was able to break the silence to hand them back to Alyssa.

"I'm finished," I said as I passed her the sheets of paper and the pen.

"Good," she said. "As your sponsor will have told you, the second part of the test is an opportunity for you to demonstrate any particular skills and abilities that you might possess. So, what have you to show me?"

I wasn't sure how to deal with this convincingly.

"I'm sorry," I replied, "but I don't think there is anything. I can tend bar well, and I mix a pretty good martini, but that's about it I'm afraid."

I tried to appear contrite, as if I were ashamed that I didn't have anything to offer her, and that wasn't far from the truth. She looked at me for a long, still moment, examining my face speculatively as if she were trying to determine whether or not I was genuine.

"Then the first test is complete," she said briskly as she rose to her feet. "I wish you the best of luck with the second and third tests. Usually they are the more straightforward of the three, but for you I fear that may not be the case."

She raised an eyebrow at me and I wondered how much she had worked out for herself. She was clearly not a stupid woman, and everything about my and Drew's behaviour must have seemed peculiar to her. I prayed that she had read between the lines and understood what I was trying to achieve here, and that she was as kind as she appeared, kind enough to allow me to fail my way out of this nightmare.

I stood from my chair as she moved towards the door, Drew following close on her heels.

"Goodbye then, Emilia," she said.

"Goodbye," I replied.

Drew didn't even look at me as he followed her out, his face as hard and strained as it had been when I last saw him. I wondered whether he would ever talk to me again, or if we would spend our time together in silence from now on. Given what had happened last time he had spoken to me, perhaps that would be for the best.

But somehow his silence was more terrible than his shouts, his contained anger more intimidating with its dark menace. One day soon it was going to break out again, and I didn't want to be in its path when that happened.

CHAPTER XII

Who is this that looks forth like the dawn,
fair as the moon, bright as the sun,
terrible as an army with banners?

- The Song of Solomon

By the time they left it must have been late morning, and Ollie and I were anticipating that we would be collected any moment for our patrol shifts. It seemed as though I hadn't had a moment to myself today, jumping from uncomfortable meeting to uncomfortable meeting, and I felt decidedly off-kilter. The day's activities so far had been busy and challenging, with a good dose of terror thrown in by Drew and disappointment thrown in by Sol.

All in all, I felt like a stranger in my own life, as though the girl I had been last week had disappeared and been replaced by someone different, someone for whom the people who mattered most to me had no affection.

But then there was Cam, I reminded myself, and Tommy. I wasn't completely bereft.

We'd geared ourselves up in the kit Tommy had brought for us, pulling on lightweight clothing and wrapping our feet in bandages and thick socks before securing them in comfortable trainers. We'd slathered ourselves in sun cream and each of us had a hat and a large bottle of water in a small pack that also contained food and, in my case, the emergency transmitter. I was loath to leave it behind in the cell where it might be discovered in our absence.

Ollie had bound up his hand so his blisters wouldn't rub against his crutch, and with our whistles round our necks we felt like we were ready to face today's walk.

In fact, as we sat side by side on the bed and waited for the guards, the windows closed tight just in case, I was wishing that they would hurry up so we could get it over with.

"You know," Ollie said, "I was expecting our confinement here to be a bit more like it was on the first day."

"What do you mean?" I asked, thinking as I looked over at him that he was pretty hot in his hiking gear.

"I mean more time left alone, less contact with the world. It seems like since the moment we got here you've had one visitor after another, like a princess in a tower receiving her courtiers. They've forgotten me here, taken me away from everyone I knew, but you know all the Silver and they all come calling. They haven't forgotten you."

"Not all of them," I said, thinking of Sol, who barely seemed to realise I existed any more. "But it won't last beyond the Casting."

"I don't know about that."

"You'll see. Cam and Tommy, they feel like they owe it to me to get me through the Casting, but they'll start to forget about me after that. If I'm here at all."

He looked away from me with a frustrated expression.

"I wish you'd stop talking like that. You threw that test, right? You've failed it?"

"I hope so. I tried to."

"Then that's the end of that," he said. "You won't get through."

I wished I had his conviction, but I didn't want to leave anything to chance and I wasn't going to believe I was safe until they told me so on Wednesday.

"I think being forgotten might be a good thing anyway," I said. "There's one Silver I'm sure we'd both rather didn't remember us."

"Benedict?" he asked.

"Yup. With things as they are at the moment, I'm not keen to get caught in the middle."

Not again, I thought.

"The sooner they forget me, the better," I said, but although I knew it was the sensible thing, my heart wasn't in it. I thought from his next question that Ollie could probably tell.

"What did you think of that performance with Ada and the Primus earlier on?" Ollie asked me.

"She blushed a lot," I said.

"She did, didn't she? And I've been thinking about that letter, you know, from the first day? You remember how the Invicti reacted when the guy driving the truck handed it to them, and how Ada reacted when she got it?"

"Yes…" I said. "So, what? You think she has a crush?"

"Maybe. She was certainly out to impress him."

I wasn't in any position to judge. After all, who could blame her? He was glorious.

"Do you miss him?" Ollie asked.

I was thrown by the question, not sure who he was talking about and not wanting to give anything away by assuming he meant Sol. I decided to play dumb.

"Who?" I asked. "Drew?"

"No. From what you've told me, I get the feeling that the bond was more about him than it was about you. No, I mean the Primus."

I missed him desperately, and seeing him this morning had only made that more apparent. But how could I tell Ollie that? How could I explain how it had felt to have his attention on me, powerful and unguarded? I'd pushed it away, not wanting to see myself as someone who would be seduced by someone like Sol, and it was exactly that rejection that had attracted him. As soon as I had wanted him too, the game was over, the prize won.

I shook my head hopelessly, unable to articulate my feelings.

I was saved by the arrival of the guards. Mark came to collect us as usual, crowing over us as usual, and Tessa drove as usual, but this time the drive was shorter. There were no comments about our new clothes and kit, so I wondered whether Tessa had warned Mark to keep his mouth shut, whether she had told him that they had come from the Primus. Either way, I was grateful that it looked like we would be able to keep them without interference, although I was still a little paranoid that they would try to search my rucksack and discover the walkie talkie.

When the truck stopped, I helped Ollie get his crutch out of the back and made to follow him.

"No, you're starting further on today," Mark said to me, blocking my exit. "This is Hop-Along's stop, not yours. You're walking the same stretch as yesterday, but you're starting at different ends of it."

Ollie smiled back at me encouragingly, looking much more comfortable now that he had proper shoes, and swung himself off towards the gates as Tessa operated the opener gadget. Whilst we waited for her to return, Mark leaned into the back of the truck towards me with one hand on the roof. There was a dark sweat stain under his arm, the warm day doing nothing to keep him presentable, and he was wheezing in the heat.

"Now," he said to me quietly, "I'm not telling your limping lothario this, but today's patrol's gonna be a bit of a race. You see, he's starting here, and you're starting thirty miles that way."

He pointed off in the direction we had been heading, the same direction we'd driven in yesterday.

"I don't care how much of that thirty miles each of your

covers," he continued, "but you both come home at the same time when you meet in the middle, wherever that is."

He was quiet for a second, biting his lip thoughtfully as he looked down at the ground.

"C'mere a minute," he said, waving me out of the back doors of the truck.

I hesitated for a moment, looking at him suspiciously, before cautiously climbing out of the truck and onto the grass. Tessa was nearly back at the truck now and Ollie had already set off on his journey away from us.

"He thinks you're still in the truck right now," Mark continued as he wrapped an arm around my shoulders. I suppressed a shudder and turned to watch Ollie as he swung himself along the path.

"You see how he moves when he thinks you're not watching?" he leered at me. "He's not telling you, cos he's a big impressive alpha male type, but look at the way he's stumbling along."

He was right. Despite the new shoes, and despite the binding on his crutch hand, Ollie was obviously finding the going tough. Every few steps he'd stretch out the fingers of the hand he was grasping the crutch with, as though he was trying to stop them from cramping. He looked unstable, wobbling on the crutch and on his good leg as he laboured along on his way.

"So this is me doing you a favour, right here," Mark said. "Every mile you cover is one less mile that poor cripple has to hobble along, and it's going to take us at least forty minutes or so to get to your start line so he's gonna have a head start. Something to think about on the journey, isn't it?"

He grinned at me, that evil grin of his I had come to loathe and dread, and shooed me back into the truck.

"Come on then," he shouted as he slammed the doors shut and thumped on the top of the truck. "Time's a-wasting!"

Every minute of the drive felt like an eternity. I wished Tessa would drive faster, knowing that the sooner I could start my patrol the sooner Ollie would be able to finish. I was pretty sure I could run comfortably in these shoes, and although I wasn't going to be able to keep up the pace for the entire distance, I thought I could probably put a decent dent in Ollie's section without too much trouble.

When the truck stopped, I made my way to the gates and into the outer ring of fencing as quickly as I could. Mark laughed with dark delight at my enthusiasm.

"Tell you what," he shouted at me as I took off at a jog. "You finish within four hours and I'll give you a fucking medal at the end!"

I ignored him, tightening the straps of my backpack as I ran, grateful that it was small enough not to bounce around too much. I'd done a fair bit of running back before the Revelation, but mostly on pavements and paths, so the uneven ground of the fields was a bit tough on my joints to begin with.

Since I'd been this way yesterday, I had the advantage of knowing the route and the way-markers I would reach. First there was the hill ahead of me, which would have the hamlet at its crest, and then there was the valley sloping down to the brook, then uphill again through the forest before coming down again through the pastureland to the flag where we had started. Beyond that would be unknown territory, but every mile of it that I could cover would be saving Ollie's injuries more aggravation. I couldn't even feel my own, the blisters no longer stinging and the pain in my muscles melting away as I stretched them into a proper stride.

It felt oddly liberating to be running out here in the sunshine, the countryside spreading out around me. Despite the fences to either side, the pace of motion I could manage under my own power gave me a sense of control that I hadn't felt for a long time. Add to that the fact that it was for a purpose, that it could help Ollie, and I couldn't have been keener for the task. Determination poured strength into my legs and they ate up the ground beneath me, carrying me uphill effortlessly towards the buildings I could see peeking over the slope ahead of me.

It seemed a surprisingly short time before I was running

past the houses, where I found a single, motionless Weeper up against the fence. I duly blew my whistle. By the time I had taken a quick swig of water and stowed the bottle back in my bag, the body was gone.

The run downhill was quicker, my feet moving fast as they raced to keep up with the momentum of my body, and soon I was leaping the stream and climbing up the other side of the valley towards the forest at its peak. I knew I would have to slow down there, the ground too treacherous with tree stumps for me to keep running, so I made the most of the open countryside while I could.

I was exhausted when I reached the tree line, the brow of my hat soaked with sweat and the sun cream hot and sticky on my skin, but I thought I must have done more than half of the distance now. My feet were feeling surprisingly good, the bandages and socks cushioning the cuts, and if it hadn't been for the uneven ground I would have continued running. But, as it was, I could only manage a slow jog, back to yesterday's routine: watching my feet most of the time, checking my surroundings every so often to make sure there were no Weepers up against the fence.

The diminished pace felt like a crawl after the speed with which I had covered the open ground, and I was impatient to get through the trees so I could start picking up speed again. The focus on my goal distracted me from the threat of the Weepers in the trees, and although I knew they were there watching me, I was too fixated on maintaining speed to spare much anxiety for them. When I contemplated finding Weepers in the cleared zone, my concern was that I might have to wait around for the Silver to come and collect their bodies, not that they might present any danger to me.

Now that I had slowed down, I started to feel the heat of the sun on my skin. It was high in the sky, so it must have been a couple of hours since I started. Feeling the minutes ticking by as I stumbled on, the restriction on my pace was agonising. I ate while I jogged to save time, pulling a couple of cereal bars from my bag and chewing them down as I navigated my way along the track. I didn't feel as though I could afford a break in the circumstances, and, despite the distance I had already covered, I was so fired with adrenaline that I didn't feel as though I needed one either.

I finally cleared the trees without incident, and saw the pastureland spreading out below. It was free from obstacles as far as I could see: no buildings, no trees and no Weepers. There was just the red flag flashing a couple of miles away, and I made it my next waypoint. Get that far, I said to myself, and everything else is a bonus.

But it was more of a struggle than I had expected. The downhill path here was rougher than the fields on the other side of the woods, the grass collected in tussocks that made it easy to twist an ankle with a single false step, and I had to pay attention to where I was putting my feet. As the ground levelled off it became more even, and by the time I reached the flag I was in a flat-out run.

By that point, I guessed that I had been on the move for about three hours, and although I was trying to ignore it I was feeling the effects, so when I heard someone say my name I thought I might be hearing things.

"Emilia," the voice said again and, slowing to a stop, I looked around to see that Ada was standing within the Farm. She was on the other side of the gates that were marked by the flag above my head. I'd had my eyes on the perimeter, checking for Weepers outside of the fence, so I hadn't seen her approach.

But then I realised that she was alone, and without a vehicle, so perhaps she had only just appeared.

I was instantly on edge. She had made me anxious the first time we had met her. There was an odd, manic inclination to her bearing, quickly covered with a civil veneer, that I found disconcerting. Suddenly I felt very alone, out here in the middle of nowhere with her.

"Yes?" I replied, audibly panting as I tried to catch my breath.

"I wonder whether we might speak for a moment."

I looked off towards the hills in the distance, wondering how far away Ollie was, and hesitated, not wanting to desert my task. I also really didn't want to talk to Ada. She creeped me out.

"I'm supposed to…" I said.

"It will only take a minute of your time," she insisted, "I assure you."

She pulled a gadget like Tessa's from her suit jacket and activated the gates. She was coming to me, I realised, as the internal gate opened and she stepped through.

"In fact," she added as she walked across the space between us and through the central gate, "I will join you in your patrol for a short distance."

I took in her cream suit and matching heels. She really wasn't dressed for hiking across the fields. Nevertheless, I nodded meekly, remembering what Martha had told us on our first day here. Besides, I didn't want to risk offending her and she seemed determined. I wasn't sure that there was any way that I could have changed her mind, and I was certain that she could have killed me in a second flat if that was what she intended.

She started walking slowly and I fell in step beside her, each pace increasing my apprehension.

"I realise," she said, "that you and your comrade are somewhat out of the loop in your little corner of my farm. I thought it might be helpful for us to talk a little so that I might enlighten you as to our way of thinking."

This all sounded worryingly ominous to me. I assumed that when she said 'we' should talk, she meant that she should talk and I should listen, so I kept my mouth shut and nodded. She continued without taking a breath, so I considered my assumption to have been correct.

"I am an old Silver," she said, "and I have been serving my Primus for hundreds of years. I have seen him in many guises, wearing many mantles, but I have followed him faithfully through the ages. It is difficult, I think, for humans to imagine that kind of faith. It's like any habit, I suppose, in that it becomes more ingrained the more that you practice it, until it becomes part of who you are."

She stopped and turned to face me for a moment.

"Are you a religious person, Emilia?"

"I was," I replied, not really sure where I stood on the question of religion after the Revelation.

"Hmm," she said contemplatively before walking on. "I don't believe that you will be aware of the religious tenets to which we hold, because I understand that they have not yet gained any kind of prevalence in the city. This is, doubtless, a function of the humility of the Primus, but nonetheless it is to be regretted."

Suddenly I understood. Ada didn't have a crush on Sol, she worshipped him. He was her god, and that light I had seen in her eyes as she looked at him this morning was religious fervour rather than infatuation. For her, he wasn't the manifestation of god on earth; he was the start and end of it, a complete deity in the flesh.

Dread started to build in my stomach as I contemplated how she might feel about me, a human who had been censured by her god.

"You see," she said as we walked on, "that kind of faith is unshakeable, a faith founded on centuries of devotion. It's something that flows through you like a guiding force, shaping your actions without your having to think about them. You know in your heart what is right and you act accordingly, your faith moving your hand to do what must be done."

She stopped and turned to me again, a terrible calm suffusing her features as a beatific smile spread across her face. Her expression was so cold and full of quiet purpose that it filled me with horror, every part of me telling me to run from her, to get away from the slow madness glinting in her eyes.

She reached out and took my hand in hers, interweaving her fingers with my own, and pulled me along beside her as she started to walk again.

"You were one of his chained," she said, "one of those

humans fortunate enough to be called upon to sustain him with your blood. Is that correct?"

I didn't answer for a moment, unsure whether this would make me better or worse in her eyes. Those crazy, crazy eyes.

At my hesitation, she squeezed my hand in hers until my knuckles ground together.

"Yes!" I gasped breathlessly.

She released the pressure instantly and the pain disappeared with it. She was apparently satisfied with my response, but now my heart was racing in my chest as I realised with terrible prescience that this encounter was going to end badly for me.

"I also understand," she continued, "that he took your blood directly from your veins. He has written me a letter on the subject, in which he explained, most eloquently, that as your blood has been touched by him it cannot be drunk by any other Silver. This, of course, is because the Primus himself is inviolate. His body is sacred, his touch a gift, and those he touches receive his favour."

I could feel this monologue taking a turn for the worse with awful inevitability.

When Sol had marked me with his kiss, he'd told me that I would be inviolate, that no one would touch me other than him. At the time, I'd put that down to the choker, but the choker would only warn others off from drinking my blood. Forbidding others from touching me had seemed like a new level of possessiveness for Sol, but now it made sense. For those who worshipped Sol, the fact that he had touched me would make me untouchable by association.

I may not have come across any acolytes who held to that in the city, but here at the Farm there was one in charge. And I was entirely in her power.

"Despite that favour," Ada continued as she stopped and turned to me once more, "you betrayed him. You betrayed the trust the Primus had placed in you, you who were so blessed to have been gifted his touch."

Her hold on my fingers started to tighten once more, and

I winced against the pain.

"He marked you," she whispered, "he held you above the other humans, and you threw your lot in with the rebels."

She was concentrating the pressure of her grip, scissoring my fingers between her own as she brought them together between the joints closest to my palm. I cried out and fell to the floor on my knees in front of her, my eyes streaming with tears at the pain.

"Please..." I gritted out between my teeth as I grimaced against the crushing force.

But she wasn't listening to me.

"But he's withdrawn his protection from you, and here you are in my charge. So I think my role here is clear: to help you to learn what happens when you touch the inviolate and then reject the sanctuary he offers."

She brought her fingers together sharply and there was a horrifying crunch. I screamed as pain shot through me then rolled hotly along my fingers, an unbearable stabbing ache that dropped me down to the ground the moment she released my hand. I cradled it towards me protectively, praying that she wouldn't touch the tender bones again as I moaned through the tears.

"What you have done is the worst kind of blasphemy," she said. "Will you remember this lesson, Emilia?"

"Yes," I groaned, utterly defeated by the pain. "Yes."

"Good," she said in an unconcerned tone. "Then my work here is done. Enjoy the rest of your walk."

CHAPTER XIII

When I raised my head Ada was gone, disappeared in an instant, off to torment some other poor human.

Although my fingers were still filled with an agonising ache, the worst of the pain had passed in the moments following the break. It was the second time in as many weeks that my hand had been broken, but this time there was no bond or brand to heal it up. I was going to have to deal with it the old-fashioned way.

I steeled my nerve and held the hand out in front of me to assess the damage. My littlest finger had escaped unharmed, but the middle three fingers of my right hand were obviously broken, misaligned and swollen. I was going to have to pull the bones back into place, but the moment I touched them the pain darted through me again with such intensity that I was blinking away the tears as I groaned and gritted my teeth against it.

I wasn't going to be able to do it myself. It was probably cowardly, but I just couldn't face the pain. I needed to get to Ollie and get back to the cell as soon as possible, and then maybe I could persuade Tessa to fetch the doctor to realign and splint the fingers for me.

There was nothing to do but pull myself up off my arse

and get moving, so I gave myself a quick pep talk, brushed the tears from my face with my good hand and started to walk. Running was out of the question when every step I took jarred the breaks and caused more pain to blossom from them liberally. Instead, I was moving at a fast but careful walk, my right hand held close against my chest by my left.

At least I had managed to cover most of the ground this morning, before our friendly local sadist had come to visit me.

I was yearning for something to distract me from the agony in my fingers, and so of course there was absolutely nothing. There wasn't a single Weeper, building, clump of trees or interesting geological feature to distract me. The route was wide, lined with open fields all the way, the only break in the uniformity provided by the hedgerows, empty roads and paths that crossed them.

It felt like a very long walk.

When Ollie eventually came into view hours later, cresting the top of a hill a few hundred yards ahead of me, I was so relieved to see him that tears began to run down my face. He had clearly had a bad day too, his movements slow and laboured, but I guessed that it was still mid-afternoon so he must have been moving at a decent pace.

"Ollie!" I shouted up to him as soon as he was in earshot.

"Emmy?" he called back. "What are you doing here?"

He picked up the tempo, swinging himself downhill at a reckless speed, but I was too exhausted, my nerves too frayed to move any further. Instead, I fell gently down onto my knees and waited for him.

"Emmy?" he said as he skidded to the ground beside me.

"Careful," I said, not wanting him to crush my mangled hand any further by hugging me. "I'm hurt."

"What happened?" he asked. "How are you here? You must have come at least twenty miles."

"Blow your whistle," I said, "and give me some food and water."

He did as I asked, sounding the whistle loudly before shrugging off his backpack and taking out his water and some chocolate. After all the running this morning, I was parched and crashing hard, craving sugar in a big way. I had intended to stop for some food and a drink shortly after the flag, but my plans had been interrupted by Ada. After that, I hadn't been brave enough to try to get into my rucksack without hurting my fingers.

There was a brief rush of air. I imagined that one of the Silver had zipped past, seen that we had blown the whistle because we were done rather than because we had spotted a Weeper, and had gone to get our ride. Or at least, I hoped so.

"Here," he said, offering me the bottle of water.

"Can you unscrew the lid for me?" I asked, nodding down towards my hands. "I have some broken fingers."

"What?" he asked. "How?"

"Water first," I insisted.

He removed the lid and I took the bottle from him with my left hand. It was only about a quarter full, but I drained it nearly to the bottom. He unwrapped the chocolate bar for me and broke it into pieces while I drank, then he handed them to me one by one as I chewed furiously.

"There's more in my pack if you want," I said, "but you'll have to get it. I don't want to take it off over my bad hand until I have to."

He shook his head, obviously not in need of anything, and waited impatiently for me to finish eating.

"So," I said, "Mark talked to me this morning. The deal is, we have to cover thirty miles between us, but it doesn't necessarily have to be fifteen each. So I ran it."

"You ran?" he asked in disbelief.

I nodded.

"The first fifteen to my flag. That took about three hours I guess, because some of it was more like a fast walk, and then I had a visit from Ada. Turns out she's some kind of fanatic."

"What?"

"You know how you thought she was in love with Sol? Well, actually she's one of the Silver that worship him, and she got fairly evangelical about it. Apparently I've committed blasphemy by touching him and betraying him, so she broke my fingers. Makes sense, right?"

I giggled then realised I was being hysterical, so I took a few deep breaths to try and calm down.

"And you carried on walking?" Ollie asked. "Are you insane?"

"No, she's the insane one. I just didn't want you to have to walk any further than you had to."

"Emmy, I'm fine. You don't have to worry about me. I wish you hadn't pushed yourself."

"Fine, are you?" I asked. "Then why are you wincing every time you put your weight on your crutch? Stop pretending like you're okay when you're not."

"Says the girl with the broken fingers," he replied.

"Well, yes, but that was after I'd already covered most of the distance. The running was the easy bit."

We sat quietly for a minute or so while I finished Ollie's water and he shared another chocolate bar with me.

"Let me see it then," he said.

"I don't want you to touch it."

"I won't."

"Do you promise?" I asked.

He laughed for a moment before realising that I was deadly serious.

"I promise," he said, "I won't touch."

"Okay."

I uncurled my arm from my body and extended the hand as far as I could. He grimaced as he saw it, the swollen joints now a worrying purple colour.

"Shit, Emmy. That does not look good."

"I need to get the bones set," I said as I pulled the hand back against myself. "Do you think Tessa will bring the doctor?"

"Yes," he replied after a moment's thought, "but not if we ask while Mark is there."

"Agreed."

I hoped that we hadn't used up all of her goodwill already,

such as it was, and prayed that we would have a chance to ask for her help.

"I'm sorry," Ollie said.

"Why are you apologising?"

"I'm just sorry this happened, and while I wasn't around to help."

"Why?" I asked. "What do you think you would have been able to do against Ada? She may be fifty shades of crazy, but she's Silver. No good would come of either of us standing up to her."

I knew that it was true with every logical part of my mind, but I was still ashamed of myself when I thought back to our meeting earlier today. She had hurt me for some imagined transgression, and I had begged her through the pain, agreeing to anything she said in order to make her leave me alone. I knew I had done what I had to do, that she would have kept on hurting me if I hadn't said what she had wanted to hear, but it hadn't been a proud moment for me, and it had reminded me of my first meeting with Drew in the cell.

Those feelings of shame and self-reproach were triggered anew by this encounter, but here at least I knew I hadn't done anything to Ada to cause the confrontation, and there was nothing I could have done to prevent it from happening. Here, I'd laid down and let her hurt me, and my ego was bruised by my inability to stand up to her. With Drew, my shame arose from my failure to roll over meekly and be subdued, convinced that I had caused his outburst.

Either way, my psyche wouldn't let me win.

My mind was running round in circles and it was getting me nowhere. I was feeling weak and tired, the pain eroding my strength, so I shuffled up next to Ollie and lay my head on his shoulder. I felt as though the heat of the afternoon sun wasn't penetrating my skin, a chill running along my limbs that made me shudder. He put his arm around me and pressed a kiss to the top of my head, pulling me close into the warmth of his body.

It wasn't long before the truck arrived to pick us up,

driving along in the same ring of fencing in which we were sitting. I hadn't thought about how they were going to get us out of here, but of course the simplest solution was to drive through the nearest set of gates and then drive out again. As the vehicle drew closer I could see that Mark was in the passenger seat, and my heart sank.

"Hello, happy hikers!" he called as he got out of the cab. "No medals for you today, but better luck tomorrow."

Ollie looked at me in confusion.

"If we do the route in under four hours," I whispered, "but I have a feeling we wouldn't like the prize, whatever it is."

I got to my feet painfully, my muscles seized up from sitting on the ground, and walked over to the back of the truck with Ollie close behind me. I was trying to hold my hand normally so that Mark wouldn't realise that it was injured. I didn't want him to get any ideas to make my day even worse, but it did have the drawback of hiding the injury from Tessa as well. I tried to catch her eye as I walked past the cab, but she was sitting in the driver's seat fiddling with the buttons on the dashboard, and she didn't look my way. If she didn't get out of the truck at the other end then it was going to be near impossible to catch a moment with her without Mark noticing.

It wasn't a long drive back to the building, maybe half an hour, and no one spoke during that time. Tessa was quiet as usual, but Mark seemed preoccupied and I wondered whether he was still feeling dazed from Sol's visit. My own attention was focussed on my fingers as I tried to minimise the effect of the juddering caused by the truck's poor suspension. From the way that he was looking at me with anxious eyes, I guessed that Ollie was thinking about my injuries too.

When we pulled up at the fence both of the guards came round to the back. Ollie nodded at me and so I got out of the truck first, moving to stand by Tessa as she fiddled with the gate opener. Meanwhile, Ollie distracted Mark by making a meal of getting to his feet: dropping his crutch, stumbling on the bumper, dropping his crutch again.

This was the best chance I was going to get.

I didn't want to risk speaking, even in a whisper, as I thought it was likely that Mark would overhear. Instead, I moved a little in front of Tessa until she looked up and met my eyes. As soon as I thought I had her attention, I lifted my hand and showed her the broken fingers, before quickly putting it back by my side again. Her glance flicked sideways towards Mark for a moment before coming back to rest on my face, and I hoped she'd got the message.

Doctor, please, I mouthed at her silently.

She looked at me for a second longer before turning back to the gate gadget. I wasn't sure whether or not she'd understood, or if she was going to help us, but I was out of time. Ollie swung his way to my side as Tessa activated the key pad for the gates. He looked at me and raised his eyebrow, glancing over towards Tessa, but I couldn't give him an answer. I offered him a hopeful smile and shrugged slightly with my left shoulder. We'd just have to wait and see if she came through for me.

"We'd better get you some more friends," Mark said as the first gate closed between us and the guards. Apparently we weren't getting a door-to-door escort today, which made me a little suspicious. Mark's words implied that there weren't any Weepers in with us yet, but I wondered whether he might be bluffing. You know, for laughs.

I scanned the enclosure as we walked through the central gate, but it looked like he'd been straight with us. There was nothing there but the building, still as clean and shining in the sunlight as it had been for Sol's visit this morning.

"Have we got time for that?" Tessa asked Mark as we walked through the final gate.

I looked over my shoulder, wondering whether this meant that Tessa was trying to find a way to help us after all, and saw that Mark's face was a mask of indecision, an agony of choices chasing through his expression. He really wanted to torment us, but there was something else fighting against that.

"He's only here for another half hour or so," she continued, her tone light and easy as if she was unconcerned either way.

She had to be talking about Sol. Mark was desperate to go and bask in his presence, so much so that it was apparently enough to take the thrill out of laughing at his human captives. I turned back towards the building and wished with every ounce of my being that he would let her divert him. I could hear their voices talking softly as we reached the cell door, but they were too far away now for me to make out their words.

I couldn't bear the suspense. My fingers were throbbing and hot, and I knew I needed the doctor. I wasn't going to ask Ollie to help me realign my snapped digits unless absolutely necessary, and there was nothing selfless about that. I wasn't trying to protect him from having to cause me pain, it was just that he wouldn't know what he was doing any more than I would, and I didn't think I would be able to stand someone fiddling around with the breaks for any longer than I had to.

He hesitated at the door to the building and I realised that he didn't know the code.

"Here," I said, starting to reach for the keypad with my right hand before quickly remembering that none of my fingers worked and switching to my left.

I punched in the numbers and hauled the door open as the locks retracted, then held it for Ollie so he could swing himself through. He gave me a confused look as he passed me, turning to face me as I closed the door behind us.

"How do you know the code?" he asked, an expression of open suspicion on his face.

"Mark told me it yesterday," I said lightly, trying to make it seem as though there was nothing else for me to tell him about it.

"They didn't walk you in?"

"Nope."

I checked the window to see if Mark and Tessa were still there, but I was just in time to watch them drive away. I guessed I would have to wait and see about the doctor, but how long should I delay before I would have to ask Ollie, I wondered? It had only been a few hours, so I was sure it would be okay for a little longer, but I certainly wasn't going to wait until tomorrow. If the doctor didn't show this evening, then I decided that we'd have to try to set the bones ourselves.

I walked across the room to sit down on the bed. Ollie propped his crutch up in the corner behind the door, hanging his hat and backpack from it before coming to join me. I could see from his expression that his mind was working away as he pondered the mystery of the code, and I hoped that he wouldn't put two and two together. We both had enough to think about already.

"There was a Weeper out there last night," he said, and I knew I was going to have to come clean.

"Yes," I said on a sigh. "Yes, there was. Look, I didn't want to tell you because I didn't want you to get worked up about it when there's nothing we can do. And anyway, it's done now."

"What's done?"

"Mark thought it would be fun to watch me race the Weeper," I said, "so he set the gates to second-long intervals and made me run through to the centre, where the Weeper was already waiting. Then he shouted me the code and I let myself inside."

I decided not to tell him about how close those last few moments had been, how close I had come to getting bitten.

He was silent for a moment, running his fingers through the curls of his hair.

"I really, really hate that dick," he said with feeling.

"Yeah," I said, "me too."

"You've got to stop doing this, Emmy."

"What?" I asked, surprised.

"Trying to protect me from this place. You ran fifteen miles today, then carried on with three broken fingers, you idiot. Are you trying to kill yourself?"

"I'm not going to die from a few broken fingers," I said dismissively, but with the way they were aching I felt like I might make a liar of myself.

"Just stop with this stubborn brave face routine," he said.

I thought that was pretty rich, given his performance with his crutch.

"I will if you will, Mr 'I can go as fast as you with only one functioning leg'."

"Fine," he said.

"Fine."

He stormed off into the bathroom to fill up his water bottle and brought it over to the bed along with some bread and cheese, which we ate in silence. After we were full of food and drink, we took our shoes and socks off, unwrapping the bandages to find that our feet were in surprisingly good shape. I was still wearing my backpack, so I started to struggle out of it, trying to shrug it off using only my left hand.

"Let me help," Ollie said.

"I can manage."

"Don't be ridiculous," he said in an exasperated tone. "Emmy, stop, just let me help."

"Fine," I said, biting the word out in frustration, but stilling as he slid the strap off my left shoulder. He helped me get my arm through it before gently doing the same with the right, holding the strap wide open so that I could pull my injured hand out without rubbing it against the backpack.

"I could have managed fine on my own," I said archly as he put the bag down on the bed behind us.

"Dear god, Emmy, don't you ever let up? You're such a pain in the neck," he said.

"No," I replied tartly, "you're thinking of the Silver."

"Well, I wouldn't know about that. Unlike some people I could mention."

I gawped at him. I couldn't believe he'd brought that up, particularly when I was still feeling raw after seeing Sol earlier today. So I said something mean.

"What are you?" I asked. "Jealous?"

He looked at me for a moment, his eyes sparking with intensity.

"Why?" he whispered as he leaned towards me. "Do you want me to be?"

The tone of his voice sent a shiver skittering over my skin, the warm scent of him washing over me and waking up desires that I hadn't acknowledged. My gaze flickered to his lips then back to his bright, grey eyes, and I watched them widen slightly as he read my expression.

Well, I thought, why the hell not?

"Emmy…"

I leaned forward, closing the gap between us, and then my lips were on his, gentle at first but then more insistent as he moved his mouth against mine. As the kiss deepened, he pulled my hat from my head and threw it behind me, bringing his hand up to my face to run his fingers through my hair to the back of my neck. His other hand found my waist and circled round to my back, grasping at my shirt as I moaned at his touch.

"Emmy," he whispered against my lips.

"Shut up."

"Emmy, there's a car."

I pulled away from him abruptly and stood up, moving over to the window to see who it was, praying that it would be the doctor. I wasn't disappointed.

"She came through," I said excitedly. "Tessa came through. She's brought Dr Tanner."

"That's great news," Ollie sighed, "but couldn't she have waited ten minutes? Hell, five probably would have done it."

"Really?" I said in a sardonic tone, not quite able to believe that he was joking about this.

"It's been a while. And who knows what kind of horrible injuries you'll have to suffer before your judgement is impaired enough to let me have another shot?"

I laughed and walked back across the room towards him, bending over to press a light kiss to his lips.

"Don't worry," I said. "We're not even nearly done yet."

His face broke into a seductive smile as I returned to the window, looking over my shoulder at him.

"You tease," he said.

Despite the circumstances, the broken fingers and the imminent Casting, I smiled happily as I watched Tessa escort Dr Tanner into the enclosure. He was wearing a crumpled shirt and carrying his usual case, together with a second bag.

And then, just as suddenly as my good mood had taken me, I started to become anxious as I realised how much this was going to hurt.

"It'll be okay," Ollie said as he joined me by the window and put an arm around my shoulders. "He'll sort it out for you, and then it'll all be fine."

"Will it?" I asked, worried that the fingers might be crushed beyond repair.

"Of course. Fingers heal really well. You'll see."

I wasn't sure I believed him, but I gave him my best brave smile as we watched them approach.

I met the doctor in the observation room as Tessa opened the outside door for him.

"Thank you," I said to her sincerely. She simply nodded at me and stepped back outside, shutting the door behind her.

"So," the doctor said as he set his bags on the table, "what is it this time? Pulled your stitches again?" he asked Ollie.

"No," he replied. "It's Emmy."

He looked at me expectantly.

"I've broken some fingers," I said, holding the hand out carefully towards him.

"And how did this happen?" he asked.

"They were, erm, crushed," I said, thinking it was probably a bad idea to say that Ada had been behind this. I didn't want to get the doctor into trouble, or to discourage him from treating me. After all, she ran this facility, and she'd wanted my fingers good and broken. I imagined that she would have preferred that they healed badly, to provide a more durable lesson in the errors of my blasphemous ways.

All in all, I decided it was better not to give Dr Tanner a reason to worry.

"I see," he said. "Crushed between several hard,

cylindrical objects?" he asked with a raised eyebrow, which made me wonder whether this was an injury he'd seen before.

"Yes," I admitted, "I'd say that was pretty accurate."

"Well, take a seat then, and let's have a look."

He sat down at the table and I claimed the seat next to him, leaving Ollie to sit opposite me. I laid my hand on the surface gingerly, wincing at the pressure on my fingers, and the doctor leaned in for a closer look.

"I'm sorry, but I'm going to have to feel the breaks so I can work out what we're dealing with."

I exchanged a nervous glance with Ollie and reached out my good hand across the table towards him. He took it in his own and I nodded at the doctor, gritting my teeth in anticipation. When he started to put pressure on the digits it was worse than I had expected, the bruised flesh screaming under his touch. I sucked in a breath and let it out raggedly as he squeezed, feeling through the swollen fingers to the bone.

"We'll have to straighten them up before we splint them," he said as he drew his hands away, "but the breaks look clean, which is a good thing. These cylindrical objects you mentioned must have twisted a little at the last moment, or the bones would just have shattered."

I sighed with relief.

"You got lucky," he continued, "trust me." As he spoke, he looked into my eyes as if he were trying to convey a message, and I knew then for certain that this wasn't the first time this had happened. I wondered what other blasphemies Ada considered to merit the punishment.

"Now," the doctor said, "I would normally like to give a local anaesthetic for this treatment, but it's being rationed for those who need it most, so I'm afraid this is going to hurt. I'll be as quick as I can, but I need you to stay as still as possible so I can get the bones set. I'll need your help, Mr Faulkner."

He stood up and pulled some splints and tape out of his bags before walking over to the outside door and knocking on it lightly.

"Doctor?" Tessa asked as she opened it to him.

"Could I borrow you for a moment, please?"

Tessa nodded and came to stand on one side of me, Ollie on the other. With the two of them looming above me I suddenly became very anxious, my heartbeat racing as the reality of the situation sank in. If it needed the two of them to hold me down, then the doctor hadn't been lying when he said this was going to hurt.

"Be strong, Emmy," Ollie whispered to me as he put his hands on my shoulders to press me down into the chair.

Tessa stepped between me and the doctor, turning her back to me as she used both hands to clamp my right wrist, thumb and little finger down onto the tabletop. Her position meant that I couldn't see my fingers, and I wondered whether that was deliberate, to save me the sight of the bones snapping back into place. I closed my eyes anyway, scrunching my face up as I anticipated the pain.

"Ready?" the doctor asked.

"Ready," I gritted out through my teeth.

It was the longest thirty seconds of my life. Credit to Dr Tanner: he pulled each of the fingers back into place with remarkable efficiency, but despite his skill I still screamed with every one, tears of pain running from my eyes. I was a snivelling mess by the time he finished, my nose running, my breath coming in gasps and my throat hoarse from yelling.

He put splints between and on each side of the three fingers then bound them all together with tape, immobilising them so that they wouldn't come out of alignment.

"Keep them still," he said, "and they'll heal well. I'll leave you some tape in case it starts to peel, but don't take out the splints, just put more tape on top if you need to. Here are some painkillers too," he said as he handed me a bottle of pills. "They're not very strong, but they're better than nothing."

"Thank you, Dr Tanner," I said, sniffing as I wiped the tears from my face and took the bottle from him. "And thank you, Tessa."

I was surprised to see what looked like the ghost of a smile crossing her face as she led the doctor out of the door.

"In the nicest possible way," he said just before he closed the door behind him, "I hope I don't see either of you again any time soon."

I couldn't have agreed more. As soon as they had left, Ollie helped me get a couple of pills out of the bottle and I swallowed them down.

"Shit," I said. "I'm glad that's over."

"Are you okay?" Ollie asked.

I nodded at him as I got to my feet.

"Surprisingly, yeah," I said, "they ache a bit, but they feel much better now they're all bound up."

"Well," he said with a glint in his eye, "it's still early, so what shall we do now?"

"I'm filthy," I said, looking down at my dirty clothes as I walked through the other room. I made my way into the bathroom to splash some water on my face and blow my nose, which was a tricky task using only my left hand.

"Shower?" he asked, following me from the observation room.

"Shower," I agreed.

"Need a hand? Might be useful, seeing as how between us we only have two that work."

I walked out of the bathroom to find him standing right in front of me.

"Er…"

"No funny business," he said, holding his hands up innocently. "I promise."

"Still…"

"It's not like I haven't already seen you naked, and anyway, freezing cold water isn't really conducive to, well, you know."

"That's not the point. I don't want you perving on me."

"Well, if I get naked at the same time then you can perv on me too," he said. "I know you enjoyed every minute of it the last time you saw me in the altogether. And the time before that."

"Did not."

"Did too. I saw you checking out my assets."

168

"They're not as impressive as you think they are, you know," I replied haughtily.

"Wait until you see them in action."

"I'm tired, long day," I said, faking a yawn. "Not in the mood."

"Really?" he asked as he took a step towards me that put him a hairsbreadth away, his face tilted down towards my own.

"Really," I whispered, so close that my lips brushed across his as I spoke.

"I bet I can get you in the mood pretty quickly," he whispered back.

"I'd like to see you try."

A sly smile spread slowly across his face and I thought he was going to kiss me, but then he leaned away from me suddenly.

"No," he said, "you're right. Long day and all. Early start tomorrow…"

"Oh, shut up," I said as I wrapped my left hand around the back of his head and pulled his mouth down to meet mine.

"Hey," he whispered against my lips in mock affront, "I said no funny business."

"You didn't mean it," I said as I rested my broken fingers carefully on his shoulder and slid my other hand up under his shirt.

"Neither did you when you said my assets weren't impressive, right?"

"Hmm," I teased, "I remain to be convinced."

"You want convincing?" he said. "Now that I can do."

"Promises, promises…"

He rested his forehead against mine and put his hands on my hips, looking deeply into my eyes as he walked me slowly backwards.

"I'll convince the pants off you," he whispered.

And then he kissed me, his lips moving urgently against mine as he pushed me back against the wall of the cell. I grabbed the bottom of his shirt with my good hand and pulled it upwards, interrupting our kiss to strip it off over his head.

"Impatient?" he asked.

I shrugged dismissively.

"Nothing I haven't seen before."

But there was no denying that it was different when I was this close to him, my fingers trailing over the contours of his chest as I felt the warmth of his skin against mine. And then I was unbuttoning his trousers and pushing them to the ground to pool at his feet, leaving him standing in just his boxers. He stepped out of the trousers and kicked them aside as he pulled me close for another kiss, more frantic this time as his hands returned to my waist and started to pull up my T-shirt. I worried for a second that he was going to forget about my broken fingers, but he didn't lose control.

He leaned away from me and gently released my left arm from the top before carefully pulling the material over my head and off my right hand, his eyes intent on his task until it was complete, but as soon as the top hit the floor he raked me with his gaze.

"You are so beautiful," he said as he pushed my hair away from my face. "I think I've wanted you since the first time you called me an idiot."

"To your face or behind your back?" I asked with a saccharine smile.

"Well, you might have some other names for me in about five minutes' time. Ten tops."

"Like 'Quickfire'?" I asked.

"I was thinking more along the lines of 'Jesus' and 'Oh, god', but whatever works for you."

And then he was kissing me again, smiling against my lips as he unfastened my trousers and slid my bra straps from my shoulders.

"Do you need me to undo it for you?" I asked as he reached behind me to unclasp my bra. "I can't imagine you've had much practice."

"Oh, really?" he said as he snapped his fingers behind my back and released the catch like magic.

Our underwear ended up on the floor a moment later and

then he was backing me into the bathroom, reaching behind me to turn on the water.

"Ready?" he asked.

I held my injured hand out of the reach of the shower and he did the same, then the water hit us in a cold rush that had me gasping for breath and laughing.

"Shit!" I screeched as I reached for the soap.

"Here," he said, "let me help."

His fingers slid across my stomach and around my waist as he joined me under the stream, kissing me, his naked body pressed against mine as he leaned me back against the wall.

"It's really fucking cold in here," he said after a moment.

"That's your excuse," I replied.

"Let's get this shower over with quickly shall we?" he said as he removed his soaked shoulder dressing.

"From what I understand," I said, "you can't do it any other way."

"Once we get out of this freezing water, I'll show you just how fast I can go."

He grabbed the shampoo and poured some into my left hand, which I quickly rubbed into my own hair and rinsed out before helping him do the same with his. We repeated with the conditioner and, after getting a little carried away helping each other with the soap, we declared ourselves clean and shut off the water.

The moment the shower stopped he pulled me into another kiss before trailing his lips down the side of my neck and onto my chest. But he didn't stop there, his hands running down my back as his mouth slowly followed the curve of my breast and the line of my stomach downwards, his warm breath raising goose bumps over my cold, wet skin.

"Ollie…" I moaned as his tongue touched my thigh, sending a shiver through me. "We don't have any protection."

He stood up slowly, kissing his way back up my body until his mouth found mine again.

"Don't worry," he whispered. "This is going to be all about you."

Then he reached behind me for the towels that hung on the back of the door of the tiny bathroom and dried me off while I helped him to do the same, with some distractions along the way.

"Bed," he said when we were as dry as we could be bothered to get.

And there he finished what he started, bringing me to the peak of ecstasy until I screamed with release and exhaustion, and then he wrapped me in his arms as the sun went down.

CHAPTER XIV

Monday

I had a moment of blissful peace when I woke, the strength of Ollie's arms around me warm and comforting. I felt as though after weeks of frantic movement, I'd found a place where I could be still.

He had kissed me, but there would be no mark left behind, because he was human, like me. However he felt about me, no one would be able to tell but him. We would never have a bond between us, or a brand, or any of the other Silver mojo to manipulate my feelings for him. What happened between the two of us was exactly that: between the two of us. And however he felt about me, being with Ollie was never going to be a matter of life or death.

It was easy and relaxed, and there was something liberating about that. We liked each other, and that was all there was to it. We weren't in love, consumed by the angst of our emotions, we just enjoyed being with each other. Unlike with Drew, there wasn't some epic love on/off switch that had been triggered. I didn't have to spend my time feeling guilty that I didn't feel more for him than I did, that I didn't have the big love. We were free to let our feelings be fluid and just do what we wanted to do.

It was… normal. And so simple.

"Morning," he mumbled as he curled a hand around my waist and pulled me close, his other hand pushing my hair back from my cheek as he softly pressed his lips to mine.

"Morning," I whispered.

But something was wrong.

"Well, well," said a self-satisfied voice from the doorway. "What have we got here then?"

Shit.

I pulled the sheet up to my armpits before turning to look over my shoulder as Ollie cuddled me close protectively, shielding me with his arms. Mark and Tessa were standing at the door to the building, and Mark looked like he was having the time of his life. Apparently we'd overslept for our patrol duty.

"Knew you'd get bored enough to stick it to her eventually," he said to Ollie.

I felt his muscles tense beside me and turned back to him quickly, worried he was going to let Mark rile him up into doing something stupid. His face was suffused with anger, his eyes fixed on Mark with a determined expression. I put my hand on his shoulder and squeezed it lightly until he broke off the stare and looked at me.

"Don't," I whispered.

He closed his eyes after a second and nodded.

"What do you say, Tessa?" Mark continued with a laugh. "Are we gonna be raising ourselves some prisoner babies in here?"

"You have five minutes," she said to us before abruptly closing the door in Mark's face.

"Shit," I said as I swung my legs out of the bed and started pulling on my clothes.

"One day," Ollie said, "I'm going to smash my fist into that man's smug, bastard face."

"No," I said, "you're not. Now hurry up and get dressed."

We got ourselves ready as quickly as we could, bandaging the blisters and re-dressing Ollie's shoulder before packing up our backpacks ready for the day's walk.

"No running today," he said to me as I quickly brushed my teeth.

I spat into the drain and rinsed my mouth out, swallowing down some of the pain pills before pulling my hair back into a messy high ponytail with difficulty and topping it off with my cap.

"Not as much running," I agreed, "but I'm going to do as much as I can."

"Emmy, please."

"Look," I said as I walked back into the cell, passing him the sun cream so he could spread it on the back of my neck while I did my face and arms, "it'll be fine. I run a lot. I've done marathons. Other than the fingers, I'm not too sore today, and the faster I can go the less you have to do. So I'm running. That's my choice, okay?"

He spread the cream over my skin then handed me back the bottle and nodded grudgingly before pressing a kiss to my lips.

"Okay," he said. "Now let's get this over with so we can go back to bed."

"Do you never think of anything else?" I asked as I passed him his crutch.

"I can, but why would I when I can spend my time remembering you naked, writhing in my arms, screaming my name…"

"Okay, okay," I said with a smile, "I get the picture."

"And what a beautiful one it is."

"You're such a deviant."

"I'm just a man who knows what he likes and is sometimes lucky enough to get it. Now come on, let's summon the guard dogs."

He knocked loudly on the outer door and Tessa opened it widely, letting us out into the empty enclosure. The day wasn't as warm as those we had seen recently, the sun peeking intermittently out from behind the clouds rather than blazing incessantly onto the dry earth. It was still early, perhaps six o'clock going by the time at which our last early shift had started, so there was still plenty of room for things to heat up.

Mark was already waiting impatiently by the truck, drumming his fingers on the roof of the cab as he smoked a cigarette. It wasn't something I'd ever seen him do before, but I supposed that it was hardly going to affect his life expectancy. Mind you, the way he wheezed and sweated, I doubted it could be helping his health.

There was disapproval in Tessa's expression as she escorted us out through the gates. I guessed that it had something to do with finding Ollie and me naked together this morning, but I wondered on what basis she would disapprove of that. Was she concerned about us being involved with each other, or was she just unimpressed that she and Mark had had to wait for us to get out of bed?

As far as Mark was concerned, I imagined that it was just another stick for him to beat us with. He was going to have an absolute field day with this one.

We ate a quick breakfast in the back of the truck and then we were dropped off at the same starting points as yesterday, Ollie first and me second. He kissed me again before he stepped out of the vehicle, his hand cupping my cheek as he smiled at me.

"Come find me, princess," he whispered.

I was determined that I would, and as fast as my body would let me.

When I eventually started my patrol, the going was harder, my muscles more sore and my broken fingers aching as I ran, but I managed to make it to the hamlet at the top of the first hill at a good speed.

As soon as I crested the rise, I could see the Weepers close up against the fence. There were hundreds of them. Hands were poking through, clenched around the chain links and railings, layered up on top of each other until about three feet from the top of the fence. They must have flung themselves up it, climbing over each other to try to get over into the next circle where I stood. A little way behind them, sightless Weepers were ambling across the cleared ground aimlessly, dropping straight to the ground the moment that they touched any of their fallen fellows. Apparently the electrified fence was still working, which was a small mercy.

I stopped dead, the nearest figures maybe a hundred feet ahead of me, and blew my whistle as quickly as I could.

Hundreds of heads swivelled in my direction, and suddenly I wasn't sure making my position known had been such a great idea. The Weeper at the head of the wandering pack lifted his face and sniffed the air deeply before throwing back his head and howling to the sky. Then he ran towards me, covering the distance with terrifying speed before slamming into the fence. He bounced straight back off it to lie still on the ground, but his cry was echoed by those behind him as they raced towards me in a wave of terrible, single-minded horror.

How many of them would it take, I wondered, to bring the fence down?

It was as though the world narrowed until there was nothing in it but me and the Weepers, the crowd charging towards me like a silent, blood-drenched army. For a moment I could do nothing but panic, fear fixing my feet to the spot, but after what felt like an age I managed to get them moving to carry me back the way I had come. I was stumbling uncertainly, terror clenching my muscles and locking them so my limbs felt ungainly and robotic. My steps were awkward, my gaze pulled back over my shoulder while I ran in the opposite direction.

And I couldn't go fast enough.

They were gaining on me.

The dark horde followed my movement, chasing me down on the other side of the fence as they tracked the deafeningly loud thuds of my urgent footsteps along the wide avenue made by the barriers to either side of me. They themselves came on with eerie quietness. They raised no noise but the gentle rustling of the scraps of their clothing as their broken limbs powered them forwards. Had I not been looking at them, I would never have believed from the sound alone that there could be so many.

Were it not for the howls, I thought, we would never hear them coming.

Within seconds, they were up against the perimeter. But, one by one, as they threw themselves against it, they each rebounded from or hung clinging to the fence.

I gasped with relief, but I didn't stop running, my feet carrying me downhill as they crashed against the metal, breaking the silence of their pursuit with the ringing clangs of their impact.

The fence seemed to be keeping them at bay for now, but I wondered how far the current would go. Surely enough interference with it would earth the charge and make it harmless? I had a moment to pray that the Silver were good at circuitry before I was swept off my feet and, after a couple of seconds of stomach wrenching dizziness, found myself back outside the enclosure.

A Silver I didn't recognise, a man with close-cut dark hair and coffee-coloured skin, stood in front of me.

"Stay," he said, and then he disappeared.

I leaned over with my hands resting on my thighs, nausea spinning up to the back of my throat, my breath coming short and ragged.

"Shit," I gasped.

Something touched my back and I jumped, spinning to look over my shoulder as my heart raced fit to bursting. My muscles tensed and I made ready to run.

"It's okay," Ollie said urgently. "Emmy, it's just me."

"Jesus," I wheezed, feeling like I was about to have a heart attack. "Fuck's sake, Ollie."

"Sorry," he said, "I didn't mean to scare you."

"Fuck," I breathed, then crouched down onto the grass with my head between my knees, trying to calm myself.

"What happened to you?" he asked.

"Weepers," I said briefly.

"Are you okay?"

I nodded, my head still hanging low, and closed my eyes.

He came and sat down beside me as my pulse slowed, my breathing gradually returning to normal. When I felt able to, I lifted my head and lay back onto the grass, my backpack digging into my ribs and spine. I was too drained to care.

We stayed like that for a couple of minutes before Ollie spoke again.

"What's going on?"

"I'm not sure," I said, raising myself up into a seated position, "but I came across a whole shitload of Weepers. There's this little village at the top of a hill, maybe three or four miles from where I started my run, and the place was crawling with them. I blew my whistle and they just started throwing themselves up against the fence."

My eyes scanned the horizon as I spoke, half expecting to see the Weepers coming towards us over the grassy hillsides that lay beyond the perimeter fences next to which we sat. I assumed that Tessa and Mark would be coming to get us, either to take us back to our patrol or to let us back into the enclosure, but I couldn't see any vehicles coming our way. Still, there wasn't really anything we could do until someone came to get us and I wasn't about to disobey the Silver who'd brought us here.

"Same here," Ollie said as he pulled off his backpack.

"What?"

"There's a stand of trees I walk through. Not that big, only a few hundred feet wide, and the Weepers are always there hiding out, but today when they heard me limping past a load of them came out into the light. Their eyes just... sort of... well, it was revolting, and then they were coming after me. But the Silver came and got them, and I was already through the trees and out the other side when suddenly I was here instead."

I carefully shrugged off my backpack and pulled out my bottle of water, holding it between my feet as I unscrewed the cap. We hadn't been out for long, but I'd been running hard and frightened half to death. Now that I'd stopped, I was suddenly feeling thirsty.

We sat quietly for a few moments as I drank, and then Ollie turned to me, looking thoughtful.

"Are there always Weepers in that village?" he asked.

"I've seen one or two there, but nothing like this. Looks like the rest of them have worked out where we are now," I said, thinking of the ones we had seen on the drive from the city, stuck in limbo between the two destinations.

"That wasn't what I was thinking," Ollie replied.

"What then?"

"Well, it's not that they haven't always known where we were, because they've always been gathering out in the woods around here."

"I suppose so," I conceded.

"The thing that's changed is the way they're behaving. It's the same thing we've seen before: they're more willing to come out into the sun to get to us. And there's some logic there that's worrying me. I mean, with all of those Weepers just outside the fence then, even if it is electrified, they'd be able to bring it down with their numbers during the night, right?"

I shrugged, pulling off my hat and stuffing it into my backpack with the water bottle.

"Maybe."

"I think definitely. Throw enough bodies at it, and one way or another it's coming down. So the Silver probably have their own patrols in the night to keep them away."

"Makes sense," I agreed.

"So what's worrying me," he continued, "is the inevitable conclusion that the Weepers know the Silver patrol in the night, so they decide to forgo their sight and make a move in the day instead. Because then we're dealing with things that think and plan, millions and millions of them, and that's just... scary."

As the implications of his words sank in, I started to feel very exposed sitting out where we were so close to the border of the Farm. Crazy though it seemed, I would be glad once we were back inside the enclosure, with solid walls and an extra three fences between us and the Weepers. As long as the guards didn't throw them in with us, of course.

"Do you think Mark will be bringing us some more friends today?" I asked.

"I hope not. With things as they are, their howls will probably bring a load of them up to the perimeter here, even if it is daylight."

"Shit," I said. "I hope we don't have to go back out there."

He shook his head.

"I have a feeling the Silver are going to be doing their own patrolling from now on."

And it looked like he might be right.

We saw dust rising in the distance and then a truck came into view, Tessa alone at the wheel. She pulled up next to us and hopped out as we got to our feet to meet her.

"No more patrolling today," she said briskly.

Ollie and I exchanged a look. I opened my mouth to ask her about the Weepers, but she cut her eyes to me sharply.

"Back inside," she said.

So we walked through the gates as she activated them and back into our cell, dutifully keying in the code and locking the door behind us. Tessa was already driving away by the time we had put our bags down inside and looked out of the window.

"Odd," Ollie said.

"She seemed a bit panicked, distracted maybe."

"Maybe it's worse than we thought."

"There weren't that many of them," I said. "I'm sure the Silver can handle them."

"Yes," Ollie agreed, "but what do they do with them after that? All they can do is put them back in the countryside and wait for them to make their way back. I mean, we've seen them with all their bones broken and still alive."

"Yes, but it's not like they can move when they're in that state."

"Maybe not," he said, "but maybe they recover. Your dickhead ex was able to heal you, and he came back without a scratch from a gunshot wound to the head. Who's to say that isn't something the Silver have in common with the Weepers? Maybe they can heal themselves too. Maybe just not the eyes."

I stepped on the heels of my trainers to pull them off my feet and kicked them into the corner of the room. I'd never thought about that possibility. Everything I'd ever been told by the Silver suggested that there was no way to kill the Weepers. Maybe Ollie was right; maybe that was because they recovered from their injuries in the same way that the Silver did.

"Shit," I said as I sat down on the bed. "I really hope that's not true."

"Me too," Ollie agreed, "but you've got to admit that it sounds plausible."

"So, what? We're just playing a waiting game here? If the Weepers are immortal like the Silver, then eventually they're going to get to us all, one way or another. And if you're right, they're going to be prepared to blind themselves to do it, so we can't even hide in the daylight. There's nowhere we can hide."

I thought about the ever-diminishing circles of protection that seemed to be offered by the presence of the Silver, remembering how close the Weepers had come to us in the woods on the truck journey to the Farm. I really didn't want to reflect on that for too long, because if we lost that last weapon in our armoury, the safety provided by proximity to the Silver, then there was no hope for us.

Well, for Ollie, at least, I thought.

Only two days left for me.

"We're in just about the safest place we could be," Ollie said.

"Really?" I asked. "Right out on the edge by the fence, no Silver within miles of us…"

"With all this electrified fencing around us," he

interrupted, "and a direct line to the Solis Invicti via your secret walkie talkie. So chill out. We're safe. Now, with patrol duty off the agenda, how shall we spend the rest of our day?"

He raised his eyebrows at me and sat down next to me on the bed.

"How about it?" he teased.

"I'm not getting caught out by Mark again. We don't know that they're not going to come back. And anyway, I've got the second test at some point today."

"You worry too much," he said, taking off his hat and skimming it across the room to join my shoes.

"And you don't worry enough," I said. "I don't know about you, but I don't want this to get out of control and end up starting the family of pet humans that Mark has always dreamed of."

"I'm not some hormone-driven teenager, you know. Despite your charms, which are many, I can restrain myself."

The problem was that, after last night, I wasn't sure that I would be able to make the same claim. I was wound tight with anxiety and I wanted something to take that away from me. I could give myself over to that temptation too easily.

I shook my head.

"Okay then," he said. "What shall we do instead?"

But now that he had made the suggestion, I couldn't stop thinking about it. My eyes roamed his face, lingering on his lips and those bright, grey eyes, and my breath started coming a little faster. After the morning I'd had, I could really do with some distracting.

What can I say? I have zero self-control.

I lifted my hand to his cheek and ran my fingers through his soft, wavy hair, leaning closer towards him to follow the movement with my eyes. His lips were right next to mine, his breath warm on my cheek, and I shuddered with anticipation.

"Emmy…" he whispered.

"Do you think, if we asked nicely, the doctor would be able to get us some protection?" I whispered back at him, grasping at straws.

The corner of his mouth turned up in a wry smile as he pulled away from me, leaning back and out of my arms.

"That would be an awkward conversation. And no, I don't think so."

"Oh."

I watched him for a moment, his eyes searching my face.

"You haven't thought about it, have you?" he asked.

I looked at him, confused.

"I don't think the Silver really believe in contraception," he added. "You know, the more humans the better."

"Oh," I said. "Right. More blood for them, I suppose."

It made sense. In fact, when I thought about it I was surprised that they hadn't yet started actively encouraging our reproduction. I wondered how long that would take, whether in a few weeks' time there would be incentives to motivate us to increase our numbers. It was a disturbing thought, but it was something I could imagine Sol getting right behind. It was practical and logical: offer to look after the mothers, and there would be more humans. On the face of it, everyone wins, but underneath it all would be a sinister note of discord.

We were their cattle, and they were farming us for blood. And how far would it go? Would we have any choice in the matter, at the end of it? I thought darkly of how humans treated their livestock: breeding for type to eliminate defects, to increase yield, for flavour…

"I mean, they've got to be thinking about the future," Ollie said. "It's like every man's dream: it's our responsibility to repopulate the Earth."

But how many men did you really need, I wondered? If things went that way, Sol would have wrapped it in an acceptable bargain for us so that we would cooperate, I had no doubt. But Ben… if he was calling the shots, or if he and Laila held sway over Sol, then things would be very different.

"Sounds like more of a nightmare to me," I said. "Anyway, this isn't a world anyone would want to bring a child into," I added, following the thought to its logical conclusion as I contemplated how desperately fraught it would be to have to look after a baby in this environment.

"No," Ollie agreed. "You're right there."

I remembered the Weepers piled up against the fence next to the hamlet this morning, their fingers intertwined with the chain link. Some of the hands had been heart-rendingly small, the little fists clenched tightly around the electrified metal, and some of the shambling walkers had been only a few feet tall. Were there some among them that were too small to do anything but crawl, I wondered? And what if they were too small even for that? How would it feel, as a mother, to see that? To know that it was a chance you took by raising a child in this place, all the time knowing that the best-case scenario was that you were rearing another donor for the Silver?

It was one thing to contemplate my own future, to imagine myself as one of those twisted things, but how could a parent function with the spectre of that possibility hanging over them? And if the worst happened, how could you carry on? But then I was hit with the certainty that it must have happened in the Revelation. After all, in that dark time, every awful thing you could imagine had happened to someone.

It didn't bear thinking about, and the image I had called to mind was enough to have me shaking my head in an effort to dislodge it before the visceral horror of it broke me. But it wouldn't budge now it had settled in, a terrible vision of tiny, innocent eyes bleeding, and I knew it would be staying with me.

"No," I said raggedly, a solid resolve clamping around my heart. "It's not going to happen. We can't... I can't risk that. It's not worth it."

"It's okay," he said. "It's not even a thing."

I sighed heavily then ran my unbroken fingers through my hair and pulled it out of its ponytail, releasing it to fall over my shoulders. Why did everything have to be so complicated all the time? Even with Ollie, when I had thought it was all so straightforward and easy.

"And besides," he said after a moment, "we can do a lot of stuff without doing... that."

"Jeez, you have such a one-track mind. This is not the time."

"I know. I'm just saying."

I had a horrible sense of unease, a creeping feeling of paranoia that was bothering me, but I couldn't work out where it was originating from. I supposed that I was feeling threatened and vulnerable out here with Ollie, the two of us apparently so close to danger. But I was also feeling strangely empty, a hollow despair sitting in my stomach.

Everything about this place was so bleak and wrong.

"Emmy," he said, "I'm just joking around. Don't come over all serious on me."

I shook my head at him in disbelief.

"How can you do it after everything that's happened today? Aren't you worried? Doesn't it get to you?"

He shrugged.

"I'm used to it. This isn't new to me. I've been living this way for weeks now, expecting to die day to day, and I just figure I have to make the most of it while I can. There's nothing we can do about it from out here anyway."

And while I had found that comforting a couple of days ago, that forced inaction, today it was weighing on me heavily. I felt itchy under my skin, uneasy and frustrated at the impotence of my position. That was aggravated by the suspicions Ollie had voiced about the Weepers. The progression he described portended gradual but inevitable encroachment onto those little slices of the world that we had carved out as safe for humans.

Maybe the rebels had it right after all: we should be shutting ourselves up underground. But how was that sustainable?

For the first time since the Revelation, I couldn't see a long-term solution here. I had believed in Sol's vision for the future. Since first I met him, I had always had confidence that the Silver would protect us, and that even if they never found a cure for the Weepers they would be able to keep them from our door indefinitely.

I'd thought that life would go on and that we would be safe.

Now I had lost that faith, and the world was stark and terrifying without it.

CHAPTER XV

Upon my bed at night
I sought him whom my soul loves;
I sought him, but found him not;
I called him, but he gave no answer.

- The Song of Solomon

There had been a new paper bag full of food on the table when we arrived back in the building, so we shared some lunch quietly, each of us lost in our own thoughts. I showered afterwards, alone, and mentally chastised myself for getting involved with Ollie so hastily when we were living in such close quarters. I'd been blasé about it, jumping in without thinking through the consequences and, particularly now that I realised just how serious those consequences could be, I was starting to feel some regret.

Thankfully, he was being relaxed about it all and giving me as much space as the building would allow us. He was sitting at the table when I came out of the bathroom, apparently sorting through our medical supplies. I had already replaced the dressings on my feet and wrist, which had been a bit of a challenge with the broken fingers, and I was wearing my cleaner pair of scrubs. After all, it didn't look like we were going to be leaving the cell again today so I wasn't expecting to need hardy clothing.

Ollie was pulling off his own bandages when I entered the observation room.

"Need a hand?" I offered.

"I'm good," he said. "I'm just going to go and wash too."

"Okay," I said with a tight smile as I took a seat opposite him.

He made as if to stand up from the table, but then hesitated and sat back in his chair.

"Do you want to talk about it?" he asked.

"I don't think so," I said. "I'm not really sure what there is to talk about yet."

"Yet?"

"I don't really know how to express it, or what I want, so I'm not sure it'll be helpful to talk."

"Do you want to try?" he asked. "I don't want this to be eating you up and you feeling like you can't talk to me about it. This isn't a big deal. If you want to step back from it, it's not a problem."

His words struck a chord with me, resonating until I felt as though I were unpicking the knot of part of my anxiety to get to its core.

"I think that's exactly what the problem is," I said. "It feels like things have changed today. I just… feel different. It feels like things need to matter more. You keep saying this isn't a big deal, but with things how they are it feels like everything should matter. And if it doesn't matter then maybe that's not enough."

"I didn't say it didn't matter," he said.

"I know, and I'm not saying it doesn't matter to me, but it's just… different."

And that was it, I realised. This was a time to be serious, and whatever was going on between us, it didn't feel serious.

It felt like a distraction, something to help us through the worst excesses of being stuck in this place. It helped me to forget the realities of our lives as they were now. It helped me to forget that the Casting was coming and that after it I would either be a Weeper or return here to spend the foreseeable future in this cell.

Just a distraction.

It recalled to my mind an unwelcome memory: a night last week on the terrace of the club, back in the city. It had been back when Drew still had the bond and I still had the brand, and I had thought Sol had still wanted me. It was what he had called me that night: a distraction. He had been the focus of my attention, the thing that pulled me on through this twisted new reality, but to him I would never be anything more than a distraction.

A toy.

And that wasn't enough.

Being with Ollie had sanded the edges off the horror and the pain, and that was a valuable thing in its own right, but it wasn't the real deal.

"This isn't going anywhere," I said, looking him in the eye.

"Well, neither are we at the moment, so where's the harm?"

I didn't have an answer for that.

"Look," he said, "I'm okay with this as it is, but I understand if you're not. So let's just put it to one side for the moment and worry about it later. Okay?"

"Okay."

"Okay then. I'm going to go shower." He stood from his seat and walked through into the cell, closing the connecting door behind him.

"No peeking!" he yelled through the wall.

I smiled at the teasing tone of his voice.

"Nothing worth looking at!" I shouted back.

His laugh filtered through the door to me and I relaxed, thinking that either way we'd be okay.

I heard an engine outside a few minutes after the water

shut off and I got up to see a car driving through the gates and into the enclosure. This must be the second test, I thought, as it pulled up at the door to leading into the observation room. Sure enough, the door opened and Drew walked in, followed by...

My mouth dropped open.

"Sean?" I asked in disbelief as I jumped to my feet. "You're alive? What the hell are you doing here? Where the fuck have you been, you bastard?"

There was a moment of stunned silence broken only by the sound of the door locking behind them. Sean was looking at me with an ashamed but determined expression, his brown eyes fixed on mine. He looked skinnier and even more drawn than he had when I had last seen him, his short, brown hair tousled as though he had been running his fingers through it anxiously.

"Hi Em," he said quietly.

"Hi Em?" I gaped. "You disappear on me, gone without a trace for a fucking year, and that's all you've got to say to me: Hi Em? Have you got any idea how fucking worried I was? The police told me you'd been borrowing money and that you'd disappeared..." I trailed off, pushing my hair back from my face, on the verge of hysteria.

"I thought you were fucking dead!" I yelled.

"You two know each other then?" Drew asked.

I turned my attention to him properly for the first time since he had walked in the door, wondering whether he was going to be dangerous today, kicking myself for having been distracted from the threat he presented. But he seemed calm and his expression was curious rather than angry, the bubbling rage from yesterday apparently under control.

"My ex-boyfriend," I said.

"There seem to be a lot of them about," Ollie said from the connecting doorway. I hadn't even heard it open.

"Oh, just don't go there, okay?" I said irritably as I sat down in one of the chairs and put my head in my hands. All I needed now was for Sol to show up and then I'd have the whole set, a parade of all my romantic mistakes for me to peruse and berate myself over at my leisure.

"Er, hi," Sean said, offering his hand to Ollie, "I'm Sean."

"I gathered," he replied as he shook it. "Oliver."

"Good to meet you."

"Er…," Ollie said, glancing at me before moving to stand behind my chair with his hands resting on its back, "I think I'll reserve judgement on that one, if you don't mind."

Sean looked between the two of us.

"Oh," he said, "I see."

It had been a difficult morning and I was feeling rubbed raw by the things I had seen, real or imagined. I was already so angry and confused that I felt as if I were going to explode, and Ollie's obviously deliberate gesture of ownership sent me over the edge.

"No, there's no Oh," I said, the pitch of my voice rising as I spoke, "and there's nothing for you to see. Ollie, sit down, and someone tell me what the hell is going on here."

Ollie did as I said without another word. Sean turned to Drew and I realised that, obviously, he was the one in charge here: the only Silver in a room full of humans.

"We've come for the second test," he said. "I didn't know that this human was someone you knew."

"Please forgive me, Secundus," Sean said to Drew, speaking quickly, his eyes wide and desperate as though he expected bad things to follow. "I saw her name come up on the list when she gave blood, together with her location, and then when they told me they needed one of us to come out here to help with someone's test… I'm sorry. I should have said, but I just needed to see her. I know it's not why I'm here, but if I could please just have a few minutes with her…"

Drew looked at me and then back to Sean, a brief flash of pain crossing his otherwise impassive face.

"She is why you're here," he said, and there was the agony in his tone, the weight of loss bearing him down. "I'm her sponsor for the Casting."

Sean's face blanched and he looked between us hopelessly.

"No," he whispered.

"Yes," I said on a sigh. "It's true."

Sean looked at Drew again, examining him closely now, and I realised that he knew what he was looking for: the silver tracing in his irises. I knew that Sean wasn't going to find anything to reassure himself there, the bond long gone, but I wondered how he was privy to those kinds of secrets. They were secrets of the Silver that I only knew because I had been caught up in the danger that they caused.

"But Em," Sean said, his expression frantic as he looked back at me, "you'll... it won't work. You can't..."

"She doesn't have any choice," Drew said quietly. "She's already signed up."

"But, Secundus, please. You know what will happen. Is there no way..."

"No," he replied sharply. "If there were any way, don't you think I would have done it?"

This was news to me. Since the bond had broken, I hadn't been aware of Drew caring at all whether or not I was going to turn into a Weeper. In fact, his behaviour towards me had been so aggressive that I'd thought he might actually welcome my end. Perhaps it was time to admit the possibility that I had been wrong and that his emotions had been firing out of his control. Perhaps he wasn't totally lost.

That would never excuse the way he had been with me, but it could maybe explain it.

"It's too late now," Drew added, his voice cracking a little as he spoke.

Frustration and despair filled Sean's expression as he opened and closed his mouth, clearly wanting to ask more of Drew, but the anxiety was evident in his eyes. He was afraid of him, and I couldn't blame him for that.

"But you agreed to sponsor her?" Sean asked hesitantly.

"Yes," Drew said, staring Sean down in a way that looked like a threat against his asking any further questions on the subject.

I, however, was feeling affronted that anyone would think

I would put myself forward for something like the Casting, that I would buy into the system, and I was still sufficiently riled up that I felt the need to defend my position.

"There were circumstances that made it necessary at the time," I said, "and there was a bond. But it's gone."

Drew glared at me, obviously irritated that I had spilled the beans, while Sean stared between me and Drew incredulously, apparently having trouble processing the news that he had been in love with me.

"If anyone outside this room finds out…" he said to Sean menacingly.

"I won't tell a soul," he replied, holding his palms up in a gesture of surrender.

"Now," Drew said. "If we could get on with this? Without the audience?"

He looked pointedly at Ollie, who shook his head and crossed his arms over his chest.

"No chance," he said. "I'm staying here."

"Oh, for god's sake," I said to him, sick of all the testosterone in the room, "just go and wait next door. The door's unlocked, and everything's fine. Okay?"

He looked at me for a moment, his eyes searching mine as though he was unsure whether or not to believe me, but then he stood from his chair.

"I'm right behind that door," he said, pointing to it emphatically, but unnecessarily. "You just yell if you need me."

I tried to stop myself, but rolled my eyes at him anyway.

I knew he was just being protective, but with things the way they were between us it was making me feel claustrophobic. But that was my problem and not his; he was just looking after me as he had promised that he would. There was no reason for me to take my frustration out on him.

I pulled myself together and offered him a quick, encouraging smile. He nodded back at me then walked through into the cell, closing the door behind him.

"So we're really doing this?" Sean asked Drew hopelessly.

He nodded and indicated that Sean should sit down. He put his briefcase, which I hadn't even noticed he had been carrying, onto the tabletop and sat down opposite me. The case was similar to Dr Tanner's: silver, hard-shelled and clinical-looking.

"Where were you?" I asked him.

Sean looked up at Drew as though he were seeking permission to speak.

"Fine," Drew said, a little impatiently but not unkindly. He moved to lean against the wall opposite the connecting door, his eyes watching us both as Sean started to speak.

"You remember my job?" he asked. "The company I worked for?"

"Er, yes. BioSilver or some… Oh, I get it," I said, interrupting myself. I felt an idiot for not having worked it out sooner.

"Yeah," he said ruefully. "It's why I started freaking out on you, getting paranoid about security. I found out what existed out there, and I just lost it. They had to take me out of the loop for a little while until I… calmed down. Then they wouldn't…"

His eyes flicked towards Drew.

"…couldn't," he corrected himself, "send me back home because of all the secrecy, and then there was the Revelation. And now here I am."

"And you do what exactly?" I asked.

"Lots of things," he said. "I do the blood testing, things like this, and I worked on the carrier test doohickey. And now, of course, we're all working on a cure. So, yeah, busy."

"How's the cure coming?" I asked, as if this were a perfectly normal conversation. How could I be angry, in the circumstances? I was scrambling for things to say, my anger ebbing away as I felt the gulf of time stretching out between us. How was I supposed to relate to him now? He was like a stranger to me.

It felt surreal to be sitting here opposite a man I had loved, a man I had thought was mixed up with loan sharks, but was actually mixed up with vampires, and talk to him as if there was nothing insane about the situation, as if no time had gone by.

"It's coming along," he said, "but it's not easy work. How are things with you?"

I raised my eyebrows at him and glanced around the room, inviting him to take in the scenic prison setting. He looked at my right hand, noting the splinted fingers, but he didn't comment on them.

"Oh," he said, "right."

"Yup."

"So, not great then?"

"Not really," I said, "no."

There was a pause for a moment before he spoke again.

"I'm so sorry for disappearing on you like that, Em. If I could have come back to you, I would have."

He reached across the table for my uninjured hand.

"I never stopped loving you," he said. "I still…"

"Woah," I interrupted as I pulled my hand from his, glancing at Drew and thinking of Ollie in the next room. "Sean, I'm sorry, but it's been more than a year. I thought you were gone. Everything's changed, I've changed, and this is…"

I shook my head, lost for words.

His face fell and I realised that he'd been building himself up for a romantic reunion, expecting that everything would go back to the way it was. He'd been standing still, stuck in the same place for over a year as a captive of the Silver. But me, I'd lived a lifetime in the past couple of weeks, let alone the past year. I wasn't the same person anymore. I didn't even recognise the girl I had been when Sean and I had been together.

I'd spent so long hating him, agonising over what I could have done differently to stop him from behaving the way he did and, ultimately, from leaving me. It had taken so long for me to stop seeing threats around every corner after the paranoia he had passed on to me. It had been months before I had managed to build up my confidence again from the rock-bottom it had hit with the shock of losing him.

When I looked at him I could still see the man I had loved: quiet and serious, caring and gentle. But I also saw in him the ghosts of the problems that had driven a wedge between us, the anxiety clawing at him and making him edgy, nervous and unpredictable.

I didn't want to move backwards, to be that frightened girl again, the wreck that he had made me when he left.

It had been another life, a time before all of this craziness had overcome us. And yes, I looked back on it fondly because it was better than where I was now, but it hadn't been better than what I had found in the interim: my life at the club, my ramshackle family, my place. I didn't miss him.

"But anyway, there's no future with me," I said to him. "Look at where I am."

"Is it forever?"

"You mean if I don't get turned into a Weeper on Wednesday? Yes, it's an indefinite sentence, so until further notice I'll be here at the Primus's pleasure."

How ironic, I thought.

Sean looked at Drew again as if seeking confirmation or approval before turning back to me.

"You know then?" he asked.

"About the Weeper thing? I know," I said.

"Part of this test is to try to work out what your absorption rate is, and whether or not you're likely to turn Weeper or Silver in the Casting."

"Okay," I said, "we could pretend that it matters, but we all know there's almost no chance of it working without the bond. So instead, why don't we just try to find a way to make it look like I've failed the test? Can you help with that?"

Sean shook his head.

"That's not how it works."

"The test is videoed," Drew said, "and the results are transmitted live to the Administrator."

I sighed. I was just going to have to rely on having failed the first test convincingly.

Drew walked around the table and came to sit next to me. Despite his slightly more approachable demeanour today, I was still far from comfortable to have him so close to me. I eyed him cautiously, but he was sitting back in his chair with his arms relaxed on his thighs, his expression defeated and placid.

"Get on with it," he said to Sean in a tone heavy with weariness.

Sean opened the case in front of him and brought out a laptop computer, together with a load of medical instruments. He opened the laptop opposite me and Drew, adjusting its position slightly as he moved the mouse on the track-pad. I realised that he was lining up the laptop's camera so that whoever was on the other end of the transmission would be able to see both Drew and me clearly.

Next, he plugged a cable into one of the computer's USB ports, the other end of which he plugged into the end of a plastic object about the size of a book with a number of different holes lined up on it, each with what looked like a sheet of paper at its base.

"It's all pretty clever stuff," Sean said as he pulled a handful of syringes from his case. "But in simple terms, I'm going to inject you with a number of different substances, and after each I'm going to take your blood to see how you react. Okay?"

I nodded.

It wasn't a very pleasant experience, but compared with the broken fingers of yesterday there wasn't much to complain about. Sean was gentle as he injected each syringe into my arm, but his eyes rested on mine just a little longer than was comfortable, his fingers lingering on my skin for more time than was necessary for the task he was performing. A few minutes after each injection, he inserted another syringe to take a small sample of blood that he then expelled into a hole in the book-sized device.

By the time he was done, which felt like hours later, I looked and felt like a human pin cushion.

"That's it?" I asked as he packed away his things.

"Yes," he said, "but I'll be back tomorrow for the third test."

He shut his case and stood at the table, ready to go, but he hesitated as he turned towards the door. His expression was frustrated for a moment then thoughtful, and finally determined as though he had resolved upon something.

"We need to get back to the city," Drew said abruptly as he got up from his seat, cutting Sean off just as he opened his mouth to speak. "Come on."

"Goodbye, Em," Sean said quickly as Drew rushed him out of the door.

"Goodbye."

And then they were gone, until tomorrow at least.

CHAPTER XVI

Ollie was lying full-length on the bed when I got back into the cell.

"Well," he said, "that was awkward."

"Yeah, well you didn't exactly help, so thanks for that."

"I'm sorry," he said as he sat up and put his feet on the ground. "I got carried away. And my pride was a tiny bit hurt. I mean, I am so much better looking than that guy."

I shook my head, feeling exasperated by the entire episode, and dug around in one of the paper bags for a bar of chocolate. I felt like I'd earned it with the amount of blood I'd just lost, not to mention the emotional trauma of the morning. When I'd crammed in some calories, I joined Ollie on the bed and told him what had just happened in the second test. Well, most of it anyway. I didn't mention Sean's declaration of love because it really wasn't something I wanted to get into.

It couldn't have been more unwelcome.

I'd always wondered how it felt to be the most popular person at the party, and now that I was suddenly in high demand I had a lot of sympathy for the pretty girls of my adolescence. I was so sick of the drama and I couldn't fathom the horrible confluence of circumstances that had brought the few men from my life together in this forsaken place at this desperate time. Sean was so out of context here that it jarred, two separate parts of my life running together in a way that felt uncomfortable and wrong.

I told Ollie how we'd met and fallen in love, how we'd moved in together, how we'd talked about getting married and having children. I'd seen a whole future stretching out ahead of me in a straight line, a narrowing of possibilities as we directed our lives towards a mutual goal, but I had been focussed on it as my happily ever after and I knew with all my heart that it was what I wanted. That dream had shattered when things had slowly but surely disintegrated as his anxiety spiralled out of control.

When I had finally moved on after he'd disappeared, finally saw a future without him in it, the line of my life seemed to expand sideways ahead of me, widening into a buffet of opportunities. I could be anyone, do anything, and go anywhere I wanted. I could remake myself. It had made me feel younger, freer and lighter without the ties that pinned me down into the conventional life I had planned.

But that version of normal didn't exist now, and Sean had known that even back then. His erratic behaviour made sense in retrospect, but I still couldn't understand why he hadn't shared any of it with me. He'd obviously been going through hell as he tried to make sense of the things he was learning, but why didn't he tell me? He couldn't have put me in any more danger by telling me about his work than he had by keeping me out of the loop.

And what a cruel irony it was that, after all of his attempts to keep me out of the world of the Silver, I had ended up embroiled in it as deeply as it was possible for me to be. We'd all had to wake up to it after the Revelation, but the bond and the brand with Drew, and the... whatever it was with Sol, those were all added extras just for me.

I wondered whether Sean knew about Sol. But then, he'd said that he hadn't even known that I was alive until I popped up in the system after my blood was taken. Maybe he hadn't seen the broadcast about the banishment of the rebels. Maybe he hadn't known that I had been one of Sol's chained, or that we had a history.

Either way, I wasn't sure that it mattered. What we'd had before all of this started was too far gone now to be salvaged. We'd moved on, orbiting away from each other, and I'd been too wounded and embittered by the experience to even consider going back.

But I was glad he was okay, nonetheless.

Ollie and I lay comfortably side by side on the bed as we talked, segueing from my history with Sean into discussion of old lovers in general, his and mine. I had only had a couple of boyfriends before Sean, neither of them particularly serious, but Ollie, perhaps unsurprisingly, had been a little more promiscuous in his affections.

We saw love very differently. He thought it was about all pleasure, a thing to be enjoyed for as long as it lasted without trying to catch or keep it, whereas I thought it should burn through the centre of your being as though it was a part of you, a thing to be cherished and nurtured.

I wondered what he would be like if we were outside of this place. I'd seen him with the rest of the rebels back in the city, cocky and concerned about his status in the group, playing up for the lads. When he was here with just me there was no one to impress, so he could do what felt right without fear of judgement. But under the gaze of his peers, he seemed like a man who would do the wrong thing to avoid censure. I wondered whether I would have been good enough for him out in the real world or if being with me would have made him an object of ridicule.

Suddenly, I didn't feel so bad about crossing over the line with Ollie. To him, what we did didn't really matter either way because it was transient, and because of that he could throw it away easily if it didn't suit it. He wasn't invested in it. But I needed something more durable than that, something that made me into more with it than I was without it. It had to be something that was necessary. Love should be hard and demanding, scouring your soul with its force, but at the same time it should satisfy every need you had, whether you were conscious of those needs or not, and whether you wanted to admit to them or not.

"Who do you think about," he asked, "when you talk that way?"

"What do you mean?"

"You're talking about love, but you're not just imagining how you think it should be. You're describing something you've actually felt. So who is it?

I'd been talking in the abstract, trying to express feelings without context, but if I was honest with myself I knew that there was someone at the root of it. There was only one person who had ever made me feel that fire, a flame that shone into the dark places of my heart and revealed everything, leaving me weak and vulnerable.

"No," I said, "it's something I started to feel, but not the whole of it."

"So you've never been in love?"

"Oh, I've been in love. Just not like that. Have you?"

He laughed.

"Not like that," he said, "no."

We lay quietly for a moment.

"So, who was it?" he asked again.

I didn't reply.

"Was it the Primus?" he asked.

"What?" I said, kicking myself for even having entertained this line of conversation. "Why do you say that?"

"You never talk about him. You talk about the others, about Drew and the bond, the brand, but you don't talk about him."

"No," I said. "I guess I don't."

"Sorry, it's just that I'm curious. I mean, he's the Primus. He seems so... different."

"He is. They all are."

But it wasn't what he had meant. I knew what he was getting at, but I was protective of those memories and unwilling to acknowledge the pointless feelings Sol provoked in me.

"Him more than the others. Is he as cold as he looks?"

"Yes," I said.

Not then, I thought, but now: yes. Now that he was dancing to the beat of Laila's drum there was no telling what he would do. No wonder he had looked so defeated the last time I had seen him at the club. He was powerless against that bond.

"I'm sorry," he said. "I don't want to dig up bad memories."

"You're not. It's just… he's changed."

"You seem to have that effect on men."

"Yes," I sighed, "apparently I do. Maybe I'm just delusional. Maybe he was always this way."

He sat up on the bed and leaned back against the wall with his legs stretched out in front of him, pulling my feet into his lap.

"What was he like then?" he insisted. "Before he changed, I mean. How did you meet?"

I resigned myself to telling him the story. After all, maybe it would do me good to talk about it.

"You remember I told you I wasn't in the safe house," I said, "because I was back at the club?"

"Yes. Where Benedict…"

"Yes," I interrupted, not wanting to talk about the deaths of my friends again. "Well, after that I set off on my own, but Drew tracked me down and brought me into the Palace. There was this conference room or something on the first floor."

"I know it," Ollie said before quickly correcting himself. "Knew it, I mean. Wood floors, up the stairs, on the right hand side as you walked into the foyer?"

"That's the one," I said. "He wanted to speak to Drew and Tommy, but they wouldn't leave me, so they brought me up there with them. I just sat there while they talked about how they were going to sort out security for the safe zone."

"Sounds like he wanted an audience to me."

"I don't know. Maybe. But I think he was more interested in Drew and Tommy than in me. It was like he wanted to put the three of us in a room together and watch them interact so he could try and work out what was going on. He didn't understand why they were behaving so oddly, which was because of the bond of course, so he wanted to put them under the microscope and study them."

"Yeah," Ollie said scathingly, "that's not cold at all."

"It actually wasn't," I said. "The point was that he was interested. And when he spoke to me it was different. When Tommy and Drew spoke to me they talked like I was a child they had to control, like I was a burden. I guess I was, really, what with the bond. I was something they needed to protect, but for Drew's sake, not mine. Sol just talked to me in the same way he talked to them. To him, I was just another person to be unravelled and deciphered."

"You liked him?"

"Not immediately. He was very… other."

It was difficult to remember how I had felt about him at that first meeting without layering the experience with the impressions of everything that had gone after it. I thought that I had been a little intimidated, but intrigued by him. But then I had been so beaten and exhausted that night, still burning with the anguish of what had happened and the frustration of my failed escape, that he hadn't been the centre of my focus. I had been too busy hating Drew.

"It seemed like he cared," I continued. "He explained the Silver bargain to me as if it mattered to him that I understood the logic behind what he was doing. I suppose he made me relate to him so I could see where he was coming from, despite our differences. It wasn't that he hadn't thought about the price of what he was imposing on us, but he made it sound like the least awful alternative."

"He sounds like a true Vulcan," Ollie said.

I raised my eyebrow at him, surprised that he was a Star Trek fan. I wondered whether it was another of the programmes his dad had enjoyed, but I didn't want to ask and risk upsetting him.

"Not at all," I said. "Yes, I think he's generally logical, but I think he manages that because he accepts his emotions, and he reads other people's as well as his own. They're like a part of his logic."

"You respect that?" he asked.

"I don't know. I suppose so, yes."

"So how did you go from that to him drinking your blood?"

How could I explain that, I wondered, when I didn't even know how it had happened myself? There had been the kiss at my admission and the mark that it had left, but that couldn't explain why I had gone back to him when the mark had faded. Then Sol had saved me from Ben's attack on the terrace of the club, but I knew that was an excuse rather than a reason. If it had just been that and nothing else, I would have been able to walk away from it. I wouldn't have been pulled back to him time and again, drawn towards him inexorably until I found myself in his arms again, his lips on my skin, his teeth in my flesh.

"There was just something there," I said hopelessly.

"So it wasn't just the chained thing?" he asked.

"No," I said quietly. "For a very short time, it was more than that. He's had a lot of chained girls, but I think what we had was different. He told me it was."

"You believed him?"

"I did," I said. Eventually, anyway. "I believe the other people who've told me the same thing. I'm not completely naïve, you know. But look, it's irrelevant now. It happened, but it's done and gone and I'm not going to waste my time agonising over it."

Not out loud at least, I thought.

"Do you think it has something to do with why you're here?" he asked.

I thought about the council that had judged us, Drew and Laila at Sol's shoulders as he decided our fate, and I wondered how much influence they each had. Laila would have known about my bond with Drew, but she also would have known about my history with Sol. After all, Ben had seen us together, and he would doubtless have passed that nugget of information on. I wouldn't be surprised if she wanted me out of the way on principle. I was probably more surprised that she or Ben hadn't just gone ahead and killed me, despite the absence of the bond.

"Maybe," I said. "Who knows? But, yeah, it's hard not to feel a bit betrayed by it. Like I said, he's changed."

"Maybe you just didn't know him," Ollie suggested.

I said nothing.

I didn't want him to be right. I couldn't face the thought that those feelings had been elicited by the remote, untouchable person that he was now. I'd seen vulnerability in him. It had been there in glimpses, the honesty that rears its head when you're labouring under the compulsion of your emotions. But now that he was apparently in love, just when he should be most exposed, it wasn't there anymore. It was gone and he had shut down, a calculating mask falling over his face and twisting his actions as though Laila's own duplicity had infected him.

It seemed that his logic was failing him too, forgetting the balance that had tempered the bargain, and I worried that he would turn us into the captive race Ben dreamed to make us. With the Weepers pressing in at our boundaries and threatening to overrun us, it felt as though the fragile sanctuary Sol had constructed so carefully here was about to break, the banks bursting to let in the flood and drown us all in its polluted waves.

"How long do you think he'll keep us here?" he asked.

"I don't know," I said. "It feels like it might be a moot point soon."

"Emmy, you're going to get through the Casting."

"Even if I do, how long will it be before the Weepers get to us in here? Do you really think the Silver are going to come running to our rescue? Because after the Casting, I'm not sure they'll care."

I was probably doing Tommy and Cam a disservice, but I just couldn't imagine that they'd keep looking out for me forever. I'd known them for just two weeks, and yes, they'd protected me, but that had been because of Drew's bond. It was gone now, he was safe, and I was out here away from the city.

Out of sight, out of mind.

They were going to forget me, and I couldn't blame them. Even if Sol was losing control, would they cross him just to save a human? I was nothing here, we were nothing, and the Silver had to worry about each other more than they had to worry about any of us.

After all, they could always breed more humans.

"One way or another," I said, "I just can't see a way out of this for us."

"So you're giving up?"

"What else is there to do? We may as well just accept that we're doomed."

"Well," he said brightly, "while you do that, shall I get some food for us?"

He scooted out from under my feet and off the bed, grabbing the paper bag with our remaining provisions in it and bringing it back to where I lay.

"Come on, Emmy," he said encouragingly, trying to cheer me up. "You can even have chocolate for dinner if you like."

I sighed and sat up so there was space for him next to me, appreciating his efforts but not sure that there was anything to be cheerful about. But, then again, it wasn't as though moping around was going to help us either.

"Fine," I said as he sat down, "but it's your own fault for making me talk about it."

"Fine. Now eat your bread and cheese like a good prisoner."

CHAPTER XVII

Tuesday

The first thing I thought when I returned to consciousness was: one day left.

The Casting was tomorrow, and then I'd know one way or another. Maybe that would be easier to bear, the certain knowledge, whatever the result was.

Ollie was still asleep with one arm flung across my stomach, his breathing soft and even against my cheek as I lay on my back. It was raining heavily outside for the first time since the day we'd arrived here. The drops were rapping hard against the windows and thudding onto the roof, then running off and slapping onto the ground as though the downpour were raising waves above us. I opened my eyes and saw that the morning light was dim, the sky outside a dark grey smudge behind the deluge of water cascading down past the window.

There was a dripping coming from somewhere in the observation room. We'd sprung a leak and, judging from the tendrils of water snaking across the floor, it had been going for some time.

"Shit," I whispered.

The air was chilled and the sound of the water all around us wasn't helping me to feel any warmer, but I was still wearing my scrubs so at least I had some protection from the cold. I slid out from under Ollie's arm and swung my legs off the bed, wondering if there was anything I could use to catch the water. In the end I picked up one of our water bottles and, taking off the cap, positioned it carefully under the drip coming from the ceiling in the furthest corner of the observation room. I couldn't see any cracks, but thought there must be one on the outside through which the water was percolating.

"What's up?" Ollie said sleepily from the bed.

"There's a leak in here," I said. "There's water all over the floor."

By the time I moved back into the cell he was sitting up in the bed rubbing his face.

"Is anything wet?" he asked.

Thankfully the corner where we had been keeping most of our belongings seemed to have escaped the flooding, but the blankets had been in the corner nearest the door, and they were absolutely sodden.

"Just these, I think," I said, holding them up. "May as well wring them out and use them to mop up the rest of the water."

So that's how we spent the first twenty minutes of our day. By the time we were done the blankets were filthy, so we washed them with soap and rinsed them as clean as we could in the shower before wringing them out for the last time and hanging them over the bathroom door and the connecting door to dry. I was freezing cold after being in contact with the water for so long, and the chill had set into my bones so deeply that it felt as though I was never going to warm up.

"The first day we need a blanket," I said irritably, "and look what happens."

I put on the only jumper I had and huddled back under the sheet, wishing for a cup of tea and desperately praying for sunshine. No one was listening.

Neither of us was feeling particularly chatty this morning,

the weather dampening our moods as well as the floor. We ate breakfast quietly, finishing the rest of the cereal bars and fruit before going back to bed to hope that when we woke again the day would be a better one.

It wasn't.

Tessa turned up a little while after we woke for the second time. She was on her own, driving the truck through the gates rather than parking outside the enclosure and walking in. I wondered whether she was trying to keep out of the rain, but when she walked into the observation room it became apparent that her motivation was a little different. She had reversed up to the door so that she could easily access the back of the truck, which was standing open to reveal four large cardboard boxes.

"One each," she said. "I'll take two."

Ollie and I lugged one of the boxes in together, unable to carry them alone because of our various injuries. When Tessa saw how much we were struggling, she grabbed the last of the boxes herself, together with two ring binders and a paper bag that had been hidden behind it. We set everything down on the table, conscious that the floor was still damp from this morning.

"No Mark today?" Ollie asked.

Tessa rolled her eyes in an uncharacteristically candid gesture.

"The Primus is here again," she said.

Ollie's eyes cut to mine. I tried to appear nonchalant, wishing that I hadn't told him as much about Sol last night, but it was difficult to remain cool.

"So," she continued, "no more patrolling."

"Is everything okay?" I asked, worried about what had happened yesterday, but she clearly wasn't prepared to talk about it.

"Everything is fine," she said in a tone of voice that closed the subject. "Sit."

We did as commanded, both taking the side of the table that was opposite the door leading outside.

"These boxes," she continued as she removed the lid of one, "contain letters from people in the city and here at the Farm asking whether their friends and family members are still alive. Your job is to read through them all, check the names they ask for against the list," she indicated the ring binders, "and write a response to each."

She pulled the lids off the other boxes and, finding the one she was looking for on the second try, lifted out a large bundle of envelopes, two thick notepads and a pack of pens. She set them all out on the desk in front of us.

"We'll collect the responses tomorrow, and every day after that. And here's some more food for you," she added, pointing to the bag. "See you tomorrow."

"Er," Ollie said to her as she made to leave, "we've got a bit of a leak in here. Any chance of some help with that?"

She followed his finger to the corner of the room, then looked down at the bottle and back up to Ollie. She shrugged dismissively and walked back outside, closing and locking the door behind her.

"I guess that's a 'no' then," he said to me as we listened to her driving away.

"Well," I said, "you were right about the patrols, so that's something."

"Yeah, not really sure it's a happy thing, though."

"No," I agreed. If we weren't patrolling any more then it just confirmed our suspicions about the encroachment of the Weepers during the daytime. That was truly not a happy thing.

I reached over to the nearest box and pulled out a letter.

Dear Silver, it read, Please, please check your records for my husband Dr Alexander Robert Carving, born on 4th August 1965. He was travelling in the Durham area at the time of the Revelation. I know this is my fifth time of writing, but I am begging you, even if you disregard all the other names in my previous letters, if you would please just tell me whether or not Alex is alive I should be so very grateful. Yours faithfully, Mrs Maria Sarah Carving, Farm block G8.

"Dear god," I said, showing it to Ollie. "What have they

been doing with these letters? Have they just been sitting in a corner somewhere, waiting for someone to look at them? This is this woman's fifth letter, and it's dated the beginning of last week. Who knows how many more she's written now?"

"Yeah," Ollie said as he picked out a letter himself, "most people wrote at least one."

"They did? I didn't even know that we could."

"Well, it's not like it was advertised, but we all know they have the list. Someone had the idea and got a response, and then the word got around and everyone was doing it. If every surviving human did that, just think how many letters that is for them to wade through. I suppose they're pretty busy."

"Not too busy to come and drink at the club and the Palace," I said acerbically.

He laughed.

"None of us were too busy for that."

I pulled out a handful of letters then grabbed one of the pads.

"Oh well," I said, "at least this way we can be useful. More useful than we were on patrol duty anyway."

I went to pick up a pen with my splinted fingers and realised somewhat belatedly that there was a flaw in this brilliant plan.

"Shit," I said.

"Right-handed?" Ollie asked.

"Yup."

"Well, no writing for you then. I'll tell you what: we can do it together, one letter at a time. It'll go faster with two of us looking up the names anyway."

I pulled one of the ring binders towards me. They were both the same, each containing a depressingly small number of loose-leaf pages with names printed alphabetically by surname next to their dates of birth.

"So this is it," I said. "This is all that's left of us here."

"I guess so," he replied.

I leafed my way through the pages. Carder, Cargill, Carver,

Carving…

"There's only one Carving listed," I said quietly, "and that's Maria."

Ollie sighed.

"I have a feeling this is going to be a real downer of a day. So, what do we say? 'Sorry, Maria, your hubby's dead'? I mean, how do we phrase that?"

I thought for a moment then dictated to him, gesturing that he should write as I spoke.

"Dear Mrs Carving, Please accept our apologies for the delay in responding to your letters. We have received a great number and are working through them as quickly as possible."

"Really?" he asked.

"Yes, really. We will."

"Okay…"

"Carry on," I said before picking up where I had left off. "We have in front of us your letter dated… and then put the date in. Was it the fifth?"

"Yep," he said.

"We regret to inform you that Dr Alexander Robert Carving's name does not appear on the list of survivors. We send you our heartfelt condolences for your loss…"

I paused to think, trying to come up with something meaningful without sounding trite.

"Er, how about: which although so common in these difficult days is felt no less keenly by each of us for the ones we love. Our sympathies are with you."

He nodded, writing quietly as I spoke.

"Yours sincerely…," I continued. "What do you think? Should we say from us?"

He shrugged.

"Yours sincerely, Oliver Faulkner and Emilia Nelson, then in brackets put: prisoners at the Farm. How's that?"

"It's a good place to start," he said.

We read letter after letter, some of them asking for just one name to be checked and some of them asking for tens of them. It was slow work, and by the time we'd been through about twenty letters we'd only managed to find one of the hundreds of names we'd looked for on the list. Ollie had been right when he'd said that today was going to be depressing.

We were just finishing a letter to a man in his nineties, whom we had to tell that none of his friends, children or grandchildren were on the list, when another car pulled up at the gates. I was glad of the distraction because I was just about ready to die with grief. All of these people had to have known that they had lost everyone they loved, but their letters were still so full of hope. I couldn't work out whether crushing that hope would break them or allow them to move on with their lives. Maybe it would depend on the individuals, but I wondered how much good we were actually doing here.

"Do you think it's your exes again?" Ollie asked as I walked over to the window. The rain was still coming down heavily, and it was so dark that even though it could only have been early afternoon we'd had to light the candles on the table to help us see the lists.

"It looks like it," I said as I recognised the model of the car.

"Well, help me get these boxes through next door so you've got some space. I'll try to make some sense of them while you have your test."

They would take up most of the space, but at least it was dry in the cell so they wouldn't get damp from being on the floor. I was guessing we'd need the table for the tests.

We had only managed to get two of the boxes repacked and moved by the time Drew and Sean came into the room, but, to my surprise, Drew stacked the remaining two on top of each other and carried them through for us.

"Thanks," Ollie said to him, his expression a picture of confusion. "So, er... I guess I'll leave you to it, then."

"There'll be some noise," Sean said, "but it's just the test."

Ollie looked at me with concern.

"I'll say 'Peanuts' if you need to come rushing in to save me, okay?"

He smiled at me and closed the connecting door behind

him quietly.

So here we were again: me, Drew and Sean, just like yesterday.

"Hi, Em," Sean said as he put his case on the table once more and pulled out his laptop.

Drew didn't say anything as we sat down in the same chairs as yesterday, but his eyes met mine briefly. He wasn't angry today. Instead, he was... I couldn't work out what he was feeling. There was a look in his eye, something inscrutable, but whatever it was, I couldn't fathom it.

"You know this is where we test your mental strength?" Sean said.

"Yes," I replied, my eyes lingering a moment longer on Drew's face before I turned to him. "So what happens?"

He pulled a load of electrodes out of his case and held them up for me to see.

"I attach these to your head and various pulse points and we test your reactions to stimuli."

"What kind of stimuli?"

"A whole range," he said. His eyes were moving over my face as he spoke, jumping from my lips to my cheeks to my hairline to my chin, but never quite coming to rest on my eyes. It was unsettling, as though he wanted to look at me but wasn't quite able to make out where I was.

I wondered whether he was feeling self conscious about the things he'd said yesterday.

"Also," he continued, "we have to do it in the dark, so I'm going to cover up the windows and blow out the candles. Okay?"

Not okay. Really, really not okay.

"In the dark?" I asked.

"Yes."

"Can Ollie be here?"

I didn't want to be in this place in the dark without Ollie beside me, especially not when Drew was here, and especially not when the horrors of the past couple of days were already piling up in my imagination. Whatever had happened with us,

Ollie was still my comfort in this place, and if the lights were going out I wanted him between me and Drew.

Sean looked at Drew, but he shook his head.

"Sorry," Sean said quietly as he came round the table to attach the electrodes to me.

He stuck them to my wrists, my head, the back of my ears and my chest. He had to reach down the front of my scrubs top to get the last ones in place, and an awkward silence fell over the room while he did so. His palpable embarrassment was excruciating, his movements fumbling and inelegant while his hands shook slightly as they stuck the pads on my skin. I felt relieved for a moment when he stepped away, but then I remembered that he was about to blow the candles out and anxiety surged through me again.

The wires leading from the electrodes all combined into a single cable that Sean plugged into his computer, which he repositioned in the same way as he had yesterday. I gathered that I was going to be recorded again.

Everything seemed to be moving very quickly as we inexorably approached the moment at which the room would go black. Sean was at the windows sticking what looked like sheets of dark card across them, one by one, and then he was back at the table, leaning over the candles.

"Ready?" he asked.

"Not really, no," I said with complete honesty, but he just laughed nervously and blew out the flames.

I blinked a few times as my eyes adjusted, and saw that the room wasn't completely dark after all. There was still a gentle light emanating from the screen of Sean's laptop, and it illuminated him eerily, the only thing in the room that was visible. He turned the screen around to face me and I saw a series of images appear, some too quick for me to register and others held on the screen for longer. At first they seemed to be showing entirely random objects and buildings. Next they were faces: children, women, men, Silver and Weepers in every combination of characteristics that you could imagine. Finally, they were scenes of violence and of love, and sometimes a little of the two.

And then the light was gone, replaced by utter darkness as the residual imprint of the screen's light pulsed in front of my unseeing eyes.

There were noises. It took me a few seconds to work out that they were coming from the laptop, played out by the speakers.

It sounded like the background noise from a café. I could hear the clinking of spoons on glasses and tables, the gentle chatter and faraway laughter of people relaxing. I strained to hear what was being said, but it was just a fraction too quiet, the bustling sounds of movement overwhelming it. There was the sound of traffic far beneath the voices, a noise I had been so used to hearing that I hadn't realised until I heard it now that it had been missing since the Revelation.

After a few minutes it faded away, replaced by piano music that rolled and rose through the length of a piece in soft waves of crescendo until the point before its apex, but then it too drifted out of the reach of my hearing, chased away by the voices of children laughing. That new sound raised the hairs along my arms and the back of my neck, the noise incongruous and empty in this hollow room, bouncing off the walls in a way that leant it a macabre edge. And then it increased in volume, the hilarity in the voices becoming manic until it edged, finally, into horrific screaming that had me clenching my hands around the sides of my chair to remind myself that I was still here, and that the noise was coming from the laptop.

It wasn't real.

But it was harder still to convince myself of that fact when the Weeper's howl exploded through the room, making me gasp with shock and stifle a scream.

"Shit," I muttered, reminding myself again that it wasn't real.

Finally, when the echoes died away, there was just a voice. It was clear and melodic, the notes crisp and almost musical. It was the most beautiful voice I had ever heard.

It was a voice I knew.

"Let him kiss me with the kisses of his mouth," it said, "for your love is better than wine, your anointing oils are fragrant, your name is perfume poured out, and so the maidens love you."

As it spoke, a scent filled the air: the smell of warm spice and cool water that was so painfully familiar. I'd yearned to have it surround me again, the intoxicating mixture igniting my senses and tingling along my skin.

"Draw me after you and let us hasten our steps," his voice enticed me. "The king has brought me into his chambers."

The words set off explosions of light in the darkness, starbursts flashing in front of my eyes.

I had to be hallucinating, I thought.

But then there was a touch at my wrist, fingertips tracing the lines of the mark of his house on my skin. I inhaled sharply, the sensation radiating through me and waking me up. It was as though every fibre of my being was suddenly alert and conscious for the first time, all directed towards that one touch, towards the sound of his voice, towards his scent.

"Set me as a seal upon your heart, as a seal upon your arm," he whispered, his words at once a seduction and a prayer, "for love is as strong as death, passion as fierce as the grave. Its flashes are flashes of fire: a raging flame."

His voice was so close that I could feel his breath on my skin. He ran his thumb across my lips in a way that made me feel dizzy, following their contours before his hand came to rest on my cheek.

"Many waters cannot quench love, neither can floods drown it. If one offered for love all the wealth of his house, it would be utterly scorned."

Then he put his lips to my own, his scent sweeping through me and knocking down all reason that stood in its way, and I was lost.

CHAPTER XVIII

My soul failed me when he spoke.
I sought him, but did not find him;
I called him, but he gave no answer.

- The Song of Solomon

I woke to find myself alone in the bed, the sheet pulled up over my shoulders. It was still light outside, but the pouring rain made it difficult at first to discern that fact.

What the hell had just happened?

Sol had been here, I thought. He'd been here, and he had kissed me, his scent wrapping around me…

For just a moment, it all seemed real. My soul soared, my heart racing with the anticipation of seeing him again, every atom of me reaching out for him.

But it hadn't been real.

Grief rolled through me. He hadn't been here. He wasn't mine. He was in love with that evil bitch Laila. I had been undergoing the third test, the test of my mental resilience.

Apparently I had none.

I thought that I must have been given some kind of hallucinogen, and after it had done its job then it, or something else, had knocked me out. On the plus side, given my reaction I imagined that I had probably failed the test. On the minus side, that reaction had been a bit embarrassing. With me hooked up to all of those electrodes, I wasn't sure exactly what Sean would have recorded, but I didn't doubt that my state would have been fairly evident. Would they know what I had been feeling or what I had been hearing? And how much of what I had heard and felt had been real anyway?

I was pretty sure I had moaned. At least once.

How mortifying.

I sat up, rubbing my face groggily, and looked around. I was the only person in this part of the building, but the connecting door was shut so I guessed that Ollie must be through in the observation room. The boxes of letters were still in here, so he hadn't taken them through with him, but it looked like he had done some good work neatening them up.

I stood up and opened the door, peering cautiously around the jamb.

"You're awake."

He was sitting at the table with the candles lit, shuffling a pack of cards. As I swung the door wider I was surprised to see that he wasn't alone: Drew was across the table from him.

"Has Sean gone?" I asked as I walked hesitantly into the room.

"Yes," Drew said, his eyes never moving from Ollie's hands as they turned and interleafed the cards.

"Oh."

I stood awkwardly in the doorway, not sure whether to come in and join them or go back into the other room and hide. They seemed oddly at ease with each other, as though they had been sitting here for long enough to become restful together.

Ollie looked at Drew and then at me, apparently just registering the atmosphere in the room.

"Shall I leave you to it?" he asked.

I looked to Drew. I didn't know why he was still here, so I wasn't sure whether or not we needed to be alone.

"That would probably help," he said, but to Ollie, not to me.

Ollie nodded and got out of his chair, leaving the cards on the table. He slipped his hand around my waist as he passed, pulling me into a quick hug before he walked into the cell and closed the door behind him.

"He seems fond of you," Drew said, reaching across the table to pick up the deck. He spun it apart in his fingers then shuffled the halves together again, watching the cards turn and fan in his hands. "Does he know about Sol?"

Apparently I had been right: my reaction in the test had been perfectly evident, and Drew knew what had caused it. Or, rather, who.

I took the seat Ollie had just vacated and leaned back in it, feeling tired and headachy and completely exasperated by the line this conversation was threatening to take.

"Why are you still here?" I asked, ignoring his question. It wasn't as though it was any of his business anymore how I felt about Sol or anyone else.

For the first time since I had come into the room, he lifted his gaze and met my eyes. He looked at me steadily, the candlelight flickering gently off the deep emerald colouring of his irises. The soft light may have made the room seem warmer and more welcoming, but it didn't do much to mellow the hardness of his expression.

"Do you love him?" he asked.

I sighed, irritated with him despite his mood, and looked away before pulling myself together to respond.

"None of this matters any more," I said. "The Casting's tomorrow. If I'm through the tests, you'll turn me into a Weeper. If I'm not, then I'll come back here and spend the rest of my life in this building with Ollie, without seeing any of you ever again."

"So it's 'Ollie' now, is it?"

I'd never expected to be having one of these familiar fights with Drew again. As far as I was concerned, there was nothing for us even to be fighting about. If he was in any way jealous, and I seriously doubted that he really was, then it could be nothing more than a ghost of emotion. It was a knee-jerk reaction, as though he had got into the habit of it, and he was finding it hard to shake.

"Drew," I said helplessly, "what do you want from me? What do you want me to say? I don't understand why you even care about this. I'm sorry that you're upset about losing the bond, but we both know I don't mean anything to you now. So what's this really about?"

"I…" he said, trailing off into silence.

He fiddled with the cards, staring down at them, his fierce concentration like that of a small child as he tried to puzzle things out.

"Look," I said, "I don't know what happened in the test, but I don't love anyone, okay? Can we just leave things there?"

"Don't you want to know?" he asked.

I was dying to know. I couldn't understand how I could have imagined it so vividly, how I could have heard him and smelled him and felt him and tasted him without him being there. I'd dabbled in some hallucinogens in my time, but nothing that powerful, nothing that could recreate reality in such a shocking full-sensory experience.

Instead of admitting that, I shrugged.

"I guess you gave me some drugs."

"Something like that. And then there was some audio at the end that spun you out."

"It was Sol?" I asked, needing to know that I hadn't imagined it all.

"Yes. An old recording."

So that much had been real at least.

"Then," he said, "you started to have a bad reaction, and the geek had to rush in with his meds. You been taking anything else today?"

I laughed at him.

"Where do you think I'm going to get drugs in here?" Then I remembered. "Oh, wait, I've got some painkillers for the broken fingers," I said, holding them up in case he had missed the splints.

"That'd do it. Ada?"

"Yeah. She doesn't like me much."

"Not surprising in the circumstances."

He shuffled the cards together for the last time before tapping their end on the table to set them straight and feeding them into a box he pulled from his pocket.

"You said his name," he added quietly.

"Sol's?"

"Yes. The meds sent you down hard, and I was carrying you through to the other room to the bed."

"Oh," I said. Frankly, I was amazed that it was all I had done, thinking I should probably count myself lucky to have escaped the episode with only that minor embarrassment. I decided not to pull on that thread any further, just in case there was more that I really didn't want to know.

"Will I have to retake the test?" I asked instead.

"No, I think he got enough."

He sat looking into one of the candle flames while I watched his face, wondering what was going on behind his eyes. He was so erratic these days, changeable and sensitive in a way that I supposed was not unusual in a person rubbed raw by bereavement. The problem was that I wasn't dead, not yet at least. I was sitting here, still alive and well, and he had been mourning my imagined loss nonetheless. But I didn't get the impression that my actual death would cause him any more pain than he was in now.

Meanwhile, we had real dead people to grieve over, real people I had known and loved: Danny, Jeff, Sarah, Alice, Ella and Mary, not to mention all of those who had lost their lives in the Revelation. The letters Ollie and I had been trawling through today only served to emphasise how devastating the scale of those deaths had been for us all. But we were getting on with things, sucking up our despair and hopelessness because there was nothing else for us to do. If we stopped fighting against it then it would consume us, and although each of us could have a bleak moment every now and then, there was the business of living to be getting on with. We carried on because we had to.

In that context, his loss of the bond just didn't feel that significant. He was moping like a sullen teenager. I didn't have time for it, not against the background of my own pain and my own fear of what tomorrow would bring.

When I signed up for this ride I was expecting today to be so very different from this reality. We'd had the bond and the brand, and they were pulling us closer together every day. We were together at the flat next to the club, sleeping in the same bed, surrounded by luxury and privilege that I hadn't fully appreciated until I was taken away to this place. We knew I would turn Silver successfully, and there was a proper reason for going to the Casting: so that Drew and Alice and I would all be safe.

Without the bond, there was no reason behind anything any more.

If that last night in the city had never happened, if the explosions hadn't been set or I hadn't been there, then maybe we would have been happy this evening. With another week to manipulate my emotions, maybe that Silver magic would have crept into my heart and brought Drew in with it. We could have been in love, but either way we would at least have liked each other. I wasn't sure that we even had that anymore.

"I'm sorry, Emmy," he said.

"What?" I said in shock, barely able to believe that the words had come out of his mouth.

"I'm sorry that I got you into this. And I'm sorry that I've dealt badly with the bond breaking."

I didn't know what to say. I wanted to tell him that it wasn't enough, and that I could never forget the way that he had terrified me. But looking at him across the table, his eyes dull and empty, he just looked wrung out and broken. I wasn't scared of him now, I just felt sad for the way he had let this destroy him.

"Okay," I said.

"And I wanted to try to explain to you why it was so important to me, not just in terms of what I felt but because of what it represented for me."

"Okay," I repeated uncertainly, not sure where this was going.

"Tommy told you that I was born Silver, that my parents were both Silver?"

I wondered about his use of the past tense, but I didn't ask.

"Yes," I said.

Tommy had also told me that the Silver didn't often have children. Between that and the difficulty they had turning humans Silver, it was almost a miracle that there were as many of them as there were. But then, I supposed that they had been around for millennia trying to reproduce, and, when they did succeed, the resulting Silver were practically immortal. It was probably a good thing that they had as much trouble as they did, I thought, or we'd be overrun.

"My parents lived in a village far up in the north of what's now Russia," he said. "My father had been there for years. He was already Silver, but he'd been fitting into the community and working with them to make them safer, healthier, wealthier and happier. My mother was just passing through on her way south, not intending to stay more than a night, but her plans changed when she saw my father. She silvered for him the moment they met."

He paused and looked at me, asking me to make the connection without his having to say it out loud. He had silvered the first time he had seen me. I wondered whether it was a genetic trait, or perhaps more accurately a defect.

"So she stayed," he continued. "Waiting centuries for him to fall in love with her. They moved around as much as they had to, because of course they weren't getting older quickly enough, but every time he moved she followed him."

He looked into the candle flame again, which seemed

brighter now that the night was starting to fall outside. After a minute or so had passed, I wondered whether or not he was going to carry on.

"Eventually, he loved her back," he said, glossing over what I would have thought was the most interesting part of the story. But then, he probably hadn't wanted to hear about how his mother had romanced his father, so maybe it wasn't a tale he knew. "And then they had me."

He sat back in his chair, and after another silence it seemed that we had reached the end of his rather abbreviated story.

"So, what?" I asked. "It's all about the bond again?"

He nodded and looked into my eyes.

"It's always about the bond, Emmy, about love. Whether we want to bear Silver or make Silver, it's all about the bond and the seal."

"The seal?" I looked at him in confusion. It had been a disorientating day, and I was feeling so dazed that I found myself wondering what aquatic mammals had to do with it.

"When the bond is reciprocated," he said.

"Ah."

And it all came flooding back to me. Again, it had been Tommy who told me about it. The bond threaded the irises with silver, but when it was returned that threading turned gold. Apparently there was a song about it and everything.

It just hadn't been on the cards for me and Drew. I wondered how his mother had managed to hold on for so many years, putting all of her heart into loving a man who didn't love her back. It was what Drew had been prepared to do for me, and I realised that he had been taking his mother as the precedent for that. He had told me that he would wait, and that if I never loved him then the bond would fade over the centuries, but that hadn't been what he had been hoping for.

And with the brand as well as the bond, he probably would have got what he had wanted. It wasn't what I had wanted, but would I have cared as long as I was happy? Would it really have mattered that it was something induced by the magic of the Silver, rather than something that was real?

Yes, I thought. Yes, it mattered.

"It'll be any day now for the Primus," he said, snapping me out of my contemplations of futures lost.

"What?"

"The seal. Laila's got her hooks in him, sure, but she's falling for him too."

I struggled to keep the emotion from my face.

It wounded me more than it had any right to. I had accepted that he had bonded to her, despite her being a vicious cow, but I suppose I had never seen her as anything other than that. In my eyes she was manipulative and cruel, and incapable of ever truly experiencing an emotion like love without twisting it into something less meaningful. I had imagined Sol eventually seeing the error of his ways and throwing her over for someone more suited for him.

Yes, someone like me, but I knew that had been a ridiculous fantasy.

But if she silvered for him too, then it was all over. They'd be tied together forever, their love sealed shut.

"Really?" I said nonchalantly, trying and failing to act as though I was unconcerned by this news.

He looked at me with a pained expression and shook his head minutely.

"What?" I asked.

"It just hurts that you still think of him that way," he said.

I closed my eyes and tried to compose myself. I was so tired of having to deal with this adolescent bullshit from him. It was love, not life, and he was too old and powerful to be this puerile.

"Drew," I said calmly, trying to contain my irritation so there was no risk that I would provoke him again. "I know you don't want me anymore. I'm stuck out here in a cage, and tomorrow I may well be a Weeper. You're still worrying about last week's problems. It's time to put them away and move on. Sol has silvered for Laila."

I really needed to take my own advice. It had just been a

shock, I told myself. It was a new piece of information that I needed to process, which I had done, and then file away. And then everything would be manageable. I hoped.

"She's been talking to Alyssa," Drew said.

"Oh?"

I wasn't surprised that Laila had been trying to interfere in the Casting, but I was perhaps a little surprised that she had been indiscreet enough to let Drew find out about it.

"How do you know that?" I asked.

"I'm the leader of the Solis Invicti, Emmy," he said in an offended tone.

I didn't think I was entirely to blame for the apparent insult. With the way he behaved he made it easy to forget that he was a man of such influence.

"So?" I asked. "What's she up to?"

"Apparently she's told the Administrator that you've been holding back from the tests because you think I regret agreeing to sponsor you. And I've been doing everything I can to give her exactly that impression, because I'd hoped that if she thought we weren't close she wouldn't let you past the selection process. You know, good relationship between sponsor and candidate being a pre-requisite."

That would explain why he had so blatantly ignored me the day Alyssa was here. Well, it might partially explain it at least.

"How did she even know I was up for the Casting?" I asked. "Isn't that supposed to be super top secret?"

"Yes. Yes it is, and I don't know. But somehow Laila's found out, and she's told Alyssa that I do have feelings for you, and that we'll have our happily ever after if she puts you through."

As he spoke his face twisted in a sort of reluctant embarrassment. It was a feeling I shared. Of course we regretted this now, but there was nothing to be done about it.

"Surely Alyssa won't listen to Laila? I got the feeling that she wasn't very happy about how Sol's changed since she's been on the scene."

He shook his head ruefully.

"I think she'll listen to her for exactly that reason. I think she misses him, and being on Laila's good side would probably help smooth things over between them."

It took a moment for the implications of his words to sink in. When they did, I felt like the floor had fallen out from under me. I'd been carrying on, just trying to focus on getting through one day at a time, and it had been easy to concentrate on the present because the week had been a real shit show. I suppose that the reality had never really settled in. I'd known there was a risk that I'd become a Weeper, and I'd kept telling myself that it might happen, but the sudden immediacy of the prospect staggered me when I realised that it was probable rather than possible.

"So, what?" I said. "You're telling me I'm screwed? You're telling me she's going to put me through at the Casting whatever the results of the tests are, just to keep Laila happy?"

"I think she might," he said quietly.

"Jesus."

I stood from my chair and started to pace around the room, the nervous energy boiling up in my agitation.

"Well," I said hopelessly, "can't you do something?"

I couldn't understand why he was just sitting there, letting this happen. Why wasn't he doing something? He might not care about me anymore, but nonetheless surely he should do something, anything?

"We're not allowed to speak to her now," he said. "She'll be in seclusion for the rest of tonight and most of tomorrow, and she won't come out until tomorrow night for the ceremony."

"Well, what about then?" I said desperately, panic raising the pitch of my voice.

He shook his head again.

"Will you stop that?" I asked as the irritation and anxiety overflowed. "Will you stop sitting there, talking and shaking your head as if you're resigned to this and go out there and do something useful? You got me into this, Drew, now get me the fuck out of it!"

"Emmy…"

"No, don't 'Emmy' me. Do you actually want this to happen? Because I've got to say it's what I've been thinking. Do you want to drain me dry and watch me turn into… into one of those… shadows?" I said, my voice quavering as I pointed out towards the perimeter fence and the Weepers beyond it. "Those terrible ghosts? Are you so unable to cope with seeing me without the bond that you want to make me into such a twisted thing?"

"No, Emmy…"

"Then fucking prove it!" I yelled.

Ollie came barrelling in from the next room, ready to go to bat for me, but when he found me standing over Drew and shouting at him as he sat placidly in his chair, he looked at a loss as to what he should do next.

They exchanged a glance.

I pushed the hair away from my face with both hands and walked back over to my side of the table, looking out of the window to watch the heavy raindrops catching the faint glow of the candles. They reflected the light briefly on their inexorable journey downwards into the dirty ground.

"You know I can't change it," he said to me. "Your name's on the list. Both of our names are on the list."

I dropped down into my chair, the fight going out of me as suddenly as it had risen, and hung my head, my elbows on my knees.

"I'm going to fucking die," I whispered, unable to believe this was happening.

Over the past couple of weeks I'd faced death so many times, but in each case the threat had arrived unseen and immediate, snatching me away and incapacitating me before I recognised it. This was different. I knew what was coming and what would happen, but I couldn't escape it. Worse still, that death wasn't coming at the hands of someone I loathed or who loathed me. At least, I thought not. Drew and I had, albeit briefly, been together. He'd protected me, held me, kissed me and loved me for long enough that he'd got under my skin.

For some reason, there was something so much worse in this death, a death by consent at the hands of someone who was unwilling. It was senseless, required not because of the sharp, honed purpose of ambition but by the rigidity of traditions that I didn't understand.

But I'd known what the terms were when I agreed to this. I knew that if I tried to get out of it, I'd be found and dragged kicking and screaming to the Casting if necessary. Actually, I thought, that would offend the Silver's sensibilities. They'd probably drug me instead so I was well-behaved and quiet through the ceremony.

I felt like the proverbial princess being fed to a Silver dragon.

Ollie sat down next to me and took my uninjured hand in his, squeezing it tight. When I met his eyes his expression was serious and anguished. I gathered that he had overhead enough to know what was going on. I looked away, not wanting to dwell on it, and saw that Drew was staring at my hand held in Ollie's.

"Tell me what'll happen tomorrow," I said.

"The ceremony?" Drew asked, his eyes moving to my face. I nodded.

"It's in two parts. The first part finishes with the Casting itself, which is when the Administrator announces who has been selected. That's at midnight in the city."

Of course it was, I thought. The Silver certainly had a flair for the dramatic.

"The second part is where the successful candidates are turned Silver."

"Or Weeper," I interjected mildly.

"Yes," he said sadly, "or Weeper. That takes place at dawn, so there'll be a few hours in between. The custom is for the turning to be in a clearing in a forest, so it'll be outside the safe zone."

"Why dawn?" I asked.

"I think you can probably guess why."

I didn't have to think very hard.

"So when we turn Weeper we'll be in the daylight, and easier to manage," I guessed.

He nodded.

"The ritual of it is important," he said, "even in these circumstances, and particularly for the older Silver. Listen carefully."

So, as the night blackened around us and took my mood with it, the three of us sat together as he told me what he thought I'd have to do, what to wear and how to act. The words seemed to echo through my head and bounce off the insides of my skull, making no impact and finding no purchase. I felt numb, absent from my mind and body.

After all, what was the point in memorising the steps? If I got it wrong then what were they going to do, kill me?

By the end of tomorrow, I thought, it would all be over anyway.

CHAPTER XIX

Wednesday

And then, all too quickly, the day was here.

Ollie got out of the bed, climbing over me to get to the floor, but I wasn't ready to face the world yet. I rolled onto my back and looked up at the ceiling, the cement slightly cracked where the building had settled unevenly into the ground.

Today was the day it would happen. Or, perhaps more accurately, it would happen in the early hours of tomorrow morning. Either way, I'd had my last night's sleep. At the end of this long day, it would end.

"Breakfast?" Ollie asked.

I would end.

I shook my head.

"Not hungry."

Drew was going to send a car to pick me up in the evening. The Casting itself didn't happen until midnight, but the whole ceremony started a little earlier. Either way, we had the day to ourselves. I couldn't stop myself from wishing it away, wishing that this was all over and done with. I knew I should be cherishing these last hours, but how could I spend them meaningfully in this place? By helping Ollie to write letters telling people their loved ones were dead?

Everything just felt so pointless or mundane when I knew the grand finale to this day would be so very dramatic.

"Are you going to get out of bed?" he asked.

"Maybe."

"I sorted out these boxes yesterday."

"I saw."

"And I sealed up the letters we wrote, ready to be collected this morning."

I said nothing, shutting my eyes against the light. It was raining again today, the drops tapping softly against the windows. At least there wasn't any water on the floor yet, I thought.

"So, that's good," he added under his breath.

I heard his footsteps padding away into the bathroom then blankly listened to him moving around for the next five minutes or so as he brushed his teeth and showered. I felt as though I was already gone, my insides emptied out and hollow.

"That water doesn't get any warmer," he said as he walked back into the room.

I listened to the rain.

"Come on, Emmy," he said. "Let's look up some names."

"Why bother?" I asked. "These people know that the people they love are dead."

"It matters to them, and if nothing else, it gives us something to do. You can't stay in bed all day, just waiting for the Casting. This isn't you."

"I think I'm allowed a few minutes to sulk about the fact that I'm about to die."

"Well," he said, "time's up. We're going to make the most of today whether you want to or not, because I'm not just going to sit around and waste these hours."

I turned my head to the side and looked at him. He was looking back with a desperate pleading in his eyes, as though he were begging me to do as he was doing and pretend that everything was okay. This wasn't easy for him either, I thought. He'd be alone here after I was gone, here in this cell with no one to talk to except the guards and the occasional Weeper.

I hoped they wouldn't put me out in the enclosure after I turned. It was exactly the kind of sick joke that I was sure Mark would find hilarious.

"Okay," I said. Yes, I thought I was entitled to be selfish today of all days, but Ollie was right: wallowing in my misery just wasn't me.

Between the two of us, we carried the boxes back through into the observation room and put them on the table.

"So," he said as he took the lids off, "I've managed to fit all the letters we have left into three of the boxes, and I've put the ones we've already replied to in the fourth. Our replies are…"

He paused, pulling out the two ring binders, the pads and the pens from the emptiest box.

"Here," he finished, brandishing a small stack of envelopes from inside one of the binders.

"Is that all?" I asked as I peered into the box to see how many of the letters we had answered. It was a pitifully small pile.

"It's a long job, so we'd better get on with it. Here," he said, handing me a letter from one of the three full boxes, "you read, I'll write."

So for the morning we worked our way slowly through a handful of the letters. I was expecting that we'd get a visit from the guards early in the day to collect the replies we'd already written, as Tessa had promised, but they never came. We ate a little food and carried on after lunch, just trying to keep busy so we could forget about what was going to happen later. It was starting to work when I came across something I really didn't want to see.

"This is Alice's handwriting," I said, putting the letter down on the table in disbelief.

"You're sure?"

I nodded.

"I recognise it from her playing cards."

She'd made the paper pack herself when she'd been in the safe house, and we'd played a few times at the club.

"She hadn't been the best artist," I continued, "so instead of drawing the picture cards she'd scribbled odd little character descriptions on them. Things like: 'Roi Guillaume was once considered the most handsome man in France until he lost an eye, so to preserve his vanity he now only lets people paint him in profile' and 'Cecil is a mummy's boy who can't tie his shoelaces without an audience'."

I guess it had kept her entertained, and she was always adding new ones or changing the ones she'd already written. Some of my best memories of her revolved around those cards. Nix had chewed the edges of a couple, but that had only added to their charm. I wondered what had happened to them. They had probably burned up in the explosions.

I didn't want to read the letter. I didn't want to know who she'd been looking for.

I realised that I'd never really asked her about her life before the Revelation and instantly felt oppressively guilty for not taking more of an interest. The thing about Alice was that she had always been superficially cheerful and optimistic, so I'd never taken her seriously as a person, even after we'd become friends. We'd had a bit of a rough start and I'd soon decided that she was silly and immature, writing her off as someone who'd had an easy time of it during the Revelation and assuming that she couldn't possibly understand what the rest of us had been through. But I never stopped to think about what she might have been leaving behind from her old life.

Were there people she'd missed, or were there things she had been fleeing? I'd been selfish enough not to have asked, and now I'd never know who she'd really been. She'd had this fixation on the Silver, this desire to be noticed and approved of. And she'd wanted to join them. I think she'd felt out of place here. She'd wanted to be more powerful, not necessarily in strength but in confidence and influence. At the heart of it, she'd wanted to make herself into something better because she didn't like who she was.

There was something heartbreaking about that quality in her. It was a vulnerability that had showed, a need for validation that was so human that it pulled people in and made it hard not to sympathise with her. But I'd never know what was at the root of that, where it came from.

There were so many things I wished that I had asked. If I'd shown even the slightest bit of interest, instead of being stuck on my own problems all the time, then maybe she would have told me more about the person under the goth Barbie exterior.

"Are you not going to read it?" Ollie asked.

I still didn't want to, but I felt as though I owed it to her.

Dear Silver, it said, *I really need to know whether or not my dad is still alive. His name is David Clement, and his date of birth is the tenth of March 1966. Please, please let me know. My name is Alice Jemima Clement, and I live at the club. Thanks.*

I scrambled for one of the ring binders and flicked through it desperately, hoping that he would be listed, as if somehow I would be able to put the pieces of Alice back together if I could only find her father and talk to him, to find out what he meant to her that his was the only name in her letter, to find out what she meant to him, and why she had been the way she was.

"No," I said, slumping back in my chair in despair as I saw that Alice's name was the only Clement listed. Her own entry was crossed through, a neat line bisecting the letters of her name and scrubbing her from the list of the living.

So she'd always be an unfinished jigsaw to me.

We should have been together today. She would have been irritating the hell out of me, clacking around in her crazy stiletto boots, getting far too overexcited about the Casting. And maybe she would have made it through, and got what she had always wanted: to be Silver. Tommy could have loved her, and she could have loved him. If she had made it through one more week, I thought, she could have lived forever.

I wiped a tear from my cheek with the back of my hand and folded the letter into its envelope.

I was keeping this one, I thought. No one would miss it.

Turning my face away from the table, I stood up without looking at Ollie and walked through to the cell. I stowed the letter away safely in my backpack beside the walkie talkie and, that task accomplished, went into the bathroom to have a proper cry in private before washing my face and returning to the observation room.

I felt so drained that I wasn't sure how I was going to make it to tonight.

Oh well, I thought darkly, I could sleep when I was dead.

"I'm sorry," Ollie said when I came back into the room. He was reading another letter, the pages spread out on the table in front of him, ticking off each name as he checked them against the list. Ticking them when they were dead, as if dying merited applause.

"She didn't deserve it," I said as I leaned against the wall by the window, thinking grimly of the horrible end the rebels had orchestrated for her.

"No," he agreed.

I wondered whether he, like me, was thinking again about my own rapidly-approaching death. I wondered whether, in the grand scheme of things, I had deserved it. I didn't believe in heaven or hell and I didn't think I would be going on to an afterlife where I would be judged as either naughty or nice and allocated my quarters accordingly. I did believe in a life well-lived, a life in which you did more good than harm, and that each of us had a responsibility to keep our own score without worrying too much about tallying up those of other people.

So what had I really contributed? I'd not created anything, no children or great artistic works. I'd not saved a life, or helped to advance technology or knowledge. I'd loved, but probably not enough, and not with enough selflessness. As a sum of a life, I wouldn't have considered that too objectionable were it not for Alice. Alice's death was my fault. In my eyes, which for the purposes of this exercise were the only ones that mattered, I was damned for that alone.

"Will you ever forgive yourself for Graham?" I asked, wondering whether Alice's death was something that time would have been able to heal.

Ollie looked up from his task, apparently surprised by the unwelcome question.

"No," he said. "I don't think so. Not really. And I don't think I'll ever forgive myself for this either."

"What?"

"What's going to happen tonight." His upbeat demeanour of this morning had vanished, tainted by my own mood. Or maybe reality was starting to settle in for both of us as the hours ticked by, every minute bringing the evening closer.

"I got you mixed up in the explosion," Ollie said. "You shouldn't have been there, and if you hadn't been then the brand wouldn't have healed you and the bond wouldn't have broken."

I shrugged.

"We don't know that. It's just a guess. It could have been entirely unrelated. Maybe it just burned out. Maybe Drew just stopped loving me, so the bond broke and took the brand with it."

"Maybe," he said, but I could see he wasn't convinced.

He wasn't looking at the list now, having entirely abandoned the letter in front of him. Instead, he was staring out of the window behind me at the rain.

I walked around the table and came to sit next to him, taking his hand in mine.

"Please don't blame yourself for this," I said. "With everything that's happened over the past couple of weeks, it's really a miracle that I've made it this far. Thanks to bloody Laila and Ben, I always would have been in danger. This way, at least it ends."

"You can't really feel that way," he said irritably. "Tell me you're not resigning yourself to this."

"I'm open to suggestions, but I think we both know I'm out of options here. Just don't blame yourself, please. God knows I made my own share of mistakes to get myself into this position."

He looked into my eyes and smiled a little, but after a moment his expression cracked as his forehead furrowed, the corners of his mouth turning down.

"Emmy…"

He leaned into me and put his arms around my body, pulling me in close and holding me tight. I wrapped my arms around his back and buried my face in his shirt, my heart feeling numb but my body still reactive enough to send tears running down my cheeks when I felt his chest start to shake with silent sobs.

"Please don't," I said, wishing we could skip the pain of the moment. If I could just stay numb and keep walking until the end, just keep going, then everything would be alright. I wouldn't feel this grief, because I wouldn't be here to witness it. I couldn't mourn my own death; I could only mourn the grief of others over it. If we could just pretend that everything was okay then I wouldn't have to see his pain and I could get through this day.

And then I'd be done.

"Ollie," I whispered. "Please. I need you to hold it together."

He took a moment to compose himself, rubbing his hands over his face as he pulled away from me. He smiled again, but there was no joy in it, his grey eyes both bright with tears and dull with sadness. I could feel the tracks of my own tears on my cheeks, but he wiped them away with his thumbs, reaching out with both hands to cup my face in his palms.

"Do you have any regrets?" he asked.

"About us?"

"Yes."

I smiled, remembering how it had been to joke and laugh with him, how he'd made me feel as though life didn't always have to be so serious. I'd needed that at the time.

"No," I said. "None. We had fun."

"We did."

His eyes searched my face, and in the split-second before his lips touched mine I had known he was going to kiss me. I didn't pull away, letting the kiss unravel to its natural end, but I wasn't going to escalate it. I may have had little to fear from pregnancy now, but I'd never felt less sexy in my life.

Everything about the moment was bleak: the setting, the circumstances and the desperation of the emotion driving it. There would be nothing redemptive about taking this further. Sleeping with Ollie wouldn't give him happier memories of me, nor would it make me feel any more alive. If anything, it would feel like a favour for the condemned, and that wasn't an experience I wanted to carry with me in my final hours.

I touched my lips to his cheek, his forehead and his mouth, once more, gently, before pulling away.

I'd rather this: a kiss between two friends who cared for each other, and who had almost been lovers, once.

CHAPTER XX

Ada arrived in the early evening and I knew that, whatever she was here for, it couldn't be good news. Clearly not a woman who was worried about how much blood she would need to consume to regain her energy, she didn't arrive by car. Instead, the first we knew of her presence was when we heard the outermost of the gates to the enclosure sliding open.

We had been sitting at the table opposite each other and working solidly on the letters all the way through the afternoon, trying to erase the spectre of this evening from our minds. When we heard the noise outside, we moved to the window to watch our visitor approach. I was disconcerted to see that she had brought the doctor with her, together with his silver case, and I wondered how she had carried him here. It made an odd mental image: the doctor piggy-backing on Ada, clinging to his briefcase as she rushed here at super-speed in her heels and skirt suit.

"She is full-blown, no holds barred, super crazy," I whispered to Ollie. "So please, please don't do or say anything that might upset her. In fact, just shut up unless she asks you a question."

"What are you saying?" he asked in mock affront.

"You know what I'm saying. Keep calm, and don't let her

rile you. Just keep your expression totally neutral."

I thought back to his various encounters with Drew and Mark and wondered if even that might be ambitious.

"In fact," I said, "why don't you just go next door and pretend to be asleep?"

He offered me a hand gesture that suggested he wasn't prepared to do as I so reasonably advised, then turned back to the window.

Unfortunately, it was no longer raining so Ada's hairdo didn't come unstuck, but I enjoyed a moment's quiet gratification when I saw that her pale heels were both sticking into the mud and getting covered in it as she walked unsteadily towards the door to the observation room. I was praying that she would slide and land on her arse, but sadly she was agile enough on her heels to make her way to the building upright.

The doctor held the door open for her as she entered, then followed her in. Dr Tanner had given me the impression that he wasn't a man whose feathers were easily ruffled, but this evening he seemed agitated and upset, which immediately put me on the alert.

"Good evening," Ada said to us both.

She gestured peremptorily towards the boxes on the table, so the doctor started moving them down off the surface and onto the floor. Ollie and I looked at each other then started to help, packing away the paper, pens and binders. When the table was clear, we lit the candles so there was some more light to chase away the gradually encroaching darkness of the evening. Ada moved one of the chairs around to its head and sat delicately, her hands resting neatly in her lap and one ankle crossed carefully behind the other. She looked as though she was the star pupil at her finishing school.

"You," she said to Ollie, "will wait in the other room."

He looked at me, but I raised my eyebrows impatiently and nodded him towards the door. This was no time for his protective nonsense. I was out of here tonight and Ada would be a complete irrelevance the moment I walked out of the door, but Ollie was going nowhere so he really needed to stay on her good side. I'd already been on the receiving end of her disapproval and I didn't want him to risk suffering the same for the sake of someone who'd be dead by dawn anyway.

I relaxed a little as he turned and left, shutting the door behind him.

Taking a seat across the corner of the table from her, I was surprised to find that I wasn't feeling particularly anxious. It was as though my impending death had lent me a feeling of invincibility. She could do what she wanted to me now because whatever she did it wasn't going to last long.

But then she smiled, and I started to doubt myself. Ada smiling couldn't be a good thing.

The doctor sat down opposite me and put his briefcase on the table, pulling out the familiar paraphernalia of his blood donation kit.

"A thought occurred to me this morning," Ada said. As she spoke, she wasn't looking at me, but at her fingernails. She pushed back the cuticle of her index finger with the thumb of her other hand, holding it out in front of her for inspection before moving onto the next one.

"I was thinking," she continued, "about your blood donation and about the letter I received from the Primus. Obviously, as we have previously discussed," she moved her gaze to my eyes for just a moment, "your blood cannot be drunk by any Silver other than him."

She glanced briefly between me, the doctor and my splinted fingers before returning to her preening. I wondered whether she was angry that he had seen to the breaks for me, for all the good it would do me now. I'd never see them heal or function properly again. I hoped that he hadn't got himself into trouble pointlessly on my account.

"However," she continued, "that being the case, why should you have been asked to donate at all?"

I didn't know where she was going with this, so I simply kept an expression of polite interest on my face as she spoke.

"Perhaps, I thought, it is to show you what you have lost by your treason, and that you must now donate as would any other person. But, if that were the case, then surely the blood could simply be disposed of, or kept here until a convenient moment could be found to take it to the city with a shipment of other necessities. Why should it be necessary for the Solis Invicti to be engaged to carry it to the city so urgently?"

She folded her hands back into her lap, apparently now satisfied with her manicure, and met my eyes.

"The only explanation I can offer is that the Primus has developed a taste for your blood, and that he wishes to see it delivered safely to him because it is something that he enjoys. This, of course, simply raises another question."

I waited patiently as she paused for dramatic effect. I resisted the urge to sigh.

"What happens," she said, "if you are the candidate for the Casting this evening? If you are no longer human, then I will no longer be in a position to provide the Primus with the blood he desires. So, in order to soften the blow should that eventuality arise, I have decided to make him a gift."

So that was it, I thought. She really was out for my blood.

"Doctor?" she said.

I knew the routine and saw no reason to argue, so I stretched out my arm and let him insert the needle. I was almost disappointed at the tame motivation for her visit. I'd been expecting some drama, a final confrontation to liven up my last day, perhaps with some Silver religious dogma thrown in my face, but apparently that wasn't on the cards. Given that on the last occasion I had spent quality time with Ada she had broken my fingers, I supposed I should have felt relieved to be getting off so lightly today.

I had to wonder whether she was right, whether Sol really did have a thing for my blood. It would answer a lot of questions, perhaps even explain why he was interested in me in the first place. It would certainly explain why, even after he'd silvered for Laila, he'd tracked me down at the club to drink from my wrist. At the time I'd thought it had been a power play, a manoeuvre to demonstrate his dominance to Drew after he'd contravened Sol's monopoly on my blood, bestowed by the choker I had worn. But now I was starting to wonder.

He'd told me that he had wanted to taste me again. Perhaps he had been telling the truth after all.

We sat in silence as the bag filled, Ada and Dr Tanner both watching it closely, the doctor clinically and Ada avariciously. I wondered what, if anything, she thought it would benefit her to give it to Sol. Was she hoping that she'd gain his favour by presenting him with such a ridiculous present, or did she just hope to escape his wrath for the fact that it was the last consignment he'd receive?

It made me think of Ollie's bizarre valentine gift, the heart with the dagger through it. I imagined Ada presenting Sol with a bag of blood as her own courting gift. But then Sol was with Laila now, and I imagined that Ada would probably think he was too sacred to touch anyway.

When the bag was full, Dr Tanner detached it from my arm and made to take out the needle.

"Oh," Ada interrupted, "I think we can probably manage another bag. After all, it is for the Primus."

The doctor looked uncertain, but after a moment's pause he reached into his briefcase and pulled out a second empty bag to replace the first. It seemed to take longer to fill this time round, the blood feeling as though it were moving more slowly in my veins, but eventually the second bag was full as well. It left me a little light-headed and dizzy, but I didn't think it would have done me any harm.

Once again, Ada stopped the doctor from removing the needle.

"We can take a third bag and she still will live," she said.

Dr Tanner opened his mouth as though he was going to protest, but I interrupted. What was the point of objecting? If I died from blood loss it would probably be more pleasant than being turned into a Weeper anyway. By all accounts the Silver transformation was horrifically painful, so I couldn't imagine that the transformation to Weeper would be any less traumatic.

"It's fine," I said, waving my free hand at him vaguely. It also happened to be the hand with the broken fingers, which might have provided a salutary reminder of what the doctor would have been risking by crossing Ada. Either way, after a brief look of regret, he attached the third bag and watched my face carefully as the blood trickled in.

Once it was about half full, I started to feel faint and cold, as though the blood flowing out of me and into the bag was taking all of my warmth with it. I looked down at the needle, following the line of the tubing snaking its way across the table past my hand. My fingernails had lost their colour, turning an odd shade of blue and purple, and my heart started racing in my chest, beating fit to burst as it struggled to pump the remaining blood around my body.

"We're losing her," Dr Tanner said.

"Wait," Ada replied. Her eyes were fixed on the bag, watching the last few fluid ounces fill it up.

"Very well," she said after another moment. "You may remove the needle."

I was having trouble focussing, blinking long and slow to try to bring the room back into focus. The pressure was removed from my arm, the tape pulled off, and I was suddenly so dizzy I felt as though I was falling out of my chair. Then my body hit the floor heavily, my left side thudding down and cracking my cheek off the concrete.

"Damn," the doctor muttered.

His face swam above me, a light flaring in my eyes as he lifted my eyelids open one by one with his thumb.

"Will she live?" Ada asked.

His fingers were at my wrists and my mind immediately jumped back to yesterday. Sol's fingertips had touched my wrist, my cheek, my lips…

"Probably," he said.

"Then come along."

"But…"

"Now!" she shouted, so loudly that the noise made my heart skip in my chest. My eyelids dropped closed and I let them stay that way. I was too tired to open them again.

Everything hurt.

I wasn't moving from this spot.

I heard the door open and shut as they left, Ada's heels clicking out across the floor. The peace after that was blissful for a moment, and I felt myself dropping off. Then there was the sound of another door opening, and I wondered idly why they were coming back.

But it was Ollie.

"Emmy? Shit, Emmy, wake up!"

I moaned gently, just wishing that he would leave me alone so I could go to sleep.

"Wake up!" he shouted again.

"Already awake," I mumbled.

"Thank Christ. Then open your eyes."

I blinked groggily and looked at him briefly before my eyelids dropped closed again, blocking out the light and shutting me in my own soporific world.

"Shit," he said again.

He slid his arms under my body and lifted me from the floor, a feeling of weightlessness enveloping me as I was raised upwards. Between that and the blood loss, I felt like I was flying. But once Ollie started moving, that illusion was well and truly shattered. His leg still hadn't fully recovered so his gait was jerky and uneven as he limped with me in his arms. His fingers dug into the side of my thigh and my arm where I had fallen to the floor, and the pressure on the tender skin felt sharp and piercing, enough to make me moan softly in the back of my throat.

"It's okay," he murmured, "we're nearly there. Just a few more steps."

He laid me down on the bed, wrapping me in the clean blankets and tucking them around me tightly. They smelled of soap, the sharp tang of citrus filling my nostrils with it summery scent.

"What happened?" he asked, his face close to mine. I opened my eyes for a second and saw that he was kneeling by the bed beside me.

"Took blood."

"How much? Too much?" he asked.

"Doc said not."

I shivered.

I felt him move away from me, then a couple of seconds later he was sitting me upright, sliding himself onto the mattress behind me so he could keep me in position. He wrapped me up in his arms and pulled the blanket back up to my chin, but I still felt freezing.

"Drink," he said.

A bottleneck touched my lips and I opened my mouth, letting the water wet my tongue. I realised how very thirsty I was, and after a couple of sips I lifted my hand and put it over his on the bottle, tipping it forward until it was empty. I supposed that I must have had a lot of fluid to replace.

He took it away and I opened my eyes to see him put it down on the floor. There was another full bottle next to me on the bed, but instead of handing it to me he held out a square of chocolate.

"Here."

I took it from him, my hands shaking so violently that it was difficult to keep a grip on it, and successfully conveyed it to my mouth. Ridiculously, it was an achievement I was proud of, but it was an uphill struggle from there onwards. It felt as though hours passed while I chewed down the chocolate bar, square by square. I was having to concentrate fiercely in order to get my jaws to work properly, but when they moved they felt alien and odd. It was as if I were operating a remote-controlled version of myself, having to think carefully about every single movement that was normally a matter of natural instinct.

It was exhausting.

When I was done with the chocolate, Ollie helped me to drink the second bottle of water then left me for a second to fill them both up again in the bathroom. By the time he returned I had curled up on my side on the bed, rolling myself into as small a ball as possible under the blankets.

"Still cold?" he asked.

I nodded.

So he climbed over me and curled himself around my back, bundling me up close to his body. I could feel his heat creeping through into me, soothing the edges off my chills and starting to warm me through. It wasn't long before I was dropping off again, and this time he let me sleep.

"Emmy," he said.

He was still at my back and so it seemed like just a moment later, but when I opened my eyes I saw that it was now full dark outside. It must have been after nine. Anxiety tightened my chest. I'd slept away my last few hours with him.

I was still feeling exhausted and groggy, but I managed to roll myself around in his arms and bury my head in his shoulder, not wanting to face what I knew would come next.

"Tessa's here to take you to the city," he said, his voice a little unsteady.

"Hmm?"

"It's alright, Mark's already there."

But that wasn't what had been worrying me. I was confused. I had thought that Drew was going to come and pick me up, or maybe Tommy or Cam. Either way, I hadn't expected one of the guards to be doing the driving.

"Emilia." Her voice came from across the room. "We have to get you ready."

This had to be Laila's doing, I thought. She wouldn't want anyone whom I might consider a friend to be driving me. I suppose she would be worried that I might be allowed to escape, but without one of the Silver with me it's not as if I would have been able to get very far. With the bond gone, I didn't think there was anyone who would risk everything to come with me now. Anyway, even if I was wrong, the others would surely find us. I was surprised Laila hadn't sent Ben to drive me so he could have one last gloat before it was all over.

I thought briefly of the walkie talkie, still shoved into the bottom of my rucksack. With Tessa already here it was too late to call in reinforcements now, but even if I did, what would I have said? Tommy and Cam weren't going to be able to save me from the Casting; our only plan had failed. Anyway, they'd just been trying to protect me from Drew, for his own sake.

At least we had managed to put that demon to rest before the end. Well, sort of. He had explained why he had been so upset, and I supposed that I could accept that. I wasn't sure that we were friends exactly, but we'd made some kind of progress, found some kind of resolution. At least I didn't think he wanted to kill me anymore.

Although he still would.

"Come on," Ollie said.

I let him roll me over onto my back and then help me up into a sitting position. Tessa looked at us quizzically.

"Ada took her blood," Ollie said. "A lot of blood, I think."

"Why?" Tessa asked bluntly, short and to the point as always.

"For Sol," I said, clearing my throat as I reached for one of the refilled water bottles and glugged a little down. "She thinks he likes it, and she didn't want him to be angry if I was the one going to the Casting."

I looked at Tessa suspiciously for a moment.

"How did you know it was me?" I asked.

She reached into the bag she was carrying and pulled out a full-length dress in emerald satin.

"They gave me this," she said, "and I didn't think it was his colour. Now let's get you clean and dressed, because we don't have much time."

I was still feeling weak and faint, my sight intermittently disappearing in a head-rush of darkness at inopportune moments. I showered as well as I could with my broken fingers, but I couldn't manage on my own so Ollie helped me to stand up under the spray. After all we'd been through we were pretty comfortable with each other, and after a moment's awkwardness I quickly got over the oddness of feeling his hands on my naked body.

With Ollie's help, I walked out of the bathroom with one of the towels wrapped around me. Tessa pointed me towards the bed so I sat down obediently as he moved back into the observation room, his head bending busily over the letters again. He caught my eye briefly before returning to his work, and I wondered how well he was doing at forgetting that this was happening tonight, that very shortly we'd be saying goodbye and leaving each other for the last time.

I was expecting that Tessa would get me dressed abruptly then bundle me into the truck, but apparently the Casting was more important than that. Although I had got the knack of washing my hair with one hand, I was unable to do anything with it to make it look tidier once it was clean. That wasn't good enough for Tessa. She fetched the other towel from the bathroom and came to stand over me as she dried my long hair carefully before teasing it out with her fingers. Once it was as neat as it could be, I sat in disbelief as she plaited it and curled the braid around my head, using clips from her own hair to pin it into place.

"It'll do," she said as she stood back to assess her handiwork.

Next, she helped me struggle into the dress. It seemed to fit okay, but it was difficult to tell without a mirror. Thankfully, whoever had chosen my Casting outfit had been sensible enough not to try to get me to walk in heels. Instead, Tessa passed me a pair of embroidered flats that matched the dress in colour and I slipped them on.

"Does it look okay?" I asked.

She shrugged, obviously about as much of a fashion expert as I was.

"The tan lines are odd," she said.

I looked down at myself and saw what she meant. On each of my upper arms there was a clear line where my skin tone changed from pale to tan, and there was a similar line in a V-shape at my neck where the scrubs top had been when I'd been sunburned on patrol. The plunging neckline of the dress fell well below it, so it must look as though I was wearing a white top underneath. My cheek and arm were really throbbing by now, so I thought I probably had some good bruises coming as well.

I must have looked a state.

I wasn't sure why I cared how I looked in the outfit I was going to die in, but I cared nonetheless. I would have felt more comfortable in jeans and a T-shirt, but if I had to wear a fancy frock I'd rather not look like an idiot in it, particularly when everyone was going to be watching. There was something to the ceremony of it too. It was like a wedding dress, I supposed: the dress in which the Silver hopefuls would go to the Casting to get the chance to be turned by their sponsors.

And this was the last thing I'd ever wear, I thought.

But it could have been worse. At least it wasn't pink.

She started to lead me towards the door from the cell out into the enclosure.

"Already?" I asked, not quite prepared to take the next step. Getting ready had been one thing, but actually leaving the building, leaving Ollie, was a different thing entirely.

"We're going to be late if we don't go now," she said.

I looked through the doorway into the observation room to see Ollie looking up at me with an expression of shock. It looked like the reality of this situation was crashing down on him in the same way as it was with me. This was the moment, the second of our last slice of time together, and nothing seemed appropriate. I wanted to make some poignant gesture, to say something meaningful, but everything felt either inadequate or overly dramatic. After all, what was my life in the scheme of things?

He got up from his chair and stood in front of me, looking down into my face with those bright grey eyes that I had hated so much in the first few days we had known each other. We might not be Silver, and we might not be in love, but there was still a bond between us that I could see in them. We'd shared this week together, this awful, horror-filled week, and we'd been there for each other. That had built something stronger than the magic that had touched Drew.

I hoped that Ollie wouldn't forget that, and that he wouldn't forget me.

But I didn't know how to express that to him, so I just put my arms around his neck, kissed him lightly on the lips and said: "Thank you."

Then it felt as though someone pressed the fast-forward button. Tessa slung my arm over her shoulder as she helped me to navigate the mud of the enclosure before loading me into the passenger seat of the car that waited outside.

Then we were gone, out through the gates, the building falling away in the distance behind us and taking Ollie with it.

CHAPTER XXI

I had been expecting Tessa's usual truck, so I was surprised that she was instead chauffeuring me in a small two-seater sports car. It seemed impractical for the rough track that skirted the inside of the Farm's boundary, but when we got to the first of the three gates leading to the outer perimeter, I understood why she'd chosen it.

As she swung the car round to face the fence, her headlights illuminated thousands of Weepers milling around outside the safety of the barriers. Some were close against the fence, but not close enough to touch, apparently having learned that electricity was a bad thing. Ollie was right: they were more sentient than we had given them credit for.

With that number of Weepers hanging around, and with night already fallen to make them fearless, they would have been all over the truck. This way, I was close to Tessa, and the ambit of the circle of safety around her was more likely to include the whole of the car. We didn't want any more bumper riders.

When we finally made it to the third gate a couple of Silver guards walked out of it in front of the car, their presence pushing the congregated Weepers away from the opening long enough to carve a path for us to drive through. As soon as they had returned to their posts, the gate falling into place behind them, the Weepers started following on behind us.

"Seatbelt on?" Tessa asked.

"Yes," I said, but I didn't have time to be anxious about why she might be asking the question. The car jumped forward, accelerating at a ridiculous speed for the small, country road, all the while jinking and swerving to avoid the Weepers that were ambling across it.

After a few minutes of panicked flinching and ducking, I opted to close my eyes and just trust that Tessa knew what she was doing. She did, and at the speed she was driving I hadn't had much time to drop off to sleep before she was shaking me awake. The headrest had probably ruined my fancy hairstyle, but that really was the least of my worries.

"We leave the car here," she said as I opened my eyes.

We were still outside the safe zone of the city, but the towers of old London were rising above us as she drove into an underground garage and parked. The place was pitch black, the only light coming from the headlights, and as soon as those winked out there was nothing to be seen at all. From the brief glimpse I had got of the place, it had appeared to be a low-ceilinged multi-storey with square pillars set at regular intervals. It had been about half full of cars, but none of them looked as though they'd suffered the usual depredations of the Weepers.

"Where are we?" I asked.

"A couple of miles away from the wall," she said. "This is a Solis Invicti building that we keep locked up tight."

"A Solis Invicti building?" I asked, confused as to why she would have access to it.

"Yes," she said. "I have something for you."

She clicked on the overhead light above the rear mirror and I saw she was holding an envelope.

"Is that…" I said.

But instead of answering, she ripped it open and poured its contents out into my uninjured hand: my parents' rings on the four silver chains. I gaped down at the treasures. I couldn't believe that she had been so thoughtful as to retrieve them for me.

"I don't know what to say," I whispered as tears welled in my eyes. "Thank you."

She just shrugged and made a circling motion with her hand to indicate that I should turn around. Once I had done so she fastened the chains for me, securing the rings once more around my neck, where they belonged. I wrapped my hand around them and clutched them tight in my palm, cementing the reality of them in my mind.

I had them back. I'd have something of theirs with me when I died, some token of them to help me get through this. I couldn't possibly express to Tessa how much that meant to me.

"Stay there," she said as she clicked the light off. "I'll come round and take you upstairs."

She got out of the car and slammed the door behind her, and then a moment later my own door opened and she was scooping me up into her arms.

"I can walk," I said.

"No."

I had a moment of increased dizziness and then I was being carried down a fully-lit corridor towards a set of double doors.

"You need your strength for tonight," she added.

She turned her back to the doors and pushed her way through them, taking us into a large space with about ten desks in it, each set with a phone, computer and the usual other workstation detritus. There was an office in the far corner of the room, separated from the open plan space by smoked glass walls, and I could see a figure moving around inside. There were a couple of chairs by the door that led into it, arranged to form a waiting area. Tessa put me down into one gently before knocking softly.

"Tessa," a familiar voice said as the door opened. "Shouldn't you be getting ready for the Casting?"

"Yes Secundus, but you asked for someone to go out to

the Farm to collect Ms Nelson?"

He peered round the doorjamb at me, apparently as surprised as I was that Tessa had been the one to bring me.

"Well, thank you for volunteering. I'll see the human safely to her sponsor."

"Sir," she said in a tone of voice that was an acknowledgement of her dismissal. She didn't look at me again, simply turning away to walk back across the office and through the double doors.

When she was gone, Drew came and sat in the seat next to me, leaning forwards to rest his elbows on his knees. He turned his head to look at me.

"What's wrong?" he asked. "What happened to your face?"

"Lost some blood and fell over," I said quietly, still feeling weak and disorientated.

Being in this building wasn't helping. With the empty desks and the office setting, it just reminded me of the makeshift hospital where Ollie had recovered after the explosions. It was so odd to see Drew running the Solis Invicti out of a place like this, almost disappointing. I mean, I knew they had to have had somewhere to work out of, but an office building? For the Silver military? It was a joke. Where were the weights rooms and the dojos?

But then I supposed that with their super powers they probably didn't need to work out.

"How much blood?" he asked.

"About three pints."

"Jesus."

I shook my head and then wished I hadn't, the movement making me feel nauseated.

"It doesn't matter anymore," I said. "Let's just get this over with. How do we do this?"

"We go quick, and we go straight there. Hold on."

He leaned in and picked me up, one arm under my knees and the other under my back. I put my arms around his neck and leaned my head gratefully against his shoulder, the familiar scent of sawdust and leather rolling over me as I closed my eyes. When I opened them again, the nausea now pulling at the back of my throat as I struggled to resist it, we were in a grand corridor that turned to the right about forty feet ahead of us. Looking over Drew's shoulder, I could see a large, heavy wooden door immediately behind us with black iron rivets and hinges crossing its rich surface. The windows running along either side of the corridor were leaded in a diamond pattern that was matched by the carpet runner under our feet: a deep red with golden crosshatching that sat on top of the pale limestone slabs.

"Where are we?" I whispered, the surroundings seeming to demand silence.

"It's an old guild hall," he said quietly. "You're going to have to walk from here."

He set me on my feet, my shoes sinking into the deep pile of the carpet, then offered me his arm. I took it gratefully, leaning on it heavily but trying to stand up straight so it didn't show.

"Why don't you have to be in evening dress?" I whispered as we walked towards the corner.

"There's a ritual for the sponsors," he replied, "remember?"

I didn't want to confess how little I had taken in of his instructions the night before, so I just nodded and pretended that I was following him.

"I have to leave you down here with the other candidates," he said as we turned the corner. The corridor opened out into a wood-panelled entrance hall filled with tapestries and paintings. The central feature was a sweeping staircase that rose up on our left, turning back on itself to reach the floor above us. To our right a set of double doors, one of which stood open, led into what looked like a small library.

"Just stay here until someone comes to get you. Don't talk to anyone, don't go anywhere and just do what they tell you. It couldn't be simpler, okay?"

I looked up at him, anxiety jumping in my stomach. I

didn't want him to leave me. I wanted someone to hold my hand through this and lead me to the end so I didn't have to be conscious of it. I wanted to let my mind wander away in the arms of the blood-loss haze and let someone else take responsibility for guiding me to my death. I didn't want to be a participant in the process.

"You'll be fine, Emmy," he whispered, and then he kissed me on the cheek and left me there, at the base of the stairway, as he climbed it up to the first floor.

I touched my cheek.

He'd kissed me.

I couldn't remember the last time he'd shown me any kind of tenderness. Not since the bond had broken. Only the problem was that it hadn't felt like affection. It had felt like pity and guilt.

I turned towards the double doors and peeked in. The room wasn't too large, perhaps thirty feet on each side, and it felt cosier and more intimate than I would have expected for a space of that size. The walls were lined with books from the ceiling down to waist height, at which point wood panelling took over. There were four small tables in the room, two on each side of the double doors, and each had four chairs positioned neatly around it. There were a few armchairs arranged against the walls in the gaps between the tables, and most of those were occupied.

I counted seven people in the room as I entered: four women and three men. They were all dressed in beautiful finery that made me feel self-conscious about my own deficient outfit and my stumbling steps. A couple of them smiled at me when I entered, but my eyes were drawn to a young man sitting in an isolated arm chair in the corner of the room. He was young, with dark hair and a goatee that made him look like a conquistador, and he had perhaps the haughtiest appearance of any person I had ever encountered. He looked me up and down as if assessing my validity as a person, and then looked away dismissively, obviously finding me wanting.

I smiled to myself a little. He reminded me of how Ollie had been when we first met.

I made my way as steadily as possible towards one of the unoccupied tables and sat down carefully, mindful of Drew's instructions not to talk to anyone. The other sponsors clearly hadn't made similar demands of their candidates or, if they had, they were being disobeyed.

"Isn't this exciting?" one of the guys said as I picked up a book at random and feigned engrossment.

"Oh, I know," a female voice responded. "I can't wait to see my sponsor. He was telling me all about the ritual they're doing. Apparently they have to do this purification thing, and then there's an oil thing, and then they dress them in these robes. I bet he'd look hot in a robe."

I took a quick glance in her direction to see who was speaking before looking back at my book, which I saw was titled 'A Social and Economic History of the Production, Importation and Applications of Wool through the Ages'. I was hoping for some pictures of sheep, but I was out of luck.

The speaker had her back to me so I wasn't able to see her face, but she was painfully thin with long, dark hair. I could see her ribs through the diaphanous back of her strapless dress, her shoulder blades and spine jutting out under her skin. I wondered whether she had always been that way or whether the Revelation had been particularly tough for her. It was always difficult to tell these days.

"Oh, god, mine too," the man replied. "He has abs like you've never seen. I'm assuming these robes will be open, right?"

"Better be," she replied.

"Oiled abs," he sighed. "Damn, you're gonna have to hold me back."

They laughed raucously and I saw the haughty conquistador roll his eyes. No one else seemed bothered by their conversation, three of the others being too embroiled in their own discussion behind me to notice. The last woman, who was also sitting alone, seemed to be doing as I was. Her book certainly looked as boring as mine from the outside. She was too far away for me to read the cover, but I hadn't heard her turn a page since I'd walked in.

"I wasn't sure about it myself," one of the girls behind me said, "but she asked so, well, yeah."

"You don't even want to be here?" the man in the group asked disdainfully.

"Seriously?" the second woman in the group said. "Do you know how much I had to go through to get one of the Silver to sponsor me?"

"Look," the first woman said, "it's not my fault. I'm not trying to take anything away from you guys, but if one of them asks you to do something you just do it, alright? What was I supposed to do?"

"Say no?" the guy said. "I mean it's not like your sponsor's even someone important."

"What? You're saying yours is?"

"Yeah," the second woman interjected quietly, "he kind of is."

"My sponsor," the man said self-importantly, "is one of the Solis Invicti."

A hush fell over the group, and I gathered that this comment had received the response he was hoping for.

Wait until they got a look at my sponsor, I thought bitterly. If they were impressed by one of the Invicti then they'd go bonkers over the Secundus.

I listened to the two groups talk a little longer, but, other than the slight reluctance expressed by the woman sitting behind me, no one seemed to be worried about turning Silver at all. Sol had made it clear that it was dangerous in his initial broadcast. He'd made it clear that there would be risks, but none of the other candidates seemed to have taken that on board. Not those that were speaking, at least.

No one else came into the room for a good half hour, so I gathered that there would only be eight of us going to the Casting. At least half of us would be rejected, and as many as four could make it through to the dawn ceremony if Alyssa considered that they had passed the tests. But the Silver weren't expecting there to be any successful turnings. They were expecting that we would all turn Weeper. How convenient that tradition dictated that the turning ceremony had to be held in a forest clearing, outside of the city where no one would be able to witness what happened.

"Candidates," a voice said from the door.

I turned to see Ben standing there, dressed in a peculiar cotton tunic and trousers. Of course he would be here, I thought, as Laila's watchdog.

"And Emilia," he added, his face splitting into a grin, "what an… interesting ensemble. I have to say, it's a genuine pleasure to see you here tonight."

He meant it, too. He must have known that I was going to be here, because apparently Laila had managed to find out that I was up for the Casting. I was also sure that he would know that Laila had spoken to Alyssa about putting me through, and he must have noticed that the bond had broken. So he knew I was going to turn Weeper at dawn, and he was just making sure he managed to fit in some gloating time before it was too late.

But the other candidates took his comment in a very different way. A couple of them were shooting me envious looks, perhaps because the Tertius knew who I was, or perhaps because they thought that the apparently welcoming way in which he spoke to me indicated that I was likely to get one of the four coveted slots at the turning ceremony. I wished that neither of those things were true. I certainly didn't think either of them was to be envied.

"So," he said, clapping his hands together gleefully, "let's get you upstairs. Here are the rules: stand where you're told to, no speaking unless spoken to, and answer only 'Yes, Primus' or 'No, Primus' if addressed. Clear?"

We all nodded at him dutifully.

"Marvellous. Well, won't this be fun?" he sighed happily. The bastard was getting far too much enjoyment out of this. "Line yourselves up, then. Single file."

I gritted my teeth together as I stood up carefully, willing myself to hold it together. I was determined not to show Ben any sign of the weakness that I was feeling, but I was still slower off the mark than every single one of the other candidates, so I just walked straight to the back of the queue, behind the other girl who had been reading. There was some scrambling at the front of the line as people jostled over their priority in the order, but things settled down fairly quickly after Ben gave a stern look to the squabblers.

He led us up the stairs in silence. When we got about halfway up I had to abandon my pride and hold onto the banister, unable to stop my head from spinning me dizzily as we climbed. Since I was at the back of the line, I didn't think anyone was likely to notice anyway.

As the route of the staircase curved around, the first floor came into view. There was a wide landing running the length of the staircase, with a wall about ten feet in front of its top. A large and imposing set of doors stood in the middle of the wall with one of the Solis Invicti posted at each side of it. I didn't recognise either of them, and assumed they must be men from Ben's unit.

"Two minutes, Tertius," one of them said to him softly.

He nodded back and paused outside the doors, bringing the line to a halt.

So we waited.

And waited.

I tried to concentrate on keeping my balance, on keeping the weight evenly distributed on my feet so I wouldn't wobble. I was still swaying a little, but it could have been worse.

Eventually, after what felt like much longer than two minutes, the double doors were dramatically flung open in front of us from within.

"Intrate candidati!" a voice rang out.

Dear god, I thought. Drew had warned me, but I really couldn't cope with Latin right now, not on top of everything else.

Ben started walking forward and we followed him one by

one into the dark room until we were positioned straight across it in a line. Once we were all inside, the doors slammed shut again behind us.

The room felt massive, but as it was illuminated only by candles it was difficult to see its true extent. Once my eyes became accustomed to the darkness, I saw that we were actually lined up across the back of it, because its focal point was to our right at the other end of the room: a raised throne, a real-life throne, with a single candelabrum set on each side of it.

It was occupied by a figure in a black, hooded cloak that covered it entirely, but I could take a fair guess as to who might be beneath it.

Between us and the throne was a third candelabrum, next to which stood a second figure in a similar cloak. In the faint glow of the candlelight I could see people lining the sides of the room. The Silver, I guessed, come to watch the show, and from the looks of things every Silver in the city was here tonight.

"Instate sponsores!" intoned the figure seated on the throne.

Eight people walked out from the crowds and lined up between the standing figure and the throne, four on each side. Presumably they were our sponsors. They were also wearing cloaks with full hoods and, to my surprise, it looked as though the raucous candidates had been right earlier about the rest of their attire. They wore dark trousers under their cloaks, which, whether the sponsors were male or female, hung open from the hoods to the floor, so that a strip of naked flesh was visible from collarbone to waist. It was a demanding look that suited some of them better than others.

The cloaked figure in the middle of the room began to speak, and I realised that it was Alyssa. After a few moments of incomprehension as I tried to follow her words, it finally dawned on me that she, too, was speaking Latin. Fluidly, and without a book, as though it had been her first language. Maybe it had been. I knew that Sol had been around in

Roman times, and given that he and Alyssa had apparently been friends it wouldn't have surprised me if she too had lived through the Roman Empire.

I supposed that I should have been scared, that I should have been anticipating my imminent death, but instead all of my energy was focussed on getting through the Casting, getting through the next few minutes until midnight had passed and the verdict was in. I could worry about turning Weeper once this ceremony was over and we were on our way out of the city, but for now I just had to make sure that I stayed on my feet to make it that far.

The indecipherable words flowed on and, in the dark surroundings, I began to feel more disorientated and sleepy. I felt my head start to nod, my body weak with the effort of staying awake, and I had to struggle to keep myself upright. My leg and arm ached from the tumble I had taken earlier, the limbs sore to the bone, but that was nothing compared with the agony of my cheekbone, which was hot with stabbing lances of pain. I wondered whether it was broken. I supposed it didn't matter. Between those injuries and the splinted fingers, I was feeling like a broken shell. In some ways it would be a relief for it to be over, to be allowed to drift away.

The enthroned figure joined in with the Latin, engaging in what sounded like natural conversation with Alyssa. As soon as I heard his voice at its normal volume my suspicions were confirmed: it was Sol, giving an audience in his guise as king. His musical tones rose and fell in cadences that were complemented by the poetry of the language, the lyrical consonants rolling off his tongue.

Then, after what seemed like an interminable amount of talking, a gong rang through the room, shocking me into alertness as my heartbeat stuttered in my chest.

Dong.

The noise echoed in a way that suggested the ceiling stretched high above our heads, and then repeated.

Dong.

Dong.

Dong.

I realised that they were striking midnight, that this was the signal for the Casting itself.

Dong.

Then the fear came. It was instant and overwhelming, a sweat breaking out across my palms and my heart racing into overdrive.

Dong.

I felt sick with nerves, my stomach rolling with waves of anxiety, and I had to breathe through my mouth to keep it at bay.

Dong.

I just had to keep it together.

Dong.

Just a little while longer.

Dong.

And then it would all be over.

Dong.

I'd be done.

Dong.

I could give up.

CHAPTER XXII

Thursday

Dong.

The last strike echoed around the room for a few seconds before silence fell. The satin of the dress was sticking to my body as my muscles rolled into balls of tension.

Just let it be over quickly, I thought.

"Insta!" Sol called.

One of the sponsors took another step forward and pulled his hood from his shoulders. He was no one I recognised, so Drew was still somewhere in the pack. I was almost certain that he would have put himself last if possible to avoid disrupting the ceremony more than necessary. All hell was going to break loose when everyone discovered that the Secundus had put forward a candidate.

It was going to go down very badly.

"Quem designas?" Sol asked the man.

The sponsor beckoned to his candidate, the skinny girl who'd thought he'd look hot in a robe. She'd been right. The candlelight glinted off sculptured abs that looked as though they'd been oiled up in preparation.

She crossed the room towards him and came to stand by his side. As he turned to her I saw that there was a symbol painted across his chest: the symbol of Solomon's house, the stylised 'SI' topped with a radiate crown. It looked as though it was painted in blood. I wondered whose.

"Hanc designo," the sponsor said.

"Istane approbatus est?" Sol asked, his voice echoing back at us through the huge room. This time it was Alyssa who answered.

"Illam repudio."

At that, the sponsor pulled the hood back over his head and returned to his original position, guiding his candidate with him. When they had stepped back he shook his head at her. She covered her face with her hands, her frail shoulders shaking with silent sobs. I wondered then whether her emaciation was the result of an illness and if she had hoped to cheat death by turning Silver.

The conquistador was up next, and there was some more Latin, but from his reaction I guessed that he had also been refused.

When the third sponsor was called forward she pointed to the girl next to me, the one who had been reading in the library.

"Hanc designo," her blood-daubed sponsor said when she reached her side, the words becoming familiar with the repetition. I still didn't know what they meant, but I guessed they were something along the lines of 'this one's mine.'

"Istane approbatus est?" Sol said. He must have been asking whether or not she'd passed the tests.

"Illi assentior," Alyssa replied.

There was a brief murmur around the room and the sponsor beamed widely at her candidate, so I guessed that it had been a yes this time. They looked at each other for a moment and then the Silver took the human's hand in hers, weaving their fingers together in a gesture that looked more tender than I might have expected. I prayed there was enough between them to make her a Silver rather than a Weeper.

More candidates were called up, one by one, until finally, as expected, I was the last one standing. There had been no other murmurs, so it seemed that the reading girl had been the only one to pass Alyssa's tests. So far.

By this point, my limbs were feeling so drained from the effort of keeping me vertical that I was panicking about covering the ground to get to Drew's side. The only sponsor left hooded was one of the two closest to the throne, the furthest away from where I stood. It looked like an insurmountable distance. I was going to make a fool of myself.

At least I wouldn't have long to be embarrassed about it.

"Insta!" Sol called for the eighth time.

The final sponsor stood forward and pulled the hood from his head, drawing it back from his long, dark hair to reveal his face. The expected gasp ran around the room as the Silver recognised Drew. There was no denying that the outfit suited him. His bare chest and stomach were pale enough to show the redness of the blood painted onto his skin, drops running down the defined indentations of his muscles.

As the volume in the room rose I felt my nervousness growing too, my hands shaking. I clutched at the rings at my neck, trying to calm myself down.

Sol sat forward in his chair and pulled his own hood from his head. In the darkness of the room his golden hair seemed to glow, his cold blue eyes staring at Drew. I couldn't quite make out his expression from this distance, but the crowd had hushed quickly as Sol looked down from his throne.

"Secunde," Sol said, his voice seeming quieter and more uncertain than it had done previously, "quam designas?"

"Scisne, Prime?" Drew replied, his tone confused. "Hanc designo," he added, reaching out his hand towards me.

But now the script had changed, and I wasn't sure what was going on. When I didn't immediately approach, Drew nodded at me encouragingly, so I made my way slowly across the floor until I stood at his side. I thanked any god that happened to be listening for the fact that I'd managed the walk without tripping or stumbling.

I'd been concentrating so hard on my feet that it wasn't until I was in place by the throne that I looked up at Sol and saw his expression.

He looked shocked. His brow was slightly furrowed as his silver-shot eyes searched my face with patent disbelief, and I realised that he hadn't been expecting to see me here. He hadn't known that Drew had put me forward for the Casting.

Laila had known and Ben had known, but they hadn't told Sol. Why hadn't they told him?

What he did know, however, was that the bond was gone. He knew that if Alyssa gave me the go-ahead I wouldn't be human this time tomorrow, and I wouldn't be Silver either.

"Emilia," he said softly to me. The look he gave me was heavy with regret I hadn't expected from him.

He was so close that I could trace the silver in his eyes in the candlelight, so close that I felt I could almost smell the fresh, spicy scent of him over the smoky, waxy aroma of the candles. I could touch him, I thought. I could just reach out and touch his skin, stroke his golden hair away from his forehead and feel his breath on my lips.

"Certe non scivi," he said to Drew. "Num scivisti, Administrator?"

Alyssa turned around and pulled her hood down too, a concerned expression on her face.

"Sane, Prime," she said.

"Num ea approbatus est?" he asked.

"Ei assentior sane."

The clamour that rose from the spectators was so loud and sudden that I started, stumbling sideways a little, having trouble keeping to my feet. Drew caught me and looped my arm around his so I could lean on him for support. I looked at him for an explanation, not knowing what was going on or where I stood.

"You're through," he said sadly over the noise of the crowd.

I knew it had been coming, but the confirmation still

thudded into my chest like a ten-tonne weight. I wrapped my spare hand around the rings at my neck once more and squeezed them tight.

Sol stood from his throne and the room quietened almost immediately. He nodded to Alyssa, his expression grim, and stepped down from his pedestal, walking around the throne and out through a door behind it. As he did so, Alyssa walked to stand beneath the throne before turning to face us. It looked as though this was some kind of handover.

Without a word from Alyssa, the unsuccessful Sponsors guided their candidates back into the crowd until I couldn't differentiate them from it, leaving just the reading girl and her sponsor with me and Drew in the centre of the room.

Alyssa turned to the other pair.

"Illam Primo offere," she said.

The Silver woman guided her candidate out of the room, following the route Sol had taken through the door behind the throne. We all stood in silence for a few minutes and I wondered what was going on. I was leaning more and more heavily on Drew, the exhaustion gradually sinking back into my bones now that the adrenaline was washing out of my system. I just wanted to lie down and sleep. I'd had enough. I just wanted it to be over.

It wasn't long before the first couple were back in the room, smiling happily as they reclaimed their places. I thought I saw a glint of silver in the sponsor's irises and fervently hoped that I wasn't imagining it.

Alyssa turned to us then and spoke the same Latin words, so Drew piloted me carefully across the floor and through the same door. The room it led into was small, an office with an antique desk and several chairs, none of which were occupied. Instead, Sol was perched on the edge of the desk, his long legs stretched out in front of him and crossed at the ankles.

"Secundus," he said in a tight tone of voice as soon as the door closed behind us, "would you like to explain this?"

"I thought you knew, Primus. You knew about the bond. You knew I wanted to put Emmy forward as a candidate."

"Yes, indeed I did, but I also understood that she had no desire to be Silver, and that it was her intention to refuse you."

"I changed my mind," I said quietly as I sat down gratefully in one of the chairs, "and then the bond broke, but it was too late to change it back."

So in a few hours' time I'd be a Weeper, I added silently.

Sol looked at me for a long, painful moment, the silver glinting through the ice-blue of his irises as if to mock me. Seeing him now, so close and with the scent of his skin lingering faintly in the air, was the cruellest torture. It was as though the universe was reminding me of what I was missing out on just before it and everything else was taken away from me.

But still, I thought, at least I had seen him one more time.

"If you attempt this," Sol said to Drew, "you know you will fail."

"And you know that the Silver won't accept a breach of the rituals," Drew said, "not even if you said they had to. I have no choice."

Anger flashed in Sol's eyes.

"Is that what you truly believe?" he asked, his tone controlled but hard. "However passively, you have chosen this, Andrew. If the bond were still in place, if your life were also on the line, would you have so easily accepted a death sentence for her? You could have fled, and then at least there may have been a chance."

"But Primus…"

"No," Sol interrupted sharply. "Whatever the odds, you have chosen this. You've chosen to bring Emilia here, to make a martyr of her."

Drew fell silent as Sol looked briefly down at the floor, his gaze unfocussed for a moment, before bringing his eyes up to meet mine. He looked at me steadily and unflinchingly, and my heart jumped in my chest. It was raw and revealing, his eyes fixed on mine so intensely that I felt as though I should look away, but I couldn't.

"That choice will be the end of me," he said quietly, his

voice sounding stripped down and bare.

I looked at him in incomprehension, not able to process what he was saying. In the end, Drew got there before I did, staring at Sol in horror as the words sank it.

"But," he said, "Laila…"

"I confess that was a ruse," Sol said as he pushed away from the desk and stepped towards me.

"What are you telling me?" I asked, knowing that I wouldn't be able to believe it until I heard him say it.

He crouched down in front of me, the god king of the Silver on his knees at my feet. It was surreal. He was every inch the Primus, his power woven into the fabric of his personality and his bearing so that he was inseparable from it, but here he was on the ground in front of a human. It was discordant, a reversal that sat uncomfortably with me, putting me at the centre of attention in a way that made me feel exposed despite the fact that he was the one making himself vulnerable.

He reached out his hand to stroke his thumb along my bruised cheek, so gently I could barely feel it, the scent of fresh spice enveloping me. But this time it wasn't my imagination. This time he was really here, his fingers on my skin and his blue-eyed gaze intent on mine.

"I'm telling you that the marks that you see in my eyes are the silver that binds me to you. Not to Laila, nor to anyone else. I'm telling you that I love you, Emilia, and that I am yours."

My heart was racing, my chest filling with elation I was attempting to suppress, because I couldn't let myself believe it. I didn't understand. After everything that had happened between us, everything he'd said to me, I couldn't make sense of this.

He loved me? How could he love me?

My mind rushed back through each of our recent encounters, trying to piece together the moments that would prove him right. I remembered the night on the balcony of the flat, the first time I had seen the silver glinting in his eyes.

It had been an evening lost in abandon and bourbon, the anonymity of the night cocooning us in a way that felt permissive enough to bring me into his arms. The darkness didn't judge us, so it was always where we found each other. It was where he had found me at the club when he was struggling under the bond, pulling me into the shadows for one last taste of my blood, for a last goodbye. But if that bond was to me rather than to Laila, if he had been trying to deny that and push it away…

The dark desperation of that final moment we had spent alone together rang true, his control breaking out from the bonds he had tied around it to give us one more embrace before it ended, one more second with his body pressed close against mine and his lips on my skin.

And now here he was: so close to me that I could barely breathe. Every inhalation invited more of him in, the smell of waterfalls and incense filling my lungs, my mind, my body, and my heart. It was taking me over until I found it hard to think, the reality of his presence so much stronger than the ghostly simulacrum I had imagined. How could I have confused that hallucination with him? The real Sol was magnetic, pulling me towards him irresistibly with every part of his being. He was the North Star, a light in the darkness, a siren calling me home, and the nostalgic pain tugging at my chest was almost too much to bear.

I longed for him to take me in his arms and hold me until my soul stilled.

But I still couldn't believe him.

"Say something," he whispered. "Tell me I am not misjudging your desire. More than that, tell me I have not misread your affection."

Was this some kind of test, some kind of game?

"You said I was just a distraction," I said numbly.

"No," he replied ruefully, "I was a distraction to you. With his brand on your skin, I knew that you would find yourself drawn to my Secundus and that you would never feel for me as the brand made you feel for him. And in the end I was right; you chose him."

I couldn't argue with that. I had been the one, in the end, who had pushed him away. I'd decided to be with Drew, to give the bond a chance, but that was when I'd thought Sol was in love with Laila. I hadn't known then what I knew now. If I'd had the slightest clue that he might want me then, even with the brand, I would have resisted it.

I would have chosen Sol.

Drew had been standing beside me quietly through this exchange, but I heard him inhale sharply and turned to see him looking down at Sol ferociously.

"You bastard," he said. "It was you, wasn't it?"

"What?" I asked, snapping my gaze away from its fixation on Sol.

I'd forgotten that Drew was still there. I looked between the two of them, disorientated and confused, not sure what was going on.

"He broke the bond," Drew said. "You healed her, didn't you, after the explosion?"

Sol stood up beside me, his absent fingers leaving my face feeling cold.

"Yes," he said. "I did."

And suddenly it all made sense: the bond breaking, the healing and the scent of Sol chasing me down into unconsciousness. The marks of Sol's teeth on my wrist sealed with silver. That's what had broken the bond and the brand: another bond had supplanted it and pushed it out.

I looked up at Drew. He was furious and despairing, his fists clenching as his face twisted into an expression of hopeless anguish.

"Why would you do that to me?" he asked. "Why would you take that away from me, especially when you know how it feels? I'm supposed to be your Secundus!"

When Sol replied he spoke quietly and evenly.

"I hope that you will choose to remain so. Emilia was seconds from death and you were not there. If I had not healed her, the three of us would not be standing here. Her death would have taken us both."

Hell of a love triangle, I thought.

"I would not have done it had it not been necessary," Sol added.

"You expect me to believe that?" Drew asked viciously. "I could have been by your side in a second. The truth is that you've been trying to take her away from me since day one, and you finally found a way to get what you wanted."

Sol was quiet for a moment.

"Yes, I wanted her," he said eventually, looking at me briefly before turning back to Drew, "and I envied you her. I am not used to being denied my desires. Unlike yours, my silvering was not entirely unexpected. And yes, I did what I considered to be necessary."

Drew just shook his head mutely. I wondered whether he would ever be able to forgive Sol for this, for saving my life and his.

I was getting sick of being talked over, and I wanted some answers of my own. If Sol was telling the truth, and I still wasn't ready to let myself believe that, then I couldn't understand why he wouldn't have told me how he felt once he knew he had freed me of the brand.

"Why did you do nothing after the bond broke?" I asked.

He turned to me, his eyes seeming to shine through the darkness of the office around us. God, how I wished it were true. How I wished he would take my face in his hands and kiss me, hold me tight against him and set the fire running under my skin.

"This bond ties my life to yours," he said. "As much as my Secundus having silvered for you was a risk to your life, if it were known that I had done the same then the risk would be multiplied a hundredfold. I have not acknowledged this bond, have ignored its existence to keep you safe until this point."

That couldn't be right, I thought, and suspicion reared its head once more.

"Safe?" I said incredulously, anger bubbling up inside me.

I was suddenly livid, my emotions spilling over irrationally and unpredictably. Part of me knew that I was only angry because it was somehow easier and less risky to react this way than it was to admit my feelings for Sol, particularly in front of Drew, just in case this was all another of Sol's ruses. I may have admitted my feelings to myself before, but never out loud and never to either of the men standing in front of me, watching and waiting for me to tell them what this meant to me.

"Seriously?" I continued. "You want me to believe that you love me, and you're telling me that you sent me to the Farm to be beaten and drained by that maniacal sadist Ada to keep me safe? Does it look to you like I was safe?"

I got to my feet and gestured at myself emphatically with my broken fingers, pointing out the smashed cheekbone and the bruises down my side. But after sitting down for a couple of minutes I was too unsteady to remain standing, the blood rushing from my head with dizzying speed and making dark spots flash in front of my eyes. I sat back down abruptly, holding onto the edges of the chair.

"Is there something wrong?" Sol asked solicitously, crouching at my feet once more.

"I also lost some blood," I said, laughing at the irony of his asking the question when he was the reason for it. "A present from Ada for you."

He raised his hand to my cheek again and gently stroked the bruise.

"I am so very sorry. I had hoped that sending you to the Farm would keep you safe from Benedict and my consort."

An irrational pang of jealousy stabbed at my stomach. Laila was still his consort, of course. Would she still be, after tonight? What was he expecting would happen here? Was he going to get me out of the dawn ceremony? Was he really going to run away with me and abandon his whole kingdom to Ben?

I shook my head and looked away, not sure what to think anymore.

"If you refuse to take my word for it, let me show you," he said. "Let me heal you."

I remembered how it had felt when Drew had healed my hand the last time it had been broken. It had been agony, the bones snapping back together with a brutal crunch. But I knew I couldn't go on for long while I was this drained, and I could stand the pain, were it not for the questions it would raise.

"And what then?" I asked. "I walk back out into the Casting miraculously better?"

"Afterwards," he promised. "You must both return to the Casting to bring it to its end, but I will come to you after it is completed."

"And after that?" Drew said irritably. "What about the dawn ceremony? Have you forgotten about that? Thanks to your consort, we can't get out of it now."

Sol took his hand from my face and turned to Drew.

"I am the Primus," he said sternly, as if that was the end of the conversation. Then his eyes met mine once more.

"I will see you very shortly," he said softly, and then he kissed my hand and helped me to my feet. "Go."

CHAPTER XXIII

My beloved speaks and says to me:
"Arise, my love, my fair one, and come away;
for now the winter is past,
the rain is over and gone."

- The Song of Solomon

Drew was walking with his back ramrod straight as he led me back out into the dark hall, my arm looped in his. There was only a single candelabrum lit now, the one standing in the centre of the room, and Alyssa was next to it. Once we had resumed our places opposite the other successful couple, she leaned over towards it and, in a single breath, blew the candles out.

Hundreds of voices started chatting around us, and I realised that it was over. The Casting was done.

How things had changed in the space of the ritual. I was trying not to celebrate too early, trying not to pre-empt what might happen next, but for the first time today I didn't think I'd be turning Weeper with the sunrise.

"I'm getting you out of here," Drew whispered beside me, and before I could protest I was swept off my feet.

There was the rush of movement that I was becoming horribly accustomed to, and then we were back in the garage under the Solis Invicti building next to a compact off-road vehicle, a single light bulb above our heads illuminating the space.

"Secundus," a voice said behind us as Drew put me on my feet.

We both turned to see who was speaking.

"I'm sorry, sir," she said, "but I can't let you take Ms Nelson out of here."

"Tessa?" he said in surprise.

She was pointing a gun directly at his head. It wouldn't kill him, but I'd seen him shot before and I knew it would put him down for a good long while.

"Sir," she said.

"What are you doing? I'm your Secundus."

"Yes sir, but I have orders from the Primus, and first and foremost I am one of his Invicti."

This was news to me.

"You're Solis Invicti?" I asked, leaning heavily on Drew's arm to steady myself, my head still reeling from the blood loss and the super-speed travelling. "Then what were you doing playing guard at the Farm?"

"She was one of your guards?" Drew asked me, apparently as surprised as I was. "You were supposed to be on duty at the city wall and the Farm perimeter," he said to her.

"I'm sorry, sir, but I had orders from the Primus to notify him if his consort or the Tertius approached Ms Nelson. And now I have orders to keep her here until he arrives."

"And you have done so, thank you, Tessa," Sol said as he appeared at her side.

"You overruled my orders?" Drew said to him, apparently furious again.

"Yes," he said. "Now leave us. We will discuss this later. You may also leave, Tessa. I will call when I have need of you."

She gave a little bow and walked across the floor and through a door set into the concrete wall at the other side of the garage from where we stood. But Drew was going nowhere. He surprised me by wrapping his arm possessively around my shoulders and standing his ground.

"Andrew," Sol said to him, more gently. "I will come to your office in ten minutes, and we will discuss this. I will meet you there."

"Drew," I said to him, desperate to talk to Sol on my own and finish what we started. "It's okay."

"No," he said, still looking at Sol, "it's not. It's too dangerous for the two of you to be alone together, for both of you. You know that, Primus."

This sudden gallantry sat oddly with me, and I wondered whether this was compensation for his failures in taking me to the Casting. Was he feeling guilty for failing to take me out of this situation, for failing to run away with me?

"Then you will wait outside and ensure we are not disturbed," Sol said to him firmly.

He looked down at me uncertainly, his green eyes full of indecision.

"Go on," I said, intending to assuage his guilt.

He looked hurt, as though the fact that I wanted to speak to Sol alone was a surprise, as if after everything that had happened his ego was still pricked by the dismissal even if the jealousy he wanted to muster wouldn't come.

But he walked away, nonetheless.

I managed to stay standing until he had followed Tessa out through the door, slamming it behind him, but then the strength finally went from my limbs, my energy falling away from me, and I was toppling towards the floor. Sol caught me, of course.

"Emilia," he breathed, his face inches from mine as he knelt on the ground with me in his arms. He lifted me up and perched me on the bonnet of the car behind us, running his fingers over the slick satin of my dress on my thighs as he looked into my eyes, the cracked ice glinting in the glare of the overhead light as if it were shining just for me. If I believed him, then I supposed that it was.

He slid his hands down to the hem of the dress at my ankles and started to hitch it up over my knees.

"Woah," I said, thinking this was moving a little quickly. Yes, we'd already slept together once, but that was in different circumstances and this felt a little abrupt. "What are you doing?"

"You need to be healed," he said, raising one hand to my face, "and the silver mark must be somewhere discreet."

"I don't want another brand," I said, thinking of what had happened when Drew had healed me this way. I didn't want my emotions to be manipulated again, to be unsure whether I was doing things because I wanted to or because I was being compelled to.

"And you will not have one," he said. "You are not on the brink of death, and this is the first time I will have healed you whilst you are not under Andrew's brand. But you are weak, and you must be strong for what will come next."

He leaned his forehead against mine and I closed my eyes, breathing in the scent of him as one of his hands slipped round to the nape of my neck and the other returned to my ankle and started to inch upwards, skimming my calf before running over the back of my knee. As he swept his fingers up and across the inside of my thigh, I shuddered and inhaled deeply, the intimate contact sending bolts of sensation through the sensitive skin.

"Sol," I whispered, my lips so close to his I could taste his breath.

"This will hurt," he said softly as his hand came to rest at the top of my thigh, his fingers spreading proprietarily over the flesh. "Will you let me take the pain away?"

More Silver magic, I thought, remembering how his kiss had turned the pain of my admission tattoos into ecstasy. But with that came more magic that would make me yearn for him, drawing me back to him for a day afterwards. For that reason,

I had sworn to myself that the next time we kissed it would be because I already longed for him, and that it would mean to me what it meant to the Silver: that he was mine and I was his.

Instead of answering him, I tipped my face upwards and touched my lips to his, tasting the dizzying addiction of his scent on my tongue. He was still for a moment and then his fingers clenched in my hair, pulling it out of its braid as his hand squeezed on my thigh and sent healing electricity buzzing through my body. His lips were moving against mine, strong and urgent. He leaned into me, pushing me backwards to lie along the car bonnet as he pressed his body between my legs and followed me down.

I was burning up. Here was the fire, the heat and the need, pulsing through me like an irresistible drumbeat of desire and lighting my body up with energy as his touch rippled through my damaged shell and made it whole again. I pulled away for a moment and sat up to strip the splints off my fingers impatiently and throw them to the ground, pushing him upright as I did so. As soon as they were free I pushed both hands through his golden hair and held his face in front of mine, studying the silver tracery in his irises, the mark of the bond. His bond to me. He looked back at me steadily, his pupils dilating to eclipse the ice-blue as I watched.

But I mistrusted the bond. I knew what it could do to people. I had seen it twist Drew around until he wanted something he had no reason to desire, beyond logic or explanation. I hoped that wasn't what was happening here, but I had to know.

"Why?" I whispered.

"Why what?"

"Why do you love me? Is it just the bond?"

He took his hand from my thigh and lifted it to my face, running his thumb across my lips.

"No," he said. "The bond is the result of it, not the cause. The first time I kissed you I was already lost to you. You fascinate me with your obstinacy. You have power in you. I want nothing more than to show you who you are, and what

291

you desire most."

He teased his fingertips along the sensitive skin at the back of my neck, and I knew exactly what I desired.

"But I cannot admit the bond," he continued, "should not even be in your company, unless you are Silver."

I had known it would be coming, but my heart still sank as he spoke. I was right back where I had been with Drew: my life and the life of the Silver who loved me both endangered by the bond. But this time it wasn't the Secundus, it was the Primus, the Silver god king.

I realised the incredible risk this presented to this new and fragmented society. If I was killed, Sol and his regime would fall with me. It may not happen this week, or this year, but even if I were to die naturally it would threaten the basis of a hierarchy that might otherwise have lasted for centuries, millennia even, and risk putting the future of the human race into the hands of Laila and Ben.

"Do I have a choice?" I whispered.

"However you feel, I will not force this on you if it is not your desire to be Silver. I can send you away from this place to one of the other safe houses with a new identity, and we can say that you died in the attempt to turn, or on your way to the dawn ceremony."

I looked at him blankly, my mind racing as I found myself unable to make this decision. He stroked his thumb across my cheek and pressed his lips to mine in a gentle kiss.

"I love you, Emmy, but I will understand if this is not what you want. I will always be yours, whether you are Silver or not, whether we are together or not. I am sorry that I can only afford you a few hours to think on it, but I can at least arrange for you to go back to your friend at the Farm for that time, if that is what you would like? I understand that you are… close?"

I wondered how much he knew, and how much Tessa had reported back to him. Did he know that Ollie and I had crossed that line? Either way, there was no censure or jealousy in his tone. He was offering me a friend to talk this through with, my only human friend left in this world.

"Yes," I said, "I'd like to go back. But you'll come in the morning?"

"I will," he said as he raised my healed fingers to his mouth and pressed a kiss against them.

He took a step backwards and I slid down from the bonnet of the car, the satin of my skirt falling back into place. But there would be a mark there, I knew: a silver handprint of possession on my thigh that would last for the next day or so until the particles of shining metal dissipated through the skin.

Sol pulled a gadget that looked like an old-school pager from his pocket and pressed a button on its face. In an instant, Tessa was standing in front of us, looking at me curiously.

"Primus?" she asked, sniffing as she looked back at me.

The mark, I thought. His kiss would have left a scent on me, a possessive mark that told the Silver world that I belonged to him and, if they credited me with the ability to turn his head, that he belonged to me. And with the silver glinting in his irises, it looked as though Tessa may have made the connection.

Stupid, I thought. I should have just suffered the pain of the healing.

"Yes," Sol said to her, "you have deduced correctly. But you are now one of only four people who know this, and you will keep it to yourself."

Her eyes widened momentarily, but then she nodded smartly.

"Of course, Primus. You know you can rely on me."

"Take care of her," he said. "You take my life with hers."

A look passed between them, a silent exchange as they measured each other, and then Tessa nodded again, apparently taking on the burden of keeping me safe.

When he was satisfied, he looked at me and squeezed my hand gently before letting go and walking towards the door, quickly and abruptly as though he were pulling off a band-aid.

"Goodnight, Emilia," he said, his eyes lingering on my face

for a moment, and then he was gone, leaving me alone in the garage with Tessa.

He loved me, I thought.

After everything we'd been through, he loved me.

She looked me up and down then shook her head.

"Shit," she said. "I wish I could wrap you up in body armour."

I felt the same way. This wasn't like it had been with Drew. This was Sol. Not only was he the Primus, but he was… Sol. The thought that I could take him down just by taking a careless step, by making a single, small mistake, made me more terrified of dying than I had ever been before in my life. My mortality was suddenly at the very front of my mind.

"Come on," she said, gesturing towards her car. "I'll feel better when you're back behind six electric fences in a reinforced concrete building."

So would I, I thought.

The city was pitch black when we drove out of the garage, and Tessa was running without lights. I gathered that she must be able to see in the dark and wondered whether it was a talent that all of the Silver shared. Either way, I was grateful not to be able to see the Weepers around us, and I guessed that avoiding them was why she'd opted not to put the headlights on. They were like moths to a flame, drawn by the promise of the meat they associated with artificial lights.

"I'm sorry," she said as she sped through the night.

"What for?" I asked, not sure how I could blame her for anything that had happened. She'd looked after me as best she could in the cell, intervening to the greatest extent possible without blowing her cover.

"I thought the Primus knew that you were the one up for the Casting. I was wrong. If I had told him when I discovered it, it might have helped."

"I thought he knew too," I said. "Don't worry."

She put her foot down on the accelerator and I gathered that we had probably cleared the centre of the city and were pushing out into the wasteland between here and the Farm.

She fell silent, apparently focussed on the road ahead of her, and I wondered how I was going to make this decision.

I could be with Sol and be Silver, or I could stay human and never see him again, knowing that when I died he'd die too. I didn't want to be Silver, to be infected with the brutality and inhumanity that seemed to have pervaded the majority of their race through the apathy that came hand in hand with immortality. But I did want to be with Sol, to feel the fire of his touch burning through my veins. I wanted his hands on my body and his scent on my skin, his words in my head and the dark hooks of addiction pulling through my heart and soul until they were all that held me together.

I wanted to abandon myself to that, to him, and to let it take me. Drew had always said that Sol would break me, but maybe he'd put me back together again as well, as someone different and new. I knew there was something at the core of me crying to be freed from its cage, and maybe that cage was a box I had constructed around it. It might have kept me safe, but until I unlocked it I wouldn't be free.

Perhaps it was time to take that part of me out into the light, to stop hiding myself with Sol in the dark and praying for liberty. In the end, I was the only one with the key to that cage, but I hadn't even realised the cage existed until he'd shown it to me.

I replayed the evening in my mind, over and over. Sol's expression as he pulled the hood from his face at the Casting, his words to me afterwards, and then his lips on mine.

I wanted to say yes.

The journey passed in a blur as the thoughts rolled through my head, and I had lost track of time when Tessa next spoke.

"Shit," she said under her breath.

"What?"

"Hold on tight," she said, and then she flicked the headlights on.

We were approaching the perimeter gate of the Farm at breakneck speed, and there was a sea of Weepers spread out in front of us. As we approached, we saw the gate open and

Silver streamed out, physically pushing the Weepers away from the entrance by speeding up and down the edge of the channel they had carved through the multitude. Tessa accelerated through the tunnel of bodies, braking and swerving abruptly as she entered the first ring of the fences.

"They're not moving back," I said as she sped around the curving path towards the second gate.

Ollie had been right: the Weepers weren't afraid of the Silver anymore. They weren't moving back when they approached, stopping only when physically propelled away. The Silver would have to break them to stop them from advancing.

We turned through the second gate, a guard waving us past as he spoke frantically into his radio, and when we straightened up the headlights illuminated a dark mass clinging up against the outermost fence in front of us.

"Is that…?" I asked, before trailing off as we closed the distance and the scene became clearer.

The Weepers had brought down the first perimeter fence. There was an incalculable number of them spread in a heap that reminded me of the video we had been shown after the Revelation, the pictures of America showing Weepers forming fluid pyramids so high that they could reach the top of skyscrapers.

And they weren't stopping there.

"Shit shit shit," Tessa muttered.

We saw the third gate opening ahead of us just as the Weepers crested the second fence and started flinging themselves down on the other side, running towards us and towards the gate. We fishtailed through it and a couple of guards slammed it shut behind us, but the Weepers were already piling up against it as Tessa accelerated away towards the enclosure, the car bumping and diving across the uneven ground. It wouldn't be long before they were over the third fence and following close on our heels.

"The cell is the safest place you could be," she said quickly as she passed me a familiar gadget. "This is the gate control.

Press the first button and the first gate will open, second button and the second gate will open, and so on. I'll stay out here and push them back. If you get in trouble, get your whistle."

She skidded to a stop close to the enclosure and flung herself out of the car, leaving the headlights on and pointed towards the building.

"Go!" she shouted at me, and then she ran back the way we had come.

I moved as quickly as I could, my legs tangling in the long skirt as I tried to get out of the low sports car. I pressed the first button as I slammed the car door behind me, and then there was a howl. It was terrifyingly close, coming from the other side of the perimeter fence close to where I was standing.

A shiver crept up the back of my neck. I looked behind me anxiously.

I could see nothing in the darkness. The lights of the car illuminated only the gate opening in front of me and the cell beyond it, and I could see nothing of the perimeter fence to the side. I knew from experience how silently the Weepers could move, how they seemed to float eerily over the ground with only their clothes rustling around them. They could be ten feet away from me and I wouldn't know about it until they were on top of me, their teeth in my flesh.

I pulled up the skirt of the dress and ran into the first ring of fences, pressing the second button as soon as I could to slam the first gate closed behind me. I listened desperately every step of the way, straining my ears for any sound, but all I could hear was the thud of my footsteps and the swishing of satin against satin.

When I was finally through the third gate I ran towards the building and pressed the fourth button, keying in the code as fast as I could.

"Emmy?" I heard Ollie call from inside.

There was another howl, closer this time, and I prayed that Ollie would hear it and know to keep quiet. Despite that, hearing his voice sent a wave of relief through me that helped me to steady my hands enough to get the keypad to work. He wrenched the door open the moment the locks tumbled, and then he was scooping me up into his arms and pushing it firmly shut behind me.

"Keep quiet," I whispered.

"You're alive," he breathed back, kissing my head as he held me close.

"For the moment."

The cell was dark, the candles unlit, and I decided it was probably a good idea to keep it that way. But I needed to find the transmitter, and I needed it now.

"What's going on?" he asked as I pulled away and rummaged in the pile of stuff in the corner of the room, trying to find my backpack. "There was this crashing sound, and then nothing for a while. Then the howls started."

"The Weepers are bringing down the fence," I said. "You were right: the Silver aren't keeping them back. We're out of time."

"Thank god," I muttered as I located the walkie talkie and started pressing whatever buttons I could find in the dark. "Cam?" I whispered into it. "Tommy?" I pressed some more buttons. "Hello? Shit, how does this work? Hello?"

"Emmy?" a voice came back, Tommy's voice.

"Tommy," I whispered, my voice tight with panic, "we could really use your help here."

"We're having some trouble of our own in the city."

"The Weepers have brought down the perimeter fence. We're in the cell, but I think they're getting closer."

"It's not just the Farm, Emmy. It's here too. We'll be with you as soon as we can. Just hold on, okay?"

The line went dead, static taking the place of Tommy's voice.

"Shit," I said, not holding out much hope that he would be here any time soon.

Then something changed and it took me a moment to work out what it was: the night had become even blacker. I stood up and looked out of the window, but I couldn't see the car headlights anymore.

"What happened?" I asked Ollie.

"They just went out," he whispered back. "I didn't see anything."

I walked to his side where he stood in the centre of the room and leaned against him. He put his arm around me and held me tight.

There was a noise. It was a crash, a metallic, fizzing noise of electricity and breaking chains.

"The fence," he whispered. "They're coming through the fence."

It came again, a sharp smack as though something were smashing through the bars and links of the fence with one, focussed punch of energy.

I thought about the Weepers at the perimeter, how they had climbed over the top. They couldn't go through it. And the fencing around our enclosure was in a dome. There was no way they would be able to get over it, but I wasn't sure that they had the strength to force their way through. A suspicion stole over me as we heard the noise again for the third and final time.

"I don't think it's Weepers," I whispered. "I think it's the Silver. Maybe Tommy and Cam…"

"Wrong again, Emilia," a voiced called through the door of the cell. It was terrifyingly familiar, creeping over my bare skin and dragging a visceral horror in its wake.

"Benedict," Ollie whispered.

"Ah," his voice came again from outside the cell, "and my young protégée. What a charming reunion. Aren't you going to invite me in?"

We said nothing, frozen to the spot in the darkness of the cell.

He laughed, a callous and sharp noise that was all the more frightening for the sobriety and sanity behind it. Cam was right: Ben knew exactly what he was doing, and exactly why he was here.

"Something very interesting happened a few minutes ago," he said, "and I thought that I simply must rush over here to bring you the news."

He paused for a moment.

"Well, aren't you going to ask me what it is?" he said when we remained silent. "I must say that your conversation is somewhat lacking tonight, Emmy." He spat my name like a curse, adopting a condescending tone as if to mock the puerility of the diminutive.

"I'll tell you anyway, shall I?" he continued as he plucked one of the bars from the window next to the door. Ollie and I stepped backwards, pressing our backs against the connecting door, but there was nowhere for us to go.

We were completely trapped.

"I was with my dear friend Laila," he rambled on, "and she was talking about her new squeeze. You know, your cx, the Primus. And then suddenly she goes all goo-goo eyed for him and silvers, right there in front of me, which I have to say rather lowered her in my estimations, but there you are."

Another two bars were wrenched from the window as though they were made of cardboard.

"But then that was it," he said. "She silvered, and nothing more."

Oh shit, I thought. He knew.

He knew Sol hadn't really silvered for Laila.

He knew that it was me.

"There was no gold in her eyes, no seal to show her love was requited, and so of course one of them had to be lying about the object of their affection. And then I thought about you, Emilia."

Two more bars popped free from the window frame.

"It's always about you, isn't it? I thought about the Primus's reaction at the Casting earlier today. And, how could I forget? About your little tryst on the terrace and the traces it left behind on you."

I stifled a scream as the glass of the window exploded inwards, punched away in a blast of force.

"And I smell it on you again tonight, his mark rolling around in the scent of old sweat and arousal. I hope it made you feel special, because you won't have long to enjoy it."

There was a series of earth-shaking detonations that sent Ollie and I to our knees as masonry tumbled down around us. When we were able to shake off the debris and see through the dust clouds by the gloomy light of the clouded moon, there was a ghostly figure standing over us in the ruins of the cell that had been demolished around us. I clenched my hand around Ollie's arm and dragged him backwards with me, stumbling awkwardly over the lumps of concrete now spread over the grass of the enclosure.

I looked up and around us, trying to catch sight of the fences that had domed our cell, but saw with terrible resignation that they were lying around us in twisted piles of metal.

"But I'm nothing if not a good sport," Ben said softly as he slowly took a few steps away, "a charitable type, so I'll give the Weepers a chance with you first. Don't worry though, I'm not going to make the same mistake as last time and leave them to finish you off. I'll be staying right here to watch proceedings."

Ollie scrambled to his feet and helped me up beside him. I looked around desperately, but there was no weapon we could grab within range, the concrete chunks all too large or too small to be of any use. We were out of options.

"There's nowhere for you to hide now, Emilia," Ben said, "but you can still run."

He put his fingers to his lips and blew, the whistle sounding out across the night. The howls of the Weepers answered him, loud and close.

"So go on," he whispered. "Run."

Do you want to read Cara Alton's story?

Join my Readers' Club and receive an exclusive short story, absolutely FREE!

www.josiejaffrey.com/subscribe

You'll also receive my monthly newsletter, including exclusive news, giveaways and offers.

***

If you enjoyed *Bound in Silver*, why not read *The Silver Bullet*? It's Book IV in the *Solis Invicti* series, and carries on right where *Bound in Silver* left off.

To think of death as a thing of beauty: that's a threshold you can't cross twice.

***

Please leave a review!

If you enjoyed *Bound in Silver*, I'd be so grateful if you would please review it. Book reviews can make a huge difference to the success of a novel, particularly those of self-published authors like me. If you have time to leave a review, even if it's just a sentence or two, then I'd really appreciate it.

***

Get in touch!

I love hearing from readers! If you'd like to contact me, you can do that through my website, Twitter, Facebook or Instagram.

ACKNOWLEDGMENTS

The author wishes to thank her lovely editing team: Jess (Queen Pedant), Zoe (the Continuity Kid) and Vicky (Team Sol).

Huge thanks, as always, are due to the author's husband for his unswerving support and tolerance.

Finally, apologies to any classicists reading if the Latin isn't quite right!

39553667R00183

Printed in Poland
by Amazon Fulfillment
Poland Sp. z o.o., Wrocław